T0414020

MASSACRE CANYON

Center Point
Large Print

Also by Wayne D. Dundee and available from
Center Point Large Print:

Dismal River
Rainrock Reckoning
The Forever Mountain
The Coldest Trail
The Gun Wolves

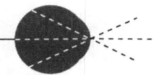

MASSACRE CANYON

A Lone McGantry Western

WAYNE D. DUNDEE

CENTER POINT LARGE PRINT
THORNDIKE, MAINE

This Center Point Large Print edition
is published in the year 2024 by arrangement with
Wolfpack Publishing.

The text of this Large Print edition is unabridged.
In other aspects, this book may vary
from the original edition.
Printed in the United States of America
on permanent paper sourced using
environmentally responsible foresting methods.
Set in 16-point Times New Roman type.

ISBN: 979-8-89164-140-2

The Library of Congress has cataloged this record
under Library of Congress Control Number: 2024900847

CHAPTER 1

The whistle stop probably had a name, Lone McGantry reckoned. But if it did, he'd either never heard it or didn't remember if he had. At any rate, none of that altered the usefulness of the place as a spot on the UP line between Sidney and North Platte for trains to stop and take on water while passengers, if there were any, had the chance to alight and stretch their legs, take on a cool drink for themselves, maybe even a quick bite of grub. The latter was Lone's intent this late summer afternoon as he approached from the west, not on a train but rather on horseback.

He was coming in on a faint southerly angle, having ridden out of Colorado and entering Nebraska just short of the panhandle hinge. The day was hot under a cloudless sky with most of the blue baked right out of it. When he'd crossed the South Platte River it had shown once again how it earned its oft-repeated description as being "a mile wide and foot deep," signaling the region's summer had been another hot, dry one.

Further evidence of this could be seen in the pale brown grass covering the treeless, endlessly rolling Sandhills that stretched off to the north

5

for as far and farther than the eye could see. This semi-arid mass of mixed-grass prairie anchored mound after mound of sand dunes that covered almost a quarter of the state. Once written off as a worthless "great inland desert," it wasn't until after the Civil War that new exploration discovered the sprawl sat atop an equally massive aquifer that provided not only pockets of much greener grass but even pools and small lakes in the lower reaches between many of the mounds.

While no such greenery or pools were visible from Lone's current route, he nevertheless knew they were out here. During his years as an army scout and on a few occasions since, Lone had traveled extensively through the heart of the Sandhills. As much as or possibly more than any other man. In that time, he'd experienced the full range of lushness and brutal ruggedness to be found within them. The only aspect he wasn't fully familiar with was the extent of cattle ranching that had spread across the vast expanse of grassland in recent years. Yet while he harbored a good deal of respect and even a kind of fondness for the place, Lone had no hankering to return any deeper into it than these fringes he was currently traveling. Those days were behind him.

While that much was clear in his mind, exactly what the days ahead otherwise held in store was something else. Lone figured to sort that out once he got back to North Platte. For most of the past year he'd been whipsawed by obligations and reactions brought on by a series of events that jarred and significantly altered the future he at one time believed to be pretty solidly mapped out. Now he faced needing to revise that map.

But, shorter term, what he needed was to swing into the watering station where he could soak up some shade, a couple cold beers, and hopefully enjoy some decent vittles he didn't have to cook for himself over a trailside campfire.

The joint wasn't much to look at—just a one-story shack slightly offset from the tracks and the hovering water tower with its cantilevered filling spout. The front was made of horizontally-stacked railroad ties with mud caulking in between. The rest, as a result of trees and lumber being so scarce to the area, was a basic sod structure with a rickety branch corral out back. Lone could see a couple horses and a milk cow milling inside the corral, and several chickens strutting about the general area. This caused him to calculate the chances for some fresh eggs or maybe a serving of chicken and dumplings being available on the inside.

When he reined up Ironsides, his big gray stallion, at one end of the hitch rail out front, there were already two saddled horses tied there. Probably belonging to wranglers from one of the nearby cattle ranches, Lone guessed, or maybe just a couple of drifters like himself. Either way, it was of no particular concern to him.

What happened a moment later, however, quickly turned into a different matter.

The front door of the station suddenly burst open and a young woman came rushing out. She was clad in a billowing wine-red skirt and an off-the-shoulder white blouse. Her face was a tangled expression of fear and anger. The dusky hue of said face and bared shoulders, combined with the long, gleaming black hair streaming out behind her, indicated she was of Mexican or perhaps Indian blood.

Lone took all of this in with a quick, sharp glance. But further appraisal of the girl was interrupted by the appearance of a man immediately filling the doorway behind her and lunging in pursuit. This second individual was tall and lean, appearing to be not very far into his twenties, with an unruly thatch of straw-colored hair, wild eyes, and teeth bared in a fierce snarl. His left cheek showed three fresh, bloody scratch marks gouged deep through pale beard stubble.

"Grab her, Tad!" somebody shouted from deeper inside the station. "Don't let that wildcat get away!"

But everything seemed to indicate the wildcat *was* going to get away. She eluded her pursuer's attempt to wrap his clawing fingers in her hair and then, propelled by long, smooth strides, increased the gap between them even more when the man momentarily staggered as his desperately reaching hands closed into nothing but empty fists.

The man referred to as "Tad" regained his balance quickly. He'd already lost precious ground, though. If the girl's determination and nimbleness held up, he stood a damn slim chance of catching her.

Only that's where Lone's unexpected presence came into play.

So intent was the girl on getting away from Tad's obviously unwanted attention that she plunged headlong, blindly, in her flight to escape him. Which was what caused her to nearly run smack up against the big gray stallion standing at one end of the hitch rail with a tall, broad-shouldered stranger mounted on his back. The sight of this pair looming directly in her path so startled the girl that she came to a skidding halt mere inches short of a collision. Drawing back sharply, it was her turn to take a faltering, half-staggering step.

This was all Tad needed to make up the ground he'd lost. Paying no heed to Lone and Ironsides, he rushed forward and grabbed once more for the girl's mane of hair, this time the fingers of both hands wrapping tightly around thick fistfuls of gleaming black.

"Now, you hip-swaying tease," he declared

harshly, "you're gonna get what you been askin' for—and more!"

So saying, he jerked the girl viciously by her hair, swinging her around a hundred and eighty degrees. She was barely able to maintain her footing. At the end of the swing, Tad released the grip of his right hand and then immediately used it to slam a clubbing blow to his captive's jaw. This knocked the girl to the ground.

For a moment, her head and shoulders were held up by Tad's left hand still buried in her hair. When he let go, she collapsed all the way flat. But she didn't stay that way for long. Pressing down with both palms, she pushed stubbornly, shakily up to her hands and knees.

Baring his teeth in a cold, menacing grin, Tad shifted around so that he was positioned on the girl's left side. Slowly drawing back one foot, he said, "You ain't worth skinnin' my knuckles on no more. But that don't mean my boots couldn't stand a little polishin'."

The foot cocked back all the way and poised to kick forward.

Before it did, however, the report of a gunshot barked loudly and a .44 slug cut the air half an inch in front of the raised foot, digging a ragged furrow in the ground and kicking up a rooster tail of dust.

Tad abruptly lowered his foot, planting it hard and flat. Twisting at the waist, he turned his face to aim a glare in Lone's direction. "What the hell! Do you know who you're interferin' with, mister?"

From where he leaned slightly forward in his saddle, Lone mirrored Tad's glare through the curl of powder smoke rising up from the muzzle of the Colt Peacemaker he held leveled steady on the surly young man. "Way I see it," he drawled, "I'm interferin' with a lowdown piece of crud who'd knock a gal to the ground an' then try to stomp her. That what you're askin'?"

A corner of Tad's upper lip peeled back in a sneer. "No, I ain't askin' nothing. Not no more. I'm tellin'. And what I'm tellin' you is that you oughta be a lot more careful about checkin' the odds before you take a notion to stick your nose into somebody else's business."

"If you're talkin' about that fat tub over in the doorway," Lone scoffed, neither his gaze nor the snout of the Colt wavering in the slightest, "then you're the one who needs to take a little more care when it comes to figurin' odds. I can see him plain enough out the corner of my eye to spot if he has the guts to go ahead and try pullin' that hogleg stuffed in his belt—instead of just fingerin' it, nervous-like, the way he is. He makes any kind of wrong move, this .44 I got already cocked and aimed will blow your gizzard halfway across those railroad tracks. Tubby might manage to plant some lead in me before I spin on him next, but none of it will matter to you—I guarantee you won't be around to see it."

Tad's smug expression started to turn not so smug.

But the heavyset man who was crowded into the station doorway, his voice when he spoke identifying him as the same hombre who'd earlier urged Tad's pursuit of the girl, was ready with some fresh encouragement. "That's a sorry-ass bluff if I ever heard one, Tad. We can put him in a crossfire and he damn well knows it. Say the word and I'll plunk that meddling fool off his horse like popping a can off a fence post."

"Not so fast, Poke," Tad objected. "I'm lookin' at this cold-eyed bastard straight on and I ain't so sure he's bluffin'. I'm also lookin' down the gullet of that Colt already in his fist, and neither you nor me even has our irons drawed."

"Something we can fix in a hurry."

Whatever Tad's response to that might have been, nobody would ever know. Because before he could say anything more, the girl at his feet suddenly shoved up onto her knees and swung one hand in a blur of motion. Within the blur could be seen the glint of shiny steel. A knife blade! It was visible for just a second and then was gone, the full six inches of its length disappearing as the girl plunged it up into her tormentor's stomach, just above the beltline.

Tad's face immediately twisted with surprise and pain. He took half a step backward, emitting a curiously mild grunt as he doubled over and his knees started to buckle.

"Tad!" wailed the husky man in the doorway. At the same time, he grabbed for the Remington revolver tucked in his waistband, the weapon he'd made noises about using but before now had only plucked at nervously.

Lone couldn't afford to hesitate and allow the big man to open fire, nor was it likely he'd be able to halt him with merely a shouted warning. His only choice was to speak once again with his Colt. Swinging his aim away from the collapsing Tad, Lone re-set his sights on the doorway and triggered a quick round. His intent was to hammer a slug into the frame of the opening, close enough to the would-be gunman to hopefully jar some better sense into him before he began throwing lead.

It worked, though not quite as planned. As the big man freed the revolver and started to raise what was now his gun hand, he took a lurching step forward and slightly to one side—directly into the path of the bullet meant only to strike close. Instead, rather than drilling into the wooden door frame, the slug slammed into the meat and bone of the big man's shoulder. The impact spun him half around, causing him to drop the Remington and topple hard against the side of the building, sputtering a string of agonized curses as he slid down.

CHAPTER 2

"Oh Lord. This is bad, real bad . . . There's gonna be hell to pay, you can bet on that."

So lamented Simon Weaver as he gazed numbly out on the scene in front of the watering station. Weaver was the station manager, a narrow-faced beanpole with a thatch of reddish-brown hair and worried, washed-out blue eyes under a puckered brow. He'd poked his head out after the shooting stopped and now stood just outside the doorway, wringing his hands and fretting like an irritable old woman.

"That'd be a pretty safe bet," Lone growled in response, "considerin' there's already been a dose of hell paid here. How about, instead of just standin' there moanin' about it, you pitch in and lend a hand to help? Go inside and get a blanket to put over this man and, while you're at it, some towels or rags to use for stoppin' the bleedin' of the other one there beside you."

Weaver's eyes touched again on the prone body of Tad and lingered there, the anguished look on his face pinching even tighter. "Get a blanket to put over . . . You mean he's dead?"

"No other word for it," Lone said flatly. He'd dismounted from Ironsides by this point and had gone over to examine the fallen man. The Indian girl—for that's what she was, Lone determined, once given the chance to appraise her more closely—remained motionless and silent beside the body, rocked back on her haunches and gazing down at the blood-stained ground with no expression on her face. Just in case she might take a notion to get busy with the knife again, Lone had gone ahead and removed it from Tad's stomach once he saw the man was dead.

Continuing to address the station man and balancing the weapon lightly in his hand as he did so, he said, "I've seen fellas survive what appeared to be worse gut sticks. But this blade must have hit something plumb serious on the inside. This hombre is a goner."

To which the heavyset wounded man, still sunk down beside the station doorway, promptly wailed, "Well he may be, but I ain't—not yet. I will be, though, if I don't get some care. I'm losing blood and I hurt like sin. I need a doctor!"

"Shut up," Lone snarled. "You go pullin' iron on me, you're lucky I left you alive. I was even tryin' to be charitable and hold off plunkin' any lead in you at all. But you ruined that with your clumsy-assed stumble into my line of fire."

More contrite but still wincing in pain, the man said, "Alls I know, no matter how it got there, is that this slug is giving me powerful misery."

Lone's eyes cut to the station man. "Damn it, mister, are you just gonna stand there? How about that blanket and some towels—maybe a belt of something to ease the wretch's pain?"

"Okay, okay." Weaver aimed a scowl at the Indian girl. "Minowi! You heard him—get up off your trouble-causin' ass and fetch what he's askin' for. Hop to it!"

Minowi didn't move, didn't look his way. Just kept staring down at the bloodied ground.

"Damn it, gal, did you hear me?" Weaver demanded. "Don't you think you're bad enough off without buckin' me to boot? The law or, worse yet, Ira Clemson comes after your red hide, I already ain't much inclined to try and speak up for you. Come to think of it, I ought not even—"

"For Christ's sake," Lone cut him off. "Can't you see this girl is in a bad way? She needs a minute to try and come to grips with what she just went through. Gettin' beat down and near stomped into the ground, then killin' in retaliation . . . Hardly things that'd go easy down the craw of most anybody."

"But she ain't like most folks. She's just a squaw who . . ." Weaver's protest faded to silence. Once again his words were interrupted by McGantry. Only this time it was the result of merely a look from the stranger, the intensity in those flinty eyes. Not to mention the hard lines of his weathered, squarish face, the breadth of his shoulders, and the coiled-spring way he carried that big frame of his. And then there was the

16

readiness he'd shown when it came to bringing into play the six-gun now re-holstered on his right hip, opposite a wicked length of Bowie knife sheathed on his left. All told, the man presented something that Simon Weaver abruptly concluded he'd best not stand arguing with. Finding his voice again, he meekly said as he turned away, "Alright. I'll go fetch those things."

A handful of minutes later, a blanket had been spread over Tad's prone body. Minowi, the Indian girl, remained silent and motionless, seemingly oblivious to all activity around her. Lone moved to the man with the bullet wound, crouching beside him and tugging open his shirt to better access the damage. Weaver hovered close, looking on with increasing concern.

"H-how bad is it?" asked the victim after taking a long pull from the bottle of whiskey Weaver had handed to him.

"Seen worse . . . seen better," Lone answered, dabbing away blood and doing some gentle probing with his fingers. More gently, he couldn't help thinking, than the damn fool deserved. "Looks like the bullet is still in there. Likely fragmented, along with some bone wreckage."

"Oh, Jesus. I ain't gonna be crippled, am I? Or will I not have to worry about that on account of lead poisoning claiming me due to the bullet fragments?"

"Calm down," Lone grated. "I can get most of

17

the bullet out, at least enough so's you'll be okay to make it to a saw bones. Far as how much arm use you might lose, I can't say."

"You've done this kind of thing before?" Weaver wanted to know.

Lone chuffed. "More than I would've liked. A time or two even on myself . . . You got a hot stove inside?"

"Sure. Always try to have some coffee and vittles warm and ready."

Lone unsheathed his Bowie and, along with the knife he'd taken from Tad's stomach, held it out to the station man. "Here. Stick these in the coals long enough for the blades to take on a rose hue. Then fetch 'em back. Bring a needle and some thread, too."

After Weaver hurried off to do as bid, the wounded man gazed up at Lone from under a puckered, sweat-beaded brow. "I sure appreciate you tending to me, mister. I'm awful sorry about pulling iron on you the way I done."

"I came out of it okay," Lone grunted, continuing to dab and press around the edges of torn flesh, aiming to stanch the blood flow. "But you'd better take another belt of that who-hit-John because you've got some more misery on the way when I go in after that bullet."

"My name's Poke, by the way. Leastways that's what folks call me. Poke Rafferty. Yours?"

"Make it McGantry. Lone McGantry."

After taking a couple big gulps and then lowering the whiskey bottle again, Rafferty slurred, "Reckon that gives us something in common. Kinda unusual names, right? Poke and Lone. Kinda unusual, ain't that right?"

"If you say so," Lone allowed. Then: "Tell me, Poke—what did I ride into the middle of here? How was it that your pal Tad was so hell bent on runnin' down that gal and threatenin' her to the point of her knifin' him?"

Poke wagged his sagging head. "Oh, it was bad business that had been building for too long. Ever since me and Tad got barred from the saloons in Ogallala and started coming here to buy our whiskey."

"Why'd you get barred from the saloons in Ogallala?"

"On account of Tad's rowdiness. Oh, he was a handful when he got wound up. A hell-raising handful. And I was supposed to keep him in check. That's what Old Man Clemson tasked me with. What a joke!" Poke took another drink. "Six of me couldn't hold Tad back when he was of a mind to let the wolf howl. Hah! All I accomplished was to keep getting into trouble along with him . . . And now he's dead and I'm in my worst trouble of all because I didn't prevent it."

Lone said, "You speak of Old Man Clemson and a minute ago Weaver mentioned the name Ira

Clemson. I take it they're one and the same?"

"You take it right," Weaver said, stepping back out through the doorway holding a broad, shallow frying pan in which rested the two sterilized knives and a ball of thread with some needles stuck in it. "And the man they add up to is Tad's father. Who also happens to be the biggest cattle rancher between here and Ogallala."

Lone grimaced. "Jesus Christ. Another rich, powerful rancher with a wild, spoiled son. Is there a rule or a law written down somewhere that requires the same damn pattern to keep showing up in so many different places?"

"I don't know about that," Weaver said. "I just know how it is hereabouts. And something else I know is that when ol' Ira learns his precious boy has been killed . . . Well, like I already said before, there's gonna be hell to pay."

"Yeah, and I just made part of the down payment," groaned Poke. "Before this is all over I may end up paying even more. Shit, it could be that all this trouble to dig out that bullet for the sake of holding off lead poisoning might only be saving me for Old Man Clemson to go ahead and finish the job anyway."

"We'll have to see about that," Lone countered. "I don't go to the trouble of patchin' a fella up merely to hand him over to the dogs. So, if those knives are ready, Weaver, hand me that big Bowie for starters."

CHAPTER 3

As Lone probed to get at the bullet in Poke's shoulder—first using the tip of the Bowie and then slicing deeper with Minowi's smaller blade—he also continued probing to hear the rest of the details on what had brought all of this on. He got most of the answers from Poke, between groans and hisses of pain. Somewhat grudgingly, Weaver provided a few more.

What it boiled down to was that Tad and Poke being barred from the town saloons not only deprived them of the liquor and gambling available in such places, but it also interfered with access to the kind of female companionship to be found in them as well. And since Tad's insatiable craving for dalliances with soiled doves drove him as strong or stronger than almost anything else, this was a particularly aggravating matter. It was inevitable then that the whiskey-buying visits to Weaver's station and the presence there of the fetching Minowi (who, Lone was surprised to hear, turned out to be Weaver's wife) would lead to fresh trouble.

"Way Tad figured it," Poke explained, the whiskey he'd guzzled not only dulling his pain but also loosening his tongue, "was that a squaw who'd been claimed from her tribe for the trade of a broke-down old mule and a sack of flour and some blankets ought to be short-time available for the trade of a little cash."

"Well he figured wrong!" Weaver had snapped back. But Lone's gut instinct immediately sensed this display of indignation was somehow lacking.

"Yeah, I guess that knife rip to his guts finally made it plain," Poke said mournfully. "I just wish you or your squaw would've got the message across one of those other times when Tad offered you money—before he decided to go ahead today and try forcing the matter."

Right after that, from the combination of pain, blood loss, and the copious amount of whiskey he'd consumed, Poke passed out. This made it easier for Lone to finish digging the slug and most of its fragments from the wound. It also pretty much ended any further conversation. Although Weaver did seem anxious to add, "What he said about me trading to get Minowi from her tribe is true. But it's also true that me and her were legally married by a preacher in town."

"Your business, mister. None of mine," Lone told him. Yet at the same time he couldn't help thinking, *If she's your wife, pal, you might try showing her a little tenderness after what she just went through* . . . But then again, what did he know about how to treat a wife, or any woman, for that matter.

Lone was almost done stitching shut Poke's wound when, from off in the distance to the west, there sounded a breathy, drawn-out train whistle. Weaver went rigid in the station doorway. "Holy shit," he exclaimed. "That's the Thursday eastbound out of Cheyenne. In all this excitement, I plumb forgot it was due. What's more,"—this as he produced a pocket watch and flipped it open to check the time—"it's running nearly an hour late. That's not good, that never happens! Oh man, what else can go wrong this day?"

As it turned out, plenty else.

Before the train arrived, however, a strange thing happened. As if animated by the sound of the whistle, Minowi abruptly ended her statue-like stillness and rose smoothly to her feet. Without the slightest glance down at the blanket-shrouded form of the man she had knifed, she came striding purposefully back toward the station. Nor did her gaze touch on Lone, Poke, or her husband, who watched her approach looking surprised and a bit dumbfounded. Brushing past him in order to step through the doorway, she said tonelessly, "I should make preparations in case there are passengers."

Lone noted her English seemed quite precise.

When the train whistle sounded again, drawing closer, Weaver shook off his dumbfounded expression and frowned first in the direction of the whistle and then cut it in closer to the body lying off one end of the hitch rail. "Jesus," he muttered. "If there *are* passengers on the train, I sure hate for them to have to step off and be faced with an upsettin' sight like that."

Finished with his stitching of Poke's wound, Lone straightened up with a grunt. "Think how Tad feels about bein' the one presentin' it to 'em."

Weaver shot him a sidelong glance. "That ain't funny."

"Wasn't meant to be. Ain't a damn thing funny about any of this." After wiping it off with one of the cloths he'd been provided, Lone re-sheathed his Bowie and then leaned over to drop Minowi's knife and the thread and needles back into the frying pan now lying on the ground beside where he'd been working. "But while we ain't got time to do anything as far as Tad," he continued, "that don't mean we can't at least get Poke here a little better situated. If you'll give me a hand, how about we get him up and inside out of the sun? For a little while, anyway. Once that train finishes its water stop and gets rollin' again, it represents the means to get him hauled to a doctor in Ogallala, somebody better suited to follow up on the patch job I did."

"Yeah. Yeah, that's a good idea," the station man agreed eagerly.

Him and Lone got Poke partially revived and up on his feet, supporting him on each side, being as careful as possible out of consideration for the

24

damaged shoulder. Inside, they seated him on a wooden chair with his back and shoulders leaned against an inner wall. Having him propped in this position, Lone bandaged the awkwardly-located wound as best he could and then knotted a towel at the back of Poke's neck and fashioned a sling to stabilize the arm. All during this, a groggy but grateful Poke insisted on thanking him repeatedly, until Lone threatened to knock him unconscious again if he didn't shut up.

When he was finally done playing doctor, Lone went back out front to where he'd left Ironsides tied at the hitch rail. As directed by a thumb jerk from Weaver, Lone led the big gray around one end of the building to where he found a hand pump and a wooden watering trough. While Ironsides drank from the trough, Lone worked the pump handle with one hand and scooped palmfuls of cool, clean water to his mouth with the other. Once his thirst had been slaked, he removed his hat, stuck his head under the pump snout, and pumped several more gushes of cold water onto the back of his neck until he felt reasonably refreshed and revitalized. After wiping his face with his bandanna and finger-combing his sopping hair back atop his head and above his ears, he replaced his hat and took Ironsides over to the greenest patch of grass he saw anywhere close by and left him to graze.

By the time Lone got back around to the front

of the station building, the incoming train had rolled in, reaching a clattering, hissing, steel-on-steel screeching halt with the engine positioned with practiced precision under the filling spout of the water tower. But it was quickly evident that taking on water wasn't the most pressing concern for anyone at the moment.

As Lone strode forward, he saw the engineer and fireman scramble hurriedly down from the massive Baldwin locomotive and approach the waiting Simon Weaver, jabbering and waving their arms excitedly. Weaver had positioned himself in front of Tad's body as if to shield it somewhat and blunt the reaction of anyone arriving on the train when they inevitably spotted it. But the two trainmen, as they continued their approach, were far more focused on relating whatever it was that had them so worked up. Lone was close enough to catch a smattering of their words and that's all he needed to hear to understand their agitation.

"Coming around that blind curve this side of Washerman's Gully . . . Hit us when we were pullin' our slowest on account of toppin' the grade. Made it easy for 'em to force us to stop . . . It was Dar Pierce and his bunch, no doubt about it. Him and that flame-haired witch Harriet Bell, ridin' right in the thick of 'em and readiest of all to spill the blood of anybody who didn't cooperate!"

For the past year and more, Lone knew, the Pierce Gang had been robbing and generally raising hell throughout north central Nebraska and southern South Dakota. Between strikes, they would lay low and avoid capture by disappearing into the barren, trackless Dakota Badlands. Until just recently, Lone had read only a few days ago in a Denver newspaper, when a posse of federal marshals had finally flushed them and driven them south, believing to be headed back to the lawless Oklahoma Indian Territory that initially spawned them. If it was truly Pierce's pack of curly wolves who had hit this train, then they indeed appeared to be headed south. If so, that might be good news for the places they left behind . . . But still potentially bad news—as witnessed by this current encounter—for anywhere they passed through on their way.

CHAPTER 4

When the results of the train robbery were tallied up, it amounted to the five gang members making off with the following: from the freight cars, five sacks of mail, six horses, eight bags of grain, one case of canned peaches, and one of canned beef. From the passengers and crew members, between four and five hundred dollars in cash, various personal items such as watches, cuff links, and a few odds and ends in the way of jewelry; plus a pair of shiny new boots that specifically caught the eye of Harriet Bell. Additionally, the gang confiscated four gun belts and accompanying pistols, five repeating rifles, and ten boxes of cartridges, mostly .44 caliber.

A further toll was taken on the persons of two individuals. A foolishly brave young brakeman was shot and killed when he made the mistake of drawing a gun on the attackers. A middle-aged businessman was only wounded, taking a slug to the meaty part of his thigh when he tried to resist giving up a family heirloom found in his travel bag.

All of this was recounted by the folks who'd been directly involved, excepting for the dead brakeman of course, as they were ushered from the train into the station building. Inasmuch as there were six passengers plus the engineer and fireman, this made for rather crowded conditions once everyone was gathered inside the public area of the station building. It also made quite a noisy scene considering how everybody was anxious to give their own version of what had happened, all at the same time. It fell to the engineer to get the throng settled down and bring things to a semblance of order, promising that each would be given a turn to speak and advising that the briefer they kept this stop the better. The sooner they made their already overdue arrival in Ogallala, he reminded them, the sooner they could tell their ordeal again and a posse would be formed to ride out with the goal of trying to right the wrongs that had been suffered.

During all of this, a quiet, somber-faced Minowi moved among the new arrivals serving biscuits and cups of either coffee or freshly-pumped cold water. No one had an appetite or wanted to take the time for anything more to eat than the biscuits.

Lone would have gladly been an exception to this, if given the opportunity. (And he still fully *did* intend to have some grub before leaving.) But first, the opportunity—for lack of a better word—presented to him instead was getting urged to have a look at the passenger with the bullet hole in his thigh; this due to the skills he'd shown treating Poke.

The former scout didn't have much choice but to grudgingly agree. As he directed the wounded man over to take a seat on one side of the room, thinking it best to gain a measure of separation from the others until he saw how bad the wound was, it occurred to Lone that the robbery in general and this wounded man in particular was for the moment at least blurring the previous incident involving Tad Clemson. When the folks from the train had filed past the blanket-shrouded body and then noted bandaged-up Poke on the inside, Weaver's terse explanation of, "We had our own spot of trouble here a little while ago," was sufficient for them to continue focusing mainly on their more personal concerns.

The patient was named Roy Whitlock, a tall, sturdy man not too far into his fifties, with flecks of gray at his temples and a steely kind of gray showing in his eyes. He ran a freighting company out of Cheyenne, he told Lone, and was on his way to Omaha for the wedding of his only daughter. There were two other men traveling with him, both of them hovering close as Lone knelt to examine the wound. One of the hoverers Whitlock introduced as his son Peter, who showed a good deal of resemblance to his dad, though not with near the steel in his gray eyes, but with a thick head of dark brown hair and a squarer cut to his jawline. The second man was a somewhat older gent, looking to have a few years on Whitlock, also tall and sturdy in build with squinted eyes set deep in a weather-seamed face. When the freighter introduced him as Jeth Howard, his lead teamster, the name caused Lone to do a double take.

"That's right," Howard said, grinning crookedly as Lone's gaze lifted and settled on him. "I was wondering when those eagle eyes of yourn might get around to recognizin' me."

"You two know each other?" Whitlock asked.

"Been a spell, but we sure did at one time," Howard replied. "That was back in the days when I was teamsterin' in an army uniform, deliverin' goods to posts back and forth along the Nebraska–Kansas line. Lone here was a civilian scout advisin' us on the safest routes to take to keep from gettin' porky-pined by Injun arrows. My hair is thinned considerable these days, all on its own—but hadn't been for Lone, there's a good chance the whole works woulda got lifted a long time back by some redskin scalpin' knife."

Whitlock's brows lifted. "In that case, I guess I'm doubly obliged to Mr. McGantry. First, for his attention to this blasted bullet hole of mine. Second, for past service keeping your hide intact so you were around to be the friend and top teamster boss I needed to make a go of my freight business."

Lone showed an exaggeratedly dubious expression. "Now hold on a minute. I'll own up to

31

whatever help I can be with this wound. But from what I recall about Sergeant Howard's rowdy ways back when, I ain't so sure I want to be held accountable for any share in keepin' his ornery ol' hide intact."

There was a short beat, and then Lone and the two older men broke into a good chuckle over the rebuttal. Whitlock's son Peter, however, clearly didn't see any humor in the moment. "Shouldn't we," he said, "be taking my father's injury more seriously?"

"Calm down, son," Whitlock was quick to say. "Nobody's saying this thing is a joke, but neither is it going to claim your old man's life. I haven't had a lot of experience with bullet wounds, thank the Lord, but even I know that much. It hurts like hell, but I also know the slug passed all the way through and that's a good thing."

"Don't know as I'd call anything about gettin' shot a 'good thing,' " Lone allowed as he undid the loose cloth wrap around Whitlock's thigh and then spread open the already slit trouser fabric underneath. This revealed a second bandage, tighter-wrapped directly on flesh, with some blood seepage showing. When this was removed Lone was able to examine the pair of ragged holes that marked the path of the bullet, entry and exit. There was some bruising and smeared blood around both. Also a gob of freshly chewed tobacco had been pressed over each one.

Lone looked up at Jeth Howard. "Your doin'?"

Jeth nodded. "Seen it done that way more'n once. Can't say it always worked, but I never saw it harm."

"Either way, if you ask me it's certainly a disgusting practice," stated Peter.

"Your opinion aside," Lone told him, "it's like Jeth said—when it's what you got to work with, it's something been done plenty. When it starts to dry, the tobacco acts like a poultice to help draw out any start of infection. In fact, since that's already done and there's no lead to dig out and no sign of fresh bleedin' or that the bullet hit bone, I'm inclined to say just re-wrap the leg with a clean bandage and leave it be until you get to a real doctor in Ogallala."

"I'm okay with that," said Whitlock. "Don't expect me to insist on more poking and prodding if you think it's not necessary."

Lone pursed his mouth. "I reckon you ain't seen the end of that, not when the doc gets hold of you. But it can wait 'til then, like I said. For now, I'm just gonna—"

Lone stopped, suddenly aware of a new presence having moved in close behind where he knelt beside Whitlock. Glancing up and around, he found Minowi standing there holding out some folds of clean cloth. "You will need these to re-bandage the wound," she said quietly.

Reaching for the fresh wraps, Lone realized

33

he and the Indian girl were exchanging direct looks for the first time. Though her expression remained impassive, he saw that her facial features were softer, prettier than he'd noticed before and there was a depth and intensity to her dark eyes that was almost startling. He thanked her and she drifted silently off again.

By the time Lone was done re-dressing Whitlock's leg, the mood elsewhere in the station had begun to change. The three other train passengers—an elderly couple on their way to visit the woman's sister in North Platte, and a failed prospector on his way back to the family farm somewhere in Iowa—were getting restless to be on their way again. A heightened degree of anxiousness seemed to be part of this, lingering effects from their own violent encounter with the robbers and now a growing awareness of the added violence that had taken place here. An unavoidable reminder of this was the wounded Poke, seated right among them, not to mention the body of the dead man they'd all walked past outside.

What was more, the engineer and the brakeman were faced off with Weaver, taking issue over a matter, and doing so in increasingly raised voices. When Lone walked over to them, he came up in time to hear the engineer stating flatly, "No way in hell! I don't want any part of gettin' caught up in how Ira Clemson is apt to react when he hears about his boy bein' kilt."

"How are you going to get caught up in anything bad?" Weaver argued. "You'll be doing a kindness by delivering the body to town like I'm asking. It's what Ira is bound to want, seeing his boy is taken to the undertaker and prepared properly for burial."

"Maybe so, maybe not," countered the engineer, a sawed-off, red-whiskered Irishman by the name of O'Gill. "But the only thing Clemson's more famous for than his fiery temper is his fierce loyalty to that wild-ass brat kid of his. There's no way of tellin' how what's happened here is gonna set him off. The safest way is for a body to stay all the way clear from any of it, and that's what I full intend to do! For the sake of myself, my passengers, and my whole blasted train, I refuse to get involved."

"What about the other hombre—the big fella sittin' over yonder with the patched-up shoulder?" Lone wanted to know.

"What about him?" O'Gill came back.

"He was ridin' with the Clemson kid and took a bullet tryin' to protect him. His shoulder is messed up kinda bad and he's lost a lot of blood. He needs to see a doctor even worse than your passenger Whitlock. You'll at least haul *him* into town for that purpose, won't you?"

O'Gill appeared to waver. But only for a moment. Then, with a firm shake of his head, he said, "No! It's all part of the same business and I won't risk steppin' into it. If I bother with that big oaf, Ira might decide to take it wrong that I *didn't* do the same for his son. I repeat, way I see it the smartest choice is to stay out of this mess altogether and that's what I mean to do."

Roy Whitlock, who had wandered over along with his son and Jeth Howard, spoke up. "Good God, man. Anybody can see that big fellow is suffering and needs medical attention."

O'Gill's face was turning bright red. "I'm sorry for that. But I had nothing to do with putting the bullet in him so it's not my problem."

"It's not ours either, Father. No need for us to get involved," said Peter Whitlock.

"Besides," O'Gill added, "there are saddled horses out front. I'm guessin' one of 'em belongs to the big fella. If he can sit up in a chair, then he oughta be able to sit his saddle. Town ain't that far, let him take his own self in on horseback."

"You're all heart," growled Lone.

Ignoring him, O'Gill turned to his fireman and said, "Go on out and tend to putting some water in that boiler, Smitty. I'll be along with our passengers—and *only* our passengers—in just a minute. We're already shamefully behind schedule through no fault of ours, I'll not be adding to it by wasting time listening to any more useless wailing."

"You'll damned well hear some more of my

36

wailing when I report this to the railroad, O'Gill," declared Weaver, his own face reddening. "You're a lily-livered disgrace to the company!"

The sawed-off Irishman dismissed him with a wave of one hand and turned to address his passengers. He'd scarcely started to speak, however, before he was interrupted by a wide-eyed Smitty bursting back in through the front door.

"Somebody had better come see this. There's three cowboys out front gathered around that dead man under the blanket, and they're mighty worked up . . . I think there's going to be trouble!"

CHAPTER 5

When Weaver turned back from looking out the window, his previously anger-flushed face had gone chalky white. "Hell's luck," he groaned. "I recognize all three of those men. They ride for Ira Clemson's C-Bar brand. They've lifted the blanket and seen who it is laying there . . . This ain't gonna be good. Not at all."

"You knew that sooner or later you were gonna have to face the music for what happened here. So now the tune has started playin'," Lone told him. "You need to go out there and 'front those rannies. Whatever mood they're in, you don't want 'em bringin' it in here among these other folks."

Weaver's eyes darted around. He licked his lips. Then, cutting his gaze back to Lone, he said, "Will you go out there with me? You can't claim you ain't already bought into a piece of this."

Lone released a ragged sigh through clenched teeth. "No, damn my lousy luck, I reckon I can't," he allowed. His right hand made a slight brushing motion at his side, flicking the keeper thong off the hammer of his holstered Colt. Glancing over his shoulder, he saw Minowi watching him from across the room where she stood in front of a heavy blanket hung ceiling-to-floor for the sake of sectioning off a cramped living quarters. Facing the front door again and taking a step toward it, the former scout said to Weaver, "Come on, let's go see what these C-Bar boys have got to say."

Outside, the sun was starting to drop in the sky and taking on a hint of reddish-orange color. The air was heavy-feeling and still, tinged with the stink of coal smoke from the locomotive. The afternoon's heat was hovering at its peak.

As Lone and Weaver emerged from the station, the three cowboys stepped back from Tad's body and fanned out some. The blanket had been smoothed back into place.

Lone's eyes swept in a quick assessment of the trio. All three wore gun belts. The accompanying hoglegs on two of them hung in well-worn holsters at just the right height for an easy downward swing of their gun hand, and each held his body in a way that suggested he had some familiarity with reaching for iron. The third, the youngest, was strapped with a newer-looking rig, the leather of the holster appearing still a little stiff and hitched up a bit too high for a smooth draw. If trouble came, he'd be the least worry, but that hardly meant he should be discounted entirely.

Standing in the middle, a muscular, cold-eyed individual with a tangle of oily black hair on full display due to his hat resting back on his shoulder blades, suspended there on a chin string, was the first to speak. "What the hell's the deal here, Weaver? Do you have any idea how much trouble you're in?"

"Now hold on a minute, Edgers. That wasn't my doing," Weaver was quick to object.

"Who then?"

"W-wait a minute now," Weaver stammered. "What you gotta understand is that Tad came 'round all liquored up and looking for more to drink . . . Everybody in the territory knows how he could be when he was liquored up and on the prod. Right?"

"The only thing we know for sure—the only thing that's gonna matter the only place it counts, and that's to the boy's pa—is Tad Clemson is layin' here dead from a knife slash to his gut." This came from the hombre standing off to Edgers' right. He had a wedge-shaped face with sharply carved features and, set deep and close on either side of a hawk's beak nose, eyes squinted so narrow they themselves bore a resemblance to knife slashes. Continuing, he said, "So, since all of it is on display right at your front door, Station Man, how is it none of your doing?"

Weaver looked desperately over at Lone. "Say something. Tell them what happened."

"I'll tell you what happened!" came a slurred voice from behind Lone and Weaver. Lone recognized immediately who it was. There was no need to look around, nor did he dare take his eyes off the C-Bar men in front of him anyway. A second later it didn't matter because the lumbering form of Poke Rafferty bulled between Lone and Weaver and went staggering toward the three cowboys. He only made it part way, though, before his knees buckled and he toppled heavily to the ground. He twisted so as not to land on his injured shoulder, but the jarring impact still sent a jolt of pain through him, causing him to cry out in agony. "I'm hurt bad, fellas! That big sonofabitch shot me and busted my shoulder to hell and gone!"

That was nearly enough to trigger a full-out blaze of gunfire. Hands dropped and fingers curled into claws, ready to wrap around pistol grips. But then came a throaty roar that split the air and shook the ground like a thunderclap. All motion froze.

Until a raspy voice spoke from the station doorway, warning loud and clear, "That was one barrel aimed at the sky. Any of you three brush-poppers make a wrong twitch, the next load will cut somebody half in two!"

Once again Lone recognized the voice behind him. At least he thought he did. But this time he couldn't hold back from risking a quick look around to make sure and to try and comprehend more fully what had just happened. Sure enough, there in the station doorway, visible through

41

the powder smoke haze of the half-discharged double-barrel shotgun he continued to hold thrust out before him, was none other than Jeth Howard. Where the blaster had come from (though it was later revealed to have been snatched down from where it was hung over the front door inside the station), Lone didn't know or care—he was just glad the old teamster had gotten his hands on it.

Snapping his face back around, Lone raked a scowl across the C-Bar men, still half-poised like bobcats with their hackles up (much as he also was). He said, "This can go either way, boys. You can try finishin' what you were ready to start, lettin' this fat slob egg you on without hearin' the full story . . . Or we can all calm down and not be in a hurry to add more killin' and bloodshed."

The youngest cowboy, the fresh-faced one with his gun hitched too high and a nervous tick tugging at the corner of his left eye, couldn't resist trying to put on a brave, tough act for his more veteran pals. "That's mighty big talk," he sneered, "comin' from a sorry-assed drifter heeled with one wore out lookin' hogleg and only one live shotgun round to back his play against the three of us."

"And you sound like just another snot-nose in a hurry to die," Lone chuffed. "Better check with your buddies, though, if you're thinkin' about settin' things back in motion. Since you're a green nub posin' the least worry, they're the ones me and the shotgun load will aim to cut down first if we're forced to do some ranny harvestin'."

"God damn it, Robby—shut your mouth and don't do nothing stupid!" barked the one called Edgers.

But from where he lay in the dirt, Rafferty wasn't ready to stay quiet. Shoving up on the elbow of his good arm, he wailed, "It was the girl! It was Weaver's damn squaw who knifed Tad. McGantry plugged me when I tried to help."

Edgers branded Lone with a hard glare. "That the way of it?"

Lone's return gaze was unflinching. "All except for the minor detail of it bein' self-defense in each case. The girl did what she did only after Tad knocked her down and tried to stomp her when she wouldn't play the whore for him. Me, I shot Tubby when he went for his gun . . . Oh yeah, and much to my regret the way he's actin' now, I also patched the ungrateful slob up and kept him from bleedin' to death."

Nobody said anything more for a long, tense beat. Gradually, however, hackles began to smooth back down.

Finally, Edgers said, "I reckon we can hold off pushin' this any harder for the time being. You should know, though, that the final say is gonna come from Ira Clemson. I'll leave it up to him to make his own call. But, self-defense or no, was I you or that squaw . . . I wouldn't count on it bein' over. Not by a long shot."

"Okay. You gave your message," Lone replied tightly. "Now here's one from me you can take back to your boss. Tell Clemson if he has any business he wants to take up with me, he can find me in Ogallala. Soon as this train rolls again, I'll be takin' it that far. When I get there, I'll be givin' a full statement on all of this to the marshal."

The wedge-faced cowboy issued a disdainful snort. "That Ogallala marshal ain't got no jurisdiction this far out. And, even if he did, it don't mean Ira'd be of any mind to give a damn. He'll do what *he* decides needs doin', no matter."

Lone's mouth pulled into a straight, tight line. "In that case, I don't see nothing left to say here. Time for you fellas to gather up your dead and wounded and take Ira's boy home to him so he can commence his decidin'."

CHAPTER 6

The year and a half since Lone had last seen Cliff Halsey appeared to have aged the man more than just the calendar-measured length of time. He was still basically clean cut and what most would consider handsome, but the harder lines worn into his face, the flecks of gray at his temples, and the stiffened way he moved his upper body due to a past shoulder injury were notable all the same. Lone's guess was that the marshal's badge now pinned to his shirt front—in place of the deputy star formerly worn there—told most of the story on these changes. Nothing could take a toll on a man, an honest one, like representing the law and keeping the peace in a rowdy cowtown. And while Ogallala was considerably tamer than in its heyday when it was known as "the Gomorrah of the Plains," it still had a ways to go before laying claim to being all the way tamed.

Nevertheless, Lone had been glad to find Halsey parked behind the desk in the marshal's office when he got to town that evening. Inasmuch as their past dealings had ended on a positive note, he figured the lawman's feelings toward him were likewise. At first, anyway. As Lone got into his reasons for coming by, however, the lines in the marshal's face began pulling steadily tighter and deeper.

45

Nor did it help any when Simon Weaver, who'd insisted on accompanying Lone, tossed in his two cents' worth.

Into the pause that came when everything had been laid out, Halsey rocked back in his chair and said, "Let me make sure I've absorbed all of this cheerful news you two have brought me . . . For starters, you're saying I need to consider that the Dar Pierce Gang is somewhere in the vicinity west of here and they hit the eastbound out of Cheyenne, which caused it to roll in so late."

Weaver's head bobbed. "That's right. Hit it, robbed it, killed the brakeman and wounded one of the passengers."

"Why ain't O'Gill in here telling me that part himself?"

"He's down at the telegraph office getting a wire off to the railroad," Weaver explained. "One of your deputies is there taking a statement from him. O'Gill says that will have to do until he comes back through again. He's wantin' to get the train rolling again right away in order to try and make up some lost time."

Halsey grunted. "There's one for the book. O'Gill not wanting to stick around and talk everybody's ear off, especially when he's got a tale like the robbery of his train to carry on about."

"I'm thinking that the push to get back on schedule is only part of it," Weaver said smugly.

"I'm thinking that not wantin' to be caught lagging in town when Ira Clemson shows up breathin' fire over what happened to his son also figures into the Irish runt's motives."

The marshal cocked one eyebrow. "Can't say as I blame him. I'd as soon not be around for that, either."

"But you *have* to be," Weaver insisted. "Among other things, you need to protect me from Ira's vengeance. That's why I left the station and came on into town."

"Why should you be so worried about Ira's wrath?" Halsey wanted to know. "According to everything you and Lone just told me, you never laid a hand on anybody. It was your woman Minowi who planted the blade in Tad."

"That's just it. She's *my* woman—my *squaw*." Weaver's tone grew strained, distraught. "Don't you see? Ira gets that temper of his fired up, I'll get blamed as being the one responsible for her. He's apt to take a notion I should pay for that— especially now that she's gone and took off!"

Halsey frowned. "That part kinda bothers me. If she's so innocent, if she used that knife in self-defense, why did she run away?"

"Come on, Cliff. For Christ's sake," said Lone, twisting his mouth sourly. "You think that gal don't know everybody sees her as nothing but a lowly squaw? Her own husband just now called her that. How could she help but figure that if the

47

high and mighty Ira Clemson came gunnin' for her she wouldn't stand a snowball's chance in Hell? And, since she *is* just a squaw, who'd give much of a damn over anything that did happen to her?"

All of this was in reference to the fact that, back at the watering station, while everyone else was focused on the confrontation with the C-Bar cowboys who'd shown up, Minowi had slipped away and disappeared. Her absence wasn't discovered until after Edgers and the others had ridden off, taking the wounded Rafferty and Tad's body with them. Once it was determined that the girl was nowhere to be found and apparently had left of her own accord, O'Gill insisted the train had to make its departure and anyone wanting to leave with it had better get aboard. In keeping with his stated intent to go make a statement to the law in Ogallala, Lone had coaxed Ironsides into a freight car and the two of them had joined the ranks of rail riders. The cowardly Weaver came along, too, abandoning the station out of fear of getting caught there alone in case any more C-Bar men returned looking for trouble.

Responding now to Lone's assessment of why Minowi had taken flight, Marshal Halsey said somewhat indignantly, "If that girl brought herself anywhere into my jurisdiction, me and my deputies would do everything we could to keep her safe, same as anybody."

"I know you would," Lone allowed. "But that don't mean Minowi believes it. And considerin' how most other folks might feel, no matter how hard you and your deputies tried to look out for her, I'd have to say she has every right to be wary."

The marshal sighed. "Yeah. I guess, in her shoes, I'd probably feel the same." He turned his attention to Weaver. "Where do you figure she ran off to? Back to her people?"

" 'Spect so. I got her at the Sioux rez up north. Ain't like she's got any friends or knows hardly anybody else hereabouts but me."

"You going after her?"

Weaver made a face. "Not likely. Apart from all this other business, she was a poor bargain right from the get-go. She could cook and clean okay, but when it came to other wifely . . . Well, never mind. The short answer is no, I ain't gonna do no chasing. Good riddance, I say, if not for the damn target she left painted on my back."

"What about your obligations at the watering station?" Halsey asked. "You just gonna leave them go?"

"I am until this business with Clemson is done and I can feel reasonably safe out there," Weaver replied. "I'll wire my boss at the railroad first thing in the morning to let him know what's going on. In the meantime, I'm sticking right here in town and counting on you to—"

"Yeah, yeah, I heard your tune the first time you sang it," the marshal interrupted irritably. "What I said about the Injun girl goes for anybody not purposely courtin' trouble in my town— it's the job of me and my deputies to keep 'em from harm. That goes for you, too, Weaver. But it don't mean I ain't got plenty else to do other than babysit one person. So part of staying out of trouble is your own responsibility."

"Don't worry about that. I aim to check into a hotel and not leave my room unless absolutely necessary," the station man assured him.

Halsey's eyes came to settle on Lone. "I know blasted well how hard it is for *you* to steer clear of trouble . . . Though sometimes, I gotta admit, for the better."

The previous encounter between Lone and Halsey had been a complex matter involving Lone first being responsible for the death of the then deputy's wrong-headed younger brother before an ironic twist of events led to the former scout rescuing Halsey's young son from a gang of ruthless kidnappers. The feelings this left between the two men was conveyed now in a brief pause filled with meaningful eye contact but minus any further words on the subject, each knowing there was no need to delve into it any deeper, certainly not in front of Weaver.

Halsey nevertheless did have the need to press Lone more on the current situation, saying, "So?

50

Are you planning on sticking around town?"

"I don't intend to run on account of Ira Clemson, if that's what you mean. But neither," Lone told him, "am I inclined to let my personal plans be interrupted for an undue amount of time waitin' to see if he has any grievance with me. I gave his men fair notice I was coming here to make an official statement on what happened at the watering station. I've made it. I figure that's all I owe anybody."

"You said you were originally on your way to North Platte. That right?"

"Uh-huh."

"I heard you eventually caught up with those varmints who raided your ranch and killed your partner. Up in Deadwood, wasn't it?"

"Uh-huh," Lone said again. "Ran afoul of a few other things in between, and this is my first time back this way. In North Platte, I got a couple matters to settle as far as that burnt-out old ranch and so forth. Then I'll need to decide what path lays ahead of me from there."

Halsey eyed him. "Let's hope your path don't end here."

Lone met his gaze. "Clemson throw that big a shadow?"

"He ain't to be taken lightly, that's for sure. He's powerful, he's mean, and more than a few of the men riding for his brand are as handy with a six-gun as a lasso." The marshal puffed out

51

his cheeks, exhaled. "But the main worry about this current situation is that Ira's always acted like the sun rises and sets in the no-good ass of that spoiled brat kid of his . . . How he'll react to Tad being killed, God only knows. It could crush him, break his heart and grind him down to nothing. I've sometimes seen strong men suffer a loss and have that happen to 'em . . . But I don't think anybody will see that from Ira. More like he'll take his heartbreak and pain and turn it back tenfold on anybody and everybody he can!"

"Jesus," murmured Weaver. "Now you're making me think it ain't even safe for me here in town. Maybe Minowi had the right idea taking off. Maybe I oughta try to catch O'Gill's train and ride it as far away from here as it will take me!"

Halsey shrugged fatalistically. "Maybe you should at that . . . But if you do stick around, I've got a hunch that all of us are going to find out plenty quick what Ira's reaction will turn out to be."

CHAPTER 7

In a shallow, grassy canyon just north of the settlement of Lodgepole, Dar Pierce took a final drag from his cigarette and then flipped the smoldering butt into the nearby campfire. At forty-five, Pierce's once handsome face was aged beyond his years. Nearly three decades of hard living and hard riding, much of it spent in harsh conditions while dodging one posse or another after forays outside the law that generally yielded takes more meager than planned, had taken their toll. Only when he smiled, which was rare, was there a hint of the rake-hell good looks from his younger days.

Pierce wasn't exactly smiling this evening, yet there was a certain smugness to his expression that came close. Close enough, at any rate, for the woman seated on the grass across the fire from him to comment, "You look like the cat who swallowed the canary."

"I don't know about no canary," Pierce replied, a corner of his mouth actually managing to curve upward a bit. "But that heated up canned beef and those peaches we got off that train sure are sitting easy in my gut. Best grub we've had in weeks."

"I can't argue with that," agreed Harriet Bell. At half Pierce's age, she, too, had been riding the owlhoot trail long enough for some hard lines to be set in her face. But there was still enough natural prettiness showing through to make them negligible, especially in the soft, pulsing glow of the firelight. Also captured and highlighted by that same glow was the thick mane of red hair that spilled about her face and shone like a ruby halo. Though to anyone in the know, Harriet's history from her owlhoot days hardly rated a halo.

Jorge Bandros, one of three men seated with Pierce and Harriet around the fire—a fair-skinned Mexican with a broad, flat face, a toothy smile, and deep blue eyes signaling the mixed blood that also accounted for his lighter complexion—chuckled knowingly. "Si. Good food, a full stomach, and a warm fire are always pleasing things. But let us not forget the most pleasing thing of all that the train and its generous passengers provided us. Money."

Beside Bandros sat a hulking man with a battered mug and one cauliflower ear testifying to time spent in his early years as a bare-knuckled boxer. During the same period, it was a shaggy, still present mop of golden blond hair that earned him the name he continued to go by to this day—"Goldy" Grissom. Responding to Bandros' remark, Grissom said, "Yeah, that train haul was bigger than any of us was counting on, that's true enough. Especially coming on it unexpected-

54

like, the way we did, and catching it chugging so invitingly slow up that grade."

"You can wet your pants over a few hundred bucks and some trinkets if you like," said the remaining man, a compact individual with seen-it-all-before eyes and a wide, full-lipped mouth perpetually drooped with indifference. A half-smoked cigarette presently hung from one corner of this mouth, bobbing up and down as he talked. "But the real truth," he continued, "is that today's haul was a mighty paltry one compared to times past. And everybody here knows it."

Pierce eyed him through smoke rising up from the campfire. "What's your point, Caldwell? You think any of us need reminding that we'd fallen on some hard luck and hard times up there in the Dakotas even before those federal hounds ran us off from what little stash we had in the Badlands? Does any good ever come from crying over spilt milk? Or is it you're trying to work up the gumption to suggest you're better suited—back then, or maybe going forward—to run this outfit smarter and better? Is that it?"

Caldwell appeared to take the challenge in stride. "Pull in you spurs, Dar. I wasn't suggesting nothing of the kind. My only point was that I don't want to see us get too complacent about these poor pay-offs. Yeah, we had a string of getting snakebit up in the Dakotas and yeah stumbling on that train out in the middle of nowhere and getting the decent haul we did was a stroke of good luck. I say we take that as an omen that our luck in general is starting to change. And since it's a long stretch before we get back on home ground in the Territory, what else I'm saying is that we should keep our eyes peeled for something bigger and better to hit on the way."

"Well hell, ain't we always on the lookout for a bigger and better haul? Don't that go without saying?" grunted Grissom.

"Of course," Caldwell conceded. "But since we'll be traveling through areas unfamiliar to us, it means we'll have to look a little sharper in order to spot any opportunities."

Bandros frowned. "But don't we want to keep moving at a pretty strong pace? For all we know there could be some of those Federales from up north still on our tail. Maybe even some kind of local posse will form to come after us on account of the train robbery we just pulled. With these extra horses we're now pulling along with us, we're leaving a mighty plain trail."

Harriet Bell rolled her eyes. "If you mental giants would take the time to ask and listen, instead of trying to think for yourselves and then yammering from the strain, you might find out that Dar already has some plans worked out to cover what we should do between here and the Territory."

Grissom scowled. "That right, Dar? You got something cooking?"

"If so, when were you going to get around to sharing it with us?" Caldwell wanted to know.

Pierce cast a somewhat annoyed glance in Harriet's direction. Then: "I was waiting until I had a few more details worked out. But since you're all so anxious, I'll tell you what I got . . . For starters, Jorge makes some good points about us needing to keep on the move because those damn feds are possibly still dogging us. That's what I hate about this flat stinking country around here—a person can be seen from miles away and there are blasted few spots, like we had in the Badlands, to duck out of sight. And yet they even found us there. Eventually."

"But that cuts both ways, right? About this flat country, I mean," said Grissom. "We can see a long way, too. And, believe me, I been watching our back trail awful tight. So far I ain't seen no bothersome sign."

"Nor have I. But keeping a sharp watch is something we all need to continue doing," Pierce advised. "As far as a fresh posse forming on account of that train hit, I don't think there's too much worry there. According to this map I got, the closest town is Ogallala, too far off to the east to even have any jurisdiction. If they *did* put something together, maybe at the urging of the railroad, they'd be at least a full day behind."

57

"But there's still all these extra horses we're pulling," insisted Bandros. "Like I said before, they make us mighty easy to track. Even after a day or so."

"Which is one of the reasons we're going to be getting rid of 'em soon," said Pierce. "Any of you ever hear of somebody called The 'Bino?" When he got nothing but blank stares, he continued. "I don't know his actual name—hell, I don't think anybody does. Maybe not even him after all this time. But he's a for-real albino, see. White as a bottle of milk from head to toe. What he also is is a trader, a buyer and seller of the kind of goods you ain't able to deal for just anywhere, if you get what I mean."

"So you figure he'll buy the spare horses?"

"I'm certain he will. The rifles, pistols, gun belts, and trinkets we've got to offer as well. It'll be at a marked-down price, naturally, due to how we acquired 'em. But it should still add a tidy sum to our traveling poke."

"You make whatever kind of deal you want," Harriet said. "But these new boots I got off that brakeman Jorge shot and killed, and this brooch I'm wearing that that other old fool took a bullet trying to hang on to—I'm claiming them for my own."

Pierce waved a hand. "Be my guest. Those boots are too small for everybody here, including you. You keep wearing 'em, you'll be hobbling worse than an old man in a day or two. And that brooch or stickpin or whatever you call it, will likely turn your skin green even sooner."

"Well it's my feet and my skin," Harriet stated with finality.

"So where do we find this 'Bino?" Grissom asked.

"About a day's ride from here. I want to head out first thing in the morning, as soon as we finish sorting through the rest of those mail sacks in order to cull out anything more of value they might hold. We'll have to cut into a corner of Colorado to get to our man."

"So then we'll follow the edge of Colorado south from there?"

"Not necessarily. Not if The 'Bino is able to confirm something for me." Pierce pulled out the makings for a fresh cigarette and began fashioning one. "You see, as I recall from when we passed a ways east of here on our way first up into the Dakotas, there was a town over near the Nebraska-Kansas border by the name of McCook where a railroad was just coming in. I don't have to tell you what a place turning into a rail head means. Growth and money. And surely a bank or two."

"I'm starting to like the sound of this," said Caldwell.

"Figured you would." Pierce hung the quirley from his lip and snapped a match to it. "If The

59

'Bino backs up how all of that has taken place, I figure it's worth us making a swing over that way before we do our final turn south."

"Be a lot of zig-zagging back and forth, though, won't it?" questioned Grissom.

Pierce cocked a brow. "So what's wrong with a little zig-zagging, especially if there *is* somebody on our tail? And that's another thing—the terrain around McCook is a lot more broken. If we have to stop and lay low for a bit, say after we hit a bank, we'll have a way better chance for doing so." He blew some smoke, then made a sour face. " 'Cause Christ knows we'll still have to face flat-assed Kansas before we finally get to the Territory."

"I like the sound of the whole thing," declared Caldwell. "Especially if we're able to land in the Territory with our pockets fat from a McCook bank so's we won't have to immediately start clawing through all the other curly wolves to scrounge for some new work."

"Watch out, Caldwell," Harriet said with a sarcastic smirk. "You almost sound like you want to land there and be complacent for a while."

CHAPTER 8

Darkness had begun to settle by the time Lone finally got the chance to sit down for the meal he'd been anticipating clear back when he first arrived at Weaver's watering station. The eating establishment he chose was the restaurant attached to the hotel where he'd booked a room after stabling Ironsides for the night at a nearby livery. When all was said and done, he was pleased to find the fare spread before him to be worth the wait. A thick, juicy steak with all the trimmings, tall glass of cold buttermilk, two slices of excellent cherry pie, and a whole carafe of steaming, fresh coffee.

What was more, it happened there was only a small crowd of other diners in the place. This provided Lone the opportunity to sit apart more or less by himself. Befitting his name, he preferred solitude over spending time in the company of most people. And the past few hours had certainly given him his fill of being tightly grouped with others, all of them strangers except for Jeth Howard.

Almost as if bidden by this thought, the former scout was just washing down his last bite of pie with a gulp of tepid coffee when he looked up and saw none other than Jeth approaching his table. Accompanying the old teamster, sporting a professionally bandaged leg and walking with the aid of a crutch, was Roy Whitlock.

"Sorry to barge in on your meal," said Jeth. "If you want, we can come back later. But, when you have a minute, we got something we'd like to talk to you about."

"No problem with right now, I just finished," Lone replied. "Sit down, take a load off. You want to order something? At least maybe some coffee?"

"No thanks. We caught a quick bite while waiting to see the doctor," answered Whitlock, settling somewhat awkwardly onto a chair in order to get his leg positioned in a reasonably comfortable way.

Indicating the leg and crutch with a tip of his head, Lone said, "I see you got fixed up right proper. Doc say everything is gonna be okay?"

"Yes, I was lucky. Bullet went through clean, didn't do any bone damage. Pretty much what we already knew. And the early treatment by you and Jeth kept it clean and protected from any start of infection. To determine that, however"—here Whitlock grimaced at the recollection—"he had to do all the additional poking and probing you warned me about."

A corner of Lone's mouth lifted. "Yeah. Never saw a sawbones yet who could resist the need to do some of that."

Jeth leaned forward, resting an elbow on the table. "Gettin' back to your original question, yeah the doc says Roy's pin is gonna heal just fine. He recommends, though, that he takes it easy for a couple days and sticks around to make sure no sign of infection shows up."

"Can you afford that? Stayin' here in town for a couple days, I mean? Don't you need to get to your daughter's wedding in Omaha?" Lone asked.

"Luckily, we allowed plenty of extra time for our trip. We meant to get to Omaha well ahead of the wedding so Peter could have a chance to take in the sights of a big city," Whitlock explained. "So we *could* afford to remain here a bit, as much as a week—though I'm still debating whether or not that's absolutely necessary."

"Speakin' of Peter, where is he?"

Whitlock twisted his mouth somewhat ruefully. "As a rambunctious young man who's never traveled much beyond Cheyenne, except for a trip to Denver once, he was eager to, er, 'see the sights' of Ogallala while here."

Grinning again, Lone said, "Uh-huh. At his age, reckon we've all gone lookin' for those sights."

Jeth grinned along, but only briefly. He seemed very earnest about something, and wanted to get to it. "Mentionin' the upcoming wedding fits, in a roundabout way, with what we came to talk to you about, Lone. You see, in the whirl of the robbery and everything that happened at the waterin' station and all, there's plenty we never got the chance to tell you. Actually, until me and Roy got the chance to hash some things over between us, there really wasn't no need to bother you with any of it. But now we're thinkin' maybe there is."

Lone's gaze passed back and forth between the two men. "Is this buildin' up to an invitation to the wedding?"

"More like a request for you to help *save* the wedding," said Whitlock, adopting Jeth's earnestness. "At least save a part of it that is very special and important to me."

"What we're gettin' at," Jeth picked up again, "is the brooch that Roy got shot tryin' to keep from the train robbers has got strong, whatycall, sentimental value. Been in his family goin' way back."

"Giving it to my daughter as a wedding gift was meant to represent several things. A gift of value and sentiment, to be sure, but also a gesture of healing. You see,"—here Whitlock's face bunched with so much emotion Lone felt he might weep—"I've been estranged from my daughter for many years. Ever since her mother and I bitterly divorced. I kept Peter, Paula took Pauline, our daughter. I haven't seen or heard from her in all this time.

"Until, a little less than a year ago, after her mother passed away, she . . . broke down, broke through. Contacted me. We exchanged a flood of letters and reached a place where we understood each other and recognized we had a blood bond and feelings like, like a father and daughter ought to have for one another. The day the letter arrived asking me to come to her wedding was one of the happiest moments of my life. I knew immediately I wanted to present her with the brooch—the heirloom my family has come to call the Whitlock Pulse, because of the way the gemstone set in it seems to breathe and throb when turned a certain way in certain lighting—as part of the ceremony."

Suddenly, Lone saw what this visit was all about. He said, "And now you want me to track down the robbers who took it—and try to get it back."

Jeth wagged his head. "Not quite."

"What then?"

"Us," declared the old teamster. "I figured the two of us—you and me—to track down the thievin' skunks and recover what they stole!"

A brooding Peter Whitlock sat at a table far back in one corner of the Crystal Palace saloon. Two men were seated with him, each also wearing brooding expressions that looked far better suited to them than to the fresh-faced younger man. Peter's companions were a coarse, hard-looking pair; unshaven, unwashed, clad in faded jeans and shirts with frayed collars and cuffs. Gun belts were strapped around their waists and while the leather of these looked about as worn as the men's clothing, the holstered pistols hanging from each had the unmistakable look of being very well maintained.

One of these hombres, who answered to the name of Lyle Vallen (often called "Big Tooth" behind his back due to his uncommonly large upper teeth that got displayed like a row of tombstones when he talked or especially when he drank too much and brayed with raucous laughter) was doing some talking now. But, even though a bottle and three glasses sat prominently on the table, Vallen wasn't drunk and the subject under discussion was clearly no laughter matter. "This is a fine goddamn howdy-do if ever I heard one," he declared.

"A crock of shit is what it is!" amended the second hardcase. His name was Hayden Hallo-way, a shorter, stockier version of Vallen also with a notable dental feature. In his case, a sizable gap between his two front teeth which sometimes caused him to whistle when he said his "esses."

In response to these laments, Peter raised his whiskey glass and took a drink, grimacing as the fiery liquid went down. Returning the glass to the tabletop with a heavy thump, he said, "You think I like this development any better than you two do? I advanced you good money to be here ready and waiting . . . and now there's nothing for you to be ready and waiting for. That's a raw deal all the way around."

"A hell of a lot rawer for us than you," Halloway grunted. "You still got daddy's money and successful business to fall back on. What have we got?"

"Yeah," Vallen agreed. "We left money-makin' opportunities back in Cheyenne to meet you here. Now here we set with a busted deal, empty pockets, and zero prospects in this pissant smudge on the prairie."

Peter's face pinched with disdain. "No good will come from picking at scabs. And neither will it help to pile a layer of cowflop on the situation—it won't cause better news to sprout up."

"What's that supposed to mean?" grunted Halloway.

"For starters, it means I know that the prospects for either of you back in Cheyenne were about as thin as those threadbare shirts you're wearing. So don't try to bullshit me," Peter stated. "It also means that the prospect may still exist for pulling off what I brought you here for—what all three of us so desperately want to succeed."

"Now who's talking bullshit," sneered Vallen. "How are we supposed to snatch that fancy stickpin away from your old man when the Dar Pierce gang already beat us to it?"

Peter's mouth spread in a slow, sly smile.

Vallen's mouth drooped in sharp contrast. "Now hold on a minute. If you're formulatin' some kind of crazy notion we snatch the doo-dad *back* from Pierce's bunch, you'd better step away from that who-hit-John real fast, sonny, before it addles your poor young brain beyond repair."

Peter lifted his glass and took another deliberate swallow. As he did so, he made a quick scan out across the central area of the saloon, making sure no one was paying any attention to him and his cohorts at their remote table. The establishment was doing a moderate business on this occasion, not bad for a week night but nothing like the raucous, hard-drinking crowds it was used to seeing on Fridays and Saturdays. Smoke hung in the air like cobwebs, especially over two other tables where games of poker were in session. A row of mismatched patrons were bellied up to the long bar and a pair of bored-looking soiled doves who'd failed to draw any interest from prospective customers leaned at the far end. The banjo player who usually did some string-strumming for the place was off sick tonight so it was quieter than usual, broken only by a low, monotonous drone of voices and the slap of the poker players' cards.

Bringing his gaze back to Vallen and Hallo-way, Peter said, "What if I were to tell you that, at this very minute, while we're having this discussion here, my father is meeting with some men he hopes to enlist to go after the Pierce gang? One of them is an old cavalry sergeant, the other is a former Indian scout who supposedly knows these plains like the back of his hand."

"So what does that mean to us?" Halloway asked.

"Don't you see? If they were to succeed—or even if they just caught up with Pierce enough to thin his ranks or perhaps merely create a diversion by confronting him—it might give you two an opening you could take advantage of." Peter's eyes gleamed with excitement. "They'd be too focused on dealing with each other to ever suspect a third faction was anywhere close at hand."

Halloway scowled. "What's a 'faction'?"

Vallen was scowling, too, but in a more thoughtful way. "So what you're suggestin' is that we follow the two birds your father is sendin' and be ready to swoop in if they catch up with and bust apart Pierce's outfit?"

"Exactly. Because this revision will obviously entail more effort and more risk than our original plan for you to simply strongarm my father," Peter said, "I'll pay you double our earlier agreement. And I'll finance horses and other supplies you'll need for going on the trail."

"How are you gonna pay for all that if the train robbers lifted you and your old man of your money, in addition to the brooch doo-dad?" Vallen asked suspiciously.

"My father already wired our bank back in Cheyenne," Peter explained. "First thing in the morning, when the local bank here opens, they will receive authorization to advance my father any amount he requires. I'll make sure I get a share of that. And if you two bring me the brooch, I will furthermore be certain you are generously rewarded even more."

"Boy, you sure want that brooch thing awful bad," observed Halloway. "It must be worth a pretty penny, eh?"

"It is. A very impressive amount. I had it secretly appraised once in Denver. My father has no idea, the old fool. He knows it has *some* value, but he views it more for the sentiment, the long-standing family heirloom and all that rot." Peter's lip curled scornfully. "Once I knew the full story, I swore it was just a matter of time before I'd claim it for myself and use it as the means to get out from under my father's thumb and escape him and his damn family business forever!"

Vallen frowned. "You'll have to excuse me if I don't see that as such a lousy deal. The only thing my old man left me was an unpaid saloon bill and a half empty jug of moonshine."

"You'd have to live it to understand," Peter countered. "But then my escape was threatened to be yanked out from under me when the crazy old bastard suddenly decided he was going to give *my brooch* to a daughter who hadn't been any part of his life for years! No way I'll ever let that happen . . . I'd rather see the Pierce gang keep the goddamn thing."

Vallen eyed him. "Only you really don't mean that."

Peter drained his glass. "Of course not. Which brings us back to the business at hand. Are you two willing to try my backup plan or not?"

Vallen and Halloway exchanged looks. When Vallen's eyes returned to Peter, he said, "What the hell. Like my old granny used to say, in for a penny, in for a pound."

"Good. I'll meet with you again in the morning after I have some money and after I've determined for sure what my father has arranged. That will leave one final understanding to be reached."

"What's that?" Halloway said.

Peter's eyes turned into hard chips of ice. "If you succeed in regaining the brooch and suddenly take a notion to try cashing it in yourselves, know this: You'll never get anywhere near the value I can through my contacts. You'd be cheating yourselves in addition to robbing me. What's more, if you *were* to swerve me in that manner . . . No matter how long it took or how much I had to spend, I'd see you hunted down and gutted like animals!"

CHAPTER 9

Lone kicked off his boots, hung his gun belt on a post of the headboard, stretched out full on the hotel bed. The room was shot with shadows, the only light coming from street lamp illumination filtering in through the curtained window, along with a warm night breeze, from outside. The former scout was naked from the waist up, having stripped off his shirt earlier when he washed and shaved at the basin over against one wall. He'd been planning on getting a bath before turning in, but the discussion with Whitlock and Jeth Howard had lasted so long he refrained from troubling the hotel staff to prepare a tub and hot water this late.

As it turned out, if he was going to be hitting the trail again right away—which seemed to be in the offing—then it hardly mattered. Though he hadn't fully agreed to taking on the mission Whitlock and Jeth put before him, his reflections ever since had been leaning more and more that way.

After all, why the hell not? Lord knew his business in North Platte had already been delayed plenty of times. Once more wouldn't make that much difference. Further, the bitter memories awaiting there and the vagueness of what would come next weren't exactly things he was looking forward to. Maybe, on some level, that's why he kept *allowing* other matters to get in the way.

And also, in contrast to the bitter memories that lay ahead, there were the bittersweet ones that lay behind. These were wrapped in the form of Tru Min Chang, the orphaned Chinese beauty he had escorted across the Nebraska panhandle to Fort Collins on the front range of the Colorado Rockies. During the trip they had grown very fond of one another, perhaps even to the point of calling it love. Before they could explore these feelings more fully, though, Lone had had to leave Tru behind for the sake of completing the unfinished business of tracking down and holding to account the human scum responsible for killing his former partner back in North Platte.

That hunt for what some might call justice, others merely vengeance—Lone didn't care which, he just wanted the guilty to pay and eventually saw to it that they did—took several bloody months. More than a year, all told, including the time he'd spent soul-searching afterward, wondering if a violent man like himself had any right to hope or expect he could be part of the life of a delicate flower like Tru. Ironically, when he finally steeled himself to go back to Fort Collins, determined to find out, he discovered the answer had already been settled for him. And for Tru. In keeping with traditions she was steeped in, to always honor the wishes of elder family members, Tru had given in to what was asked of her by the uncle she'd gone to Fort Collins to live with—her late father's brother, her only remaining family. In Lone's lengthy absence, and with no certainty he would ever return, Tru had agreed to wed a young Chinese man, the son of a close friend to the uncle.

The deed was done by the time Lone got back there. So all he could do was accept it. Extend to Tru and her new husband his best wishes for a happy future and then move on. Not that it was that easy . . . Not on the inside, not the gnawing questions, the wondering about what might have been . . . But it wasn't his nature to pine and fret uselessly over something irretrievably lost. He'd lost enough in his time—"Lone" fitting him in more ways than just a name others had hung on him—to have learned that lesson well. You held your feelings, kept them deep, and moved on. That's all a body could do.

But none of that answered the current question about moving on from Ogallala. And it had little to do with the uncertainties of what lay ahead or the finality of what was behind . . . Except maybe for the odd thought of how the deep, soulful eyes of Minowi, when Lone had caught her looking at him back at the watering station, somehow reminded him of the way Tru at times used to look at him.

No, the main factor bogging down his indecision about leaving town had to do with the lingering potential threat from Ira Clemson. Another delay in making it to North Platte for the sake of aiding his old friend Jeth and trying to bring a measure of justice to the likable Roy Whitlock probably would have been a quick, easy choice if not for all the talk about the impending wrath due from the powerful, grief-stricken rancher. If such wrath came and part of it was meant for him—despite what he'd told Marshal Halsey about having made his statement and feeling like he owed nothing more—Lone didn't like the thought of anybody, least of all himself, thinking he rode away from trouble instead of staying and facing it. Not even if the reason for leaving likely involved charging into more trouble at the behest of an old and a new friend.

The thought, not for the first time, echoed through his head: *How the hell do I keep getting myself into these situations?*

Luckily, the day had been long enough and tiring enough, and the bed embracingly comfortable enough, so that Lone did not toss and turn the way he'd figured he might. He fell quickly into a deep sleep. As deep, that was, as someone who spends most of their time in the wild, as he did, ever allows themselves.

Which was why, at the earliest sound of

stamping hooves and loud voices coming through the window from the street outside, he came instantly awake. In a single smooth motion, his legs swung over the side of the bed, his arm snaked out to grab the Colt from its holster hanging on the headboard post, and he glided to his feet. Moving silently, not taking time to pull on his boots, he went to the open window and stood off-center to gaze down on the street below.

They came from left to right in his field of vision. Twenty riders boiling down the middle of the street, dragging a dust cloud with them that swirled and churned, blurring their features and dimming the already meager lighting thrown by the street lamps on either side. As they reined to a halt and the dust cloud rolled on by and dissipated, Lone could more clearly make out the individual horsemen. All were heavily armed. Several of them brandished rifles, four or five up near the head of the pack held burning torches in raised fists.

At the lead was a stocky man of fifty or so, spikes of white hair poking out above his ears from under the brim of a high-crowned black hat. Black also dominated much of the rest of his attire; black leather vest, black gun belt, black gloves fitted snugly on his hands. If mood was a color, then the glowering expression his face conveyed more of the same—maybe deeper and darker than any of the rest. It wasn't hard to guess that here was none other than Ira Clemson.

Cocking his head back and lifting his face slightly, he shouted down the length of the murky, quiet street. "Citizens of Ogallala! Marshal Halsey! Everybody . . . Hear me, and listen good!"

In the tense pause that followed, the only sounds were that of a few horses blowing softly and shifting their feet, the accompanying creak of saddle leather. And then came the muted, unhurried tramp of human feet as Marshal Cliff Halsey and two of his deputies reverse-melted out of the shadows and moved into the street up ahead of Clemson and his men. They fanned out into a triangle, with Halsey at the point nearest Clemson. Each of the deputies stood with the butt of a shotgun braced on one hip.

Casually hooking his thumbs on either side of his belt buckle, Halsey squinted up at the rancher and said, "Evenin', Ira. Been expecting you. Gotta say, though, I wasn't figuring you'd show up leading quite such a parade."

"The purpose of this 'parade,' as you call it, is to send a message," Clemson responded. "I mean business."

Halsey gave a faint nod. "You usually do. Meaning business, I expect, is what's made you so successful."

"This is a different kind of business, and you know it. You know damn well why I'm here!"

Clemson's eyes blazed, catching extra brightness from one of the flickering torches that bracketed him. "My son is lying dead back at the ranch, gutted like something sliced open for fish bait! I want the vermin responsible. I know they're here in town. All you have to do is hand them over. What they did to Tad was out of your jurisdiction, and the same will hold for what I do to them."

Halsey's tone and expression remained flat. "There's only one problem with that, Ira. If whoever you're talking about—"

"Don't try getting cute with me, Halsey. You know damn well who I'm talking about!" bellowed Clemson. "Simon Weaver and his squaw wife from the railroad watering station. And some big stranger called McGantry who sided with 'em. I hold all three of 'em to blame!"

Edgers, the muscular wrangler who'd showed up earlier back at the watering station, spoke up from where he sat a horse just off to one side of his boss. "The squaw did the knifin' and the other two backed her play. Then, when Poke Rafferty tried to help, McGantry shot him for his trouble. Poke was an eye witness to it all."

Watching and listening from his window, Lone could see a restless, angry ripple pass through the pack of C-Bar riders. They'd come here for a purpose and now, as the talking heated up, they were growing anxious to get to it. Blood had been spilled within their ranks, and men

78

who rode for the same brand tended to stick together mighty tight, no matter what. A knot of increasing certainty started to form in Lone's gut—a certainty that it was going to take more than words before this was ended.

Ignoring Edgers' remark, Marshal Halsey stayed focused on Clemson and said, "The fact remains that if you're right about those folks being here in town, then that *does* put 'em in my jurisdiction and makes me responsible for 'em. There's the problem. I'm not in the habit of handing anybody under my watch over to a mob out for blood."

"You're right about one thing. I'm damn sure out for blood," Clemson declared. "I aim to wring every drop from those to blame for my boy, and then nail their skulls to the gate arch of my ranch!"

"Seems to me you're throwing that word blame around mighty freely, Ira. Do you think, for one minute, some of it maybe oughta land on Tad himself?"

"Watch your mouth, Halsey. I won't have my poor, murdered boy spoke ill of. I'm warning you."

But Halsey wouldn't back down. "Where was your warning—*to Tad*—when he kept ripping and tearing all over the countryside and you only continued making excuses and spending money to smooth over the worst of the problems he caused? Why do you think I had to bar him from coming into town? Anybody with eyes could see it was just a matter of time before he pushed the wrong person too far and there'd be a bullet or a knife on the other end that your money wouldn't be able to save him from."

"God damn you—I'm warning you for the last time!"

Lone swore under his breath as he thumbed back the hammer of his Colt and used its barrel to part the thin curtains a bit wider. This was it, it was going to pop any minute now and there was no stopping it.

Sure enough, it erupted a second later. The only surprise was who opened the ball. Lone was keeping a close eye on Edgers and, mounted next to him, the narrow-faced hombre who'd also been at the watering station earlier. Since they were positioned up near the boss and Edgers had already done some spouting off, Lone figured them for two of Clemson's top toughs and the likeliest ones to spearhead trouble. Or maybe Clemson himself. What the former scout forgot was the twitchy-eyed young hothead who'd also been at the watering station and had shown signs there of an eagerness for trigger pulling.

He showed the same thing again now, only this time no one—including Lone—noticed him in time to slow his hand. "The marshal is as much to blame as anybody! If he hadn't barred Tad from town then him and Poke never would've had to go near that whiskey-peddlin' squaw!" the hothead howled from halfway back in the pack. At the same time, he was pulling the pistol from his high-hitched holster and extending his arm to take aim at Halsey.

It was only the awkward placement and the stiffness of the new holster that slowed the kid's draw enough for Lone to have a chance to react. And barely, at that. Nothing fancy, just point and fire at body mass. The kid got his shot off, too, but it came at the same time he was jolted by Lone's slug pounding into him. The kid's bullet sailed half a foot wide of Marshal Halsey's head. He never knew the result of his shot—or anything else, ever again—because he was dead before he spilled from his saddle and toppled to the ground.

And then all Hell broke loose.

CHAPTER 10

The street that had only minutes ago been filled with clouds of churning brown dust kicked up by the arriving horsemen now turned quickly to a bluish-gray fog of powder smoke as guns began cracking and roaring in an exchange of sizzling lead. Several other C-Bar riders immediately attempted to follow through on what the hotheaded kid started, drawing guns and snapping off rounds even as their mounts bucked and reared in startled response to the sudden chaos. Halsey and his deputies scattered to either side of the street, scrambling for cover in doorway recesses or behind water troughs or barrels, frantically returning fire as they did so.

From his window, Lone didn't hesitate to aid them further. Having a good vantage point and able to take more careful aim, he knocked two more men off their horses. He was trying to get a bead on Clemson, figuring if he could cut off the head of the snake then the rest of the reptile might start to wither. But the swerving, shifting shapes of men and horses were in such turmoil that not even his considerable skill as a marksman could keep up. Once he missed clean when the rancher made an unexpected twist in his saddle; a second time another rider cut suddenly in the way just as Lone pulled the trigger. This unfortunate individual got the top of his head blown off for his trouble. More unfortunate still, the man happened to be one of the torch bearers whose outflung arm as he went down sent what amounted to a flaming missile crashing against the wood frame front of one of the businesses on the opposite side of the street.

Flames quickly spread in a wider pattern and began licking hungrily up the front of the building and across the boardwalk. Lone cursed this inadvertent piece of bad luck but there was nothing he could do to alter it except try to help bring the raging gunfight to an end so attention could be put to extinguishing the fire before it spread worse.

But that was easier said than done. There were too many C-Bar riders—and lawmen—focused on nothing but continuing the gunfight.

The shotguns of Halsey's deputies boomed and more C-Bar men fell. Then Lone saw one of the deputies go into a flailing spin and fall, too, never to get back up again.

The marshal himself was taking heavy fire, pinned down behind a watering trough and barely able to get off any return shots of his own. More and more horsemen were abandoning their mounts and taking cover at various spots along the boardwalks, not shooting so wildly now, working their way more carefully toward the two remaining lawmen. But that hardly meant they stopped shooting altogether and, in particular, three or four of them had figured out they had more than just the lawmen sending lead their way. Bullets suddenly began ripping through the curtain of Lone's window and chipping away the wood frame around it.

The former scout ducked low, grimacing. He hated giving up the vantage point but it was evident that trying to maintain it much longer would be suicide. The opening was simply too narrow to allow any maneuverability. Still, he stubbornly wanted at least one more crack at Clemson before falling back entirely.

Preventing an immediate such attempt, however, was the fact he'd emptied the cylinder of his Colt. Staying low, he turned and crab-walked a few feet deeper into the room. Tossing the empty .44 onto the mattress, he reached instead toward the shadowy lump he had earlier placed on the seat of an upholstered chair pushed against the wall at the foot of the bed. Lying across the top of this lump—his saddlebags and possibles pack—was his Winchester Yellowboy repeater. Seizing this, he spun back around and returned to the window.

His brief absence no longer offering a target, the shooting up at the window had ceased. This gave Lone the chance to stealthily peek over the sill for a quick re-appraisal of what was happening in the street below. Not much had changed, of course, except that black smoke was rolling thicker from the building fire and mingling with the powder smoke to create an even denser haze over the scene. In fact, it appeared like another torch or two had been thrown—purposely this time, Lone guessed—so there were more fires starting to burn. But in spite of the haze there was still a healthy exchange of gunfire taking place and he could discern that both Halsey and his remaining deputy were managing to trigger their share of it. Yet the marshal continued to be precariously pinned down.

Somewhere farther down the street a fire bell was ringing. Through the stutter of gunfire, Lone could hear the excited buzz of distant voices—citizens alarmed by the fire and smoke, no doubt, but being held at bay by the shooting.

Lone's gaze swept frantically, looking for some sign of Ira Clemson. Most of the C-Bar men had dismounted by this point, some by choice and some with the help of a bullet. Either way, there was no hint of Clemson . . . Until, only a split second before he disappeared under the board-walk overhang directly below Lone's window, the former scout finally caught a glimpse of him. He was bracketed by Edgers and the nameless hombre with the narrow face, the two of them protectively hurrying the powerful rancher in off the bullet-riddled street.

For a moment Lone felt the pinch of frustration and dismay at missing his desired target by such a narrow margin. But then the realization hit him: If the three men had disappeared directly beneath him, that meant they had ducked into the front lobby of this very hotel!

Shoving away from the window, he rose to his full height and wheeled for the door. He didn't take time for his boots or shirt. But he did pause long enough to grab his Colt off the bed, jam it into the holster of the gun belt hanging on the headboard post, then snag the belt and sling it over his shoulder as he bolted out into the hallway.

He'd taken only a few steps before things turned suddenly, unnervingly quieter. The intervening rooms and closed doors muted most of the sound of the shooting outside.

But just ahead, the door to one of the rooms had been thrown open and a half-emerged man was standing there, looking warily around. It was Jeth Howard. He was clad in bright red long-handled underwear, boots, and hat. And he was holding the same double-barreled Greener shotgun he'd used back at the watering station.

When he saw Lone, he said, "What in blazes is goin' on out in the street? Sounds like a war."

"It is," Lone told him. "That big rancher, Clemson, showed up lookin' to avenge his son. Brought an army with him. He wants the hides of the Injun girl, Weaver, and yours truly. The marshal and a couple of his boys are tellin' 'em no."

"Tough odds."

"Uh-huh. I did a little objectin' of my own from the window of my room. Now I'm headed down to do a little more, only closer." Lone paused, indicating Jeth's shotgun with a tip of his head. "That thing loaded?"

"Ain't carryin' it around for no walkin' stick."

"You interested in *un*-loadin' it some?"

"Only got two more shells in addition to what's already packed. Wouldn't say no to the chance to burn up what I got, though."

Lone nodded. "Good. I got reason to think the boss man, Clemson, is in the lobby downstairs. I'm thinkin' if I can get to him and make him pull in his horns, permanent-like if I have to . . . well, maybe the rest won't be so eager to continue."

Now it was Jeth who nodded. "Sort of like cuttin' down a war chief and causin' the rest of his bunch to turn back on account of they think their medicine went bad."

"Something like that."

"Sounds worth a try. Let's take a crack at it."

Half a minute later, the two men were squatting behind the curve of a polished wood banister that reached down along the right side of the open stairway leading to the lobby below. The sound of shooting had grown louder again now—from out in the street and also from the lobby itself. Lone's range of vision did not cover the full area down there. He could see one end of the check-in desk off to the left, the front door straight ahead, only a portion of the lounge area that he knew was off to the right. It made sense that the three men he'd seen enter would be positioned over that way, firing from the front window. Farther to the right, out on the street, was the position of the lawmen they were gunning for.

Lone held up three fingers and then gave a thumb jerk to the right, indicating to Jeth how many they'd be going against and where he figured they were. Then, leaning closer, he added in a whisper, "I'll go first and do what I can with this repeater. If they're stubborn about it and I have to duck for cover, that should give you an opening to step down and go to work with that street sweeper of yours."

"Leave me your gun belt," Jeth whispered back. "I only got four rounds for this blaster, remember. In case things don't go quick, I may need more lead to throw."

Lone made the transfer before easing forward to the lip of the top step. One of the shooters below was talking excitedly between trigger pulls. Lone thought the voice sounded like Edgers.

"Those stinkin' law dogs can't last much longer! If we don't fill 'em full of lead first, the fires will soon be burnin' 'em out!"

That only added to Lone's anger and resolve. Mouth twisting into a grimace, he started down the carpeted steps, bent forward at the waist to gain some shielding from the thick, sloping banister. Halfway down, the full spread of the lounge area became visible and he saw that his recollection of its layout had been accurate. What was more, the three men who'd taken refuge there were positioned almost exactly as he'd calculated.

The lounge featured four upholstered chairs and a long couch, all interspersed with some small tables adorned with ashtrays and a couple potted plants—its purpose to provide guests a roomier, more comfortable setting than their cramped rooms for visiting or perhaps just relaxing with a cigar and a newspaper.

The arrangement remained mostly undisturbed, except for the couch having been pushed over and turned up on its side in front of the broad front window. Ragged gaps of the window's decorative glass had been broken away. Edgers and the narrow-faced hombre were squatted down behind the couch, sporadically shooting out through the gaps in the glass, aiming at an angle toward where the two lawmen were located. Edgers was using a long-barreled Remington revolver; Narrow Face a Henry repeating rifle. Although he held a pistol in one hand, Clemson wasn't currently doing any shooting. He was a few feet behind his men, dropped down on one knee beside one of the chairs, the arm holding the pistol resting across its cushioned back rest.

Lone reached the bottom of the steps and pressed in behind the big anchor post at the end of the banister. So far none of the three had taken any notice of him. He could brace his Yellowboy across the top of the post and easily kill Clemson with one shot, before he ever knew what hit him. When he'd been trying to get a bead on the man from up in the window that had been his goal— kill the boss in front of his men and hope that would take the fight out of them. But now Lone's mind raced with a different thought, weighing the option of trying to take Clemson alive and giving him the chance to call off his men. Not having to kill a man in cold blood if there was a way to avoid it also factored in.

Lone made his choice. Steadying the Yellow-boy's muzzle atop the post, he called out, "I'm only saying this once, Clemson—freeze or take a bullet!"

The boss rancher reacted as hoped for. He stayed motionless, only his suddenly widened eyes rolling as far as they could to one side, straining to look around and back at who had given the command.

But it was a different story for Edgers and Narrow Face. They were too keyed up, pumped too full of adrenaline by the flames and smoke and sizzling bullets to show good sense. Their response was to immediately wheel about and swing their guns with them.

"McGantry!" Edgers spat, almost as if he'd been expecting it before his glare ever fell on Lone. And as he said the name he was making a wild thrust with the Remington, taking desperate aim.

Lone shifted the sights of the Yellowboy from Clemson to Edgers and stroked the trigger. The muscular cowboy reacted to the punch of the slug, hunching his shoulders and lifting up on his toes. His body trembled but he refused to let go of the Remington, fighting to hang on, to steady it. Lone shot him again and this time he went down flat and hard.

Jacking a fresh shell and taking that second shot had cost Lone time—time enough for Narrow Face to get off a shot of his own. He'd have gotten it off quicker and maybe more accurately if he hadn't clunked the butt of his rifle on the window sill when starting to make his turn. The big anchor post Lone was behind played a part, too, shielding him and taking the hammering *whap!* of the slug. A gritty cloud of cracked varnish and splintered wood burst out like the post had coughed.

Before either Lone or Narrow Face could squeeze their triggers again, Jeth Howard came bounding down the stairs and beat them to it. The shotgun gripped in his hands roared, momentarily drowning out the sound of gunfire from the street. The twelve gauge load it hurled caught Narrow Face dead center, lifting him off his feet and hurling him out the shattered window and onto the boardwalk like a bundle of bloody rags.

CHAPTER 11

Cliff Halsey leaned wearily back in his desk chair and emitted a long, ragged sigh. "What a hell of a mess." His voice was hoarse, also ragged sounding. "Seven men dead, four wounded . . . Half a dozen buildings fire damaged and as many additional injuries, mostly minor thank God, suffered getting the blazes under control . . . All on account of one spoiled, snot-nosed little puke who never amounted to—or ever would have—a pinch of shit."

There were five other men gathered in the marshal's office with Halsey. Lone and Jeth Howard were there; Evan Porter, the surviving deputy of the pair who'd stood so bravely with Halsey against the pack of C-Bar riders; Norman Clairmont, the city attorney; and Adam Bagby, owner and editor of the Ogallala Star. Each man was soot-streaked, sweat-stained, bleary-eyed, and exhausted looking from their participation, along with the dozens of anonymous townsfolk who'd come swarming, in an hours-long fight to beat down the fires.

This had immediately followed the surrender of Ira Clemson to Lone and Jeth after they'd killed his two top gunnies in the hotel lounge. The ranch boss had wilted in defeat, responding to demands (at gunpoint) to call off the rest of his men before turning sullen and silent as he was cuffed and put behind bars. The second the shooting stopped, people had begun pouring onto the scene to engage the new battle of getting the fires under control.

Outside now, dawn was only an hour or so away. The street was empty, cleared of debris and fallen bodies, both the dead and those only wounded or injured. All flames had been extinguished, leaving just a few smoldering patches and the curls of gray-black smoke rising up from them. A general gray murkiness hung in the air, holding within it the stink of charred wood and burnt paint. Three volunteers remained on watch along the stretch where the fires had burned, vigilant until daylight activity returned to the street, making sure no seemingly dormant hot spots unexpectedly flared again before then.

Speaking in response to the marshal's remark about the cause of it all, attorney Clairmont said, "Tempting as it may be to lay everything that transpired at the feet of young Tad and be able to consider it finished because he is conveniently dead, I think there remain subsequent actions and responsibilities that can't easily be ignored."

Halsey scowled. "Who said anything about ignoring anything? Ain't Ira Clemson behind bars back in our cell block—waiting to be held responsible in a court of law for his actions? Ain't that where you're gonna come in?"

"To be sure," replied Clairmont. "But how successfully I'll be able to proceed—now that you've released all the other C-Bar men, the ones still alive that is—causes me concern."

"I didn't release those men of any and all responsibility for what happened here. I simply sent 'em back to the ranch," Halsey argued. "Number one, I don't have room to effectively jail all of 'em. Number two, it seemed like a good idea to get 'em out of town and away from citizens whose tempers were rightly on edge after seeing their town threatened to be burnt down. I didn't need another mob battle or half-assed necktie party to start up before all the smoke even cleared. And number three, there are animals and chores and families back at the C-Bar who don't deserve to be suddenly left in the lurch because Ira's temper tantrum led off all the hands."

"You realize, of course, that especially right about now most folks here in town don't give a hang about any inconveniences suffered at the C-Bar," pointed out editor Bagby.

"And do you really trust that those wranglers you let go are going to stick around or even bother to return to the ranch at all?" questioned Clairmont. "Whether they do or not, the problem it presents to me—from a legal standpoint—is that turning them loose while keeping Ira behind bars introduces a question of prejudice that will no doubt come up if and when he stands trial."

"Oh, he'll be standing trial," Halsey said with grim assurance. "I already, yesterday, wired the U.S. Marshals office regarding the train robbery that took place. I expect somebody from the railroad did the same. At first light, I'll send another wire about this latest trouble, since part of it also reaches beyond my jurisdiction. So you can bet they'll be sending somebody. And he'll likely take charge of the whole thing—both cases." He let his gaze settle heavily on Clairmont. "So any problems you got with how I handled things, counselor, you'll be able to take up with him."

"Now hold on a minute, Cliff," huffed the attorney. "There was nothing personal meant by what I said. It's my job to consider the legal ramifications, that's all."

"Like I said, you can take up whatever you need to with the U.S. Marshal."

"There's something everybody needs to understand," Deputy Porter spoke up abruptly. "I was in full agreement with Cliff when it came to letting those wranglers go back to the ranch. At the time, it seemed the smartest thing. But don't ever think we're forgetting it was a C-Bar rider—maybe one of the dead ones, maybe one of the ones we let go—who was behind killing my partner, Deputy Ben Hartzall. U.S. Marshal or no, singling out that particular varmint, in case he *is* still alive, is something me and Cliff plan on taking care of ourselves."

The intensity of his statement left everybody quiet for a long beat.

Taking the opportunity, Lone straightened up from where he'd been leaning against a wall and said, "Sounds like you fellas are gonna have your hands plenty full in the days and weeks to come. Can't rightly say I'm gonna miss stickin' around for it, but that's the case for me and Jeth both. Happens that as soon as we can get on the other side of a good scrubbin' and some clean duds and take on a few supplies, we'll be hittin' the trail out of here."

Clairmont looked alarmed. "Wait a minute. If there's a trial, you'll be needed as a key witness to what happened out at the watering station as well as the recent—"

"I already gave a detailed statement to the marshal about the watering station," Lone cut him off. "Comes to what just happened here, you don't need me to add nothing. I've got better things to do than wait for a trial that'll take who knows how long to even get scheduled."

"Not that I'm saying you ain't got every right to light out," said Halsey, "but you mind saying what it is that's so urgent?"

"Got to do with the train robbery," answered Jeth. "I was on that train. Me and the fella I'm travelin' with, Roy Whitlock, the passenger who was shot in the leg, got money took. What's more, Roy also lost something more special to him than money—a piece of jewelry that's been in his family since a time way back in the old country. He's asked me and Lone to try and retrieve it for him."

Porter's brows pinched together. "Just you two figure to go against the whole Dar Pierce gang?"

"Didn't say that. Said we're goin' to try and retrieve the doo-dad." Jeth shrugged. "Body looks hard enough and has a little luck, he can sometimes find different ways to do a thing."

"Well, if any two men *could* take on the Pierce gang—based on your performance here against the C-Bar raiders," said Bagby, "then I reckon it could be the pair of you."

"I'll second that," allowed Halsey. "Hadn't been for the 'performance' of Lone and Jeth taking down Ira's key men and then getting the drop on the ranch boss himself . . . well, I don't know how things would have turned out. Most likely for the worst. I don't want to think about how close me and Evan were to the brink of not being able to hold out much longer."

"*Don't* think about it then," grated Lone. "You'd've figured out a way to turn things back against those peckerwoods."

"Maybe, maybe not," Halsey said stubbornly. "But I ain't so sure of it that I'll hold off heaping on another thanks to both of you. Furthermore, I ain't forgetting another time, Lone, when you also stepped in and pulled a certain person—

98

somebody very dear to me—back from a different brink."

Here the marshal paused to cut a hard glare over at Clairmont. "Which is my way of saying to you, counselor, that if Lone and Jeth want to ride out of here, then they've earned every damn right to leave whenever they please."

CHAPTER 12

"If they're headed south for the Territory, like everybody figures, then we oughta be cuttin' their sign in the next two, three hours, don't you reckon?" queried Jeth Howard.

Riding alongside him, Lone replied, "Sounds about right. We've been holdin' a good, steady pace. I'd say we're near even with that waterin' station now off to our north. That bein' the case, then drawin' even with the point farther west where they hit your train, should be comin' before long."

"Uh-huh. So if Pierce and his bunch rode south from there, then we're bound to T-bone their sign."

"Don't hardly see how we can miss it," Lone allowed. "To keep goin' south, they've got to cross the river. Five riders and the six-horse string they stole off the train means comin' out of the water they'll chew up the bank pretty good. Blind man'd be able to spot it."

The two men were riding along the south edge of the South Platte River, moving west. The sun overhead in a cloudless sky was a ways past its noon peak. Lone was mounted on Ironsides, Jeth a sleek black gelding that he'd picked out for himself.

As soon as Roy Whitlock had been able to make arrangements in order to secure funds from a local bank, he'd provided the pair the means to outfit themselves with whatever they needed. For Lone this meant merely the replenishing of a few basic supplies. For Jeth, who'd been picked clean of everything but the clothes on his back by the bank robbers, it meant a wide range of replacement acquisitions. Though a pack animal was briefly considered, in the end they decided against one, opting instead to travel faster and lighter and forage, if necessary, for any additional needs that might crop up.

A need both men acknowledged they would require before continuing very far was to stop and get some rest. Each had only slept a handful of minutes the previous night before the C-Bar raiders showed up in the street outside their hotel rooms. From there they'd been swept into a literal non-stop series of events on top of an already full day that lasted through until dawn— the gun battle, fighting the fires, agreeing in the aftermath to accept Whitlock's mission, settling things with the town officials, and starting to make preparations.

True, there'd been a couple hours after leaving the marshal's office and before Whitlock's funds were ready when they could have tried to grab a snatch of sleep. But that likely would have been a restless, frustrating attempt that gained little or nothing. They were still too keyed up from what they'd just been through and already contemplating what they were about to undertake next. Better, for the time being, to keep in motion, stay busy. Full, proper rest would have to wait until the right time.

The right time, Lone and Jeth had agreed, wouldn't be until after they'd cut initial sign of the Pierce gang and were started on their trail south.

Back in Ogallala, while Lone and Jeth were completing preparations before heading out, Peter Whitlock had been finalizing arrangements with Vallen and Halloway ahead of their own departure. The meeting between the three took place in an empty lot behind an abandoned building at the seedier end of town, well removed from anywhere Peter's father might take note.

Having attained a share of the funding his father received, as expected, Peter had paid off his hirelings in order for them to take on supplies and otherwise get ready for their task. He noted sourly that none of their purchases seemed to have included much in the way of improved attire for themselves. If anything, only evidence of a hangover and a fresh layer of disgruntlement appeared to have been added.

"While we was getting ourselves set up this morning," Vallen announced, "we heard talk most everywhere we went about these two hombres you're sending us after."

"I'm not sending you after *two hombres,*" Peter countered, his tone taking on a skeptical edginess. "I'm sending you after an object—a *brooch* that I've given you a clear description of. Remember?"

"What I *don't* remember," Vallen came back, "is you saying anything about how much bark it sounds like those two have still got on 'em. You know, that *old* teamster and *old* army scout, the way you described 'em."

"Only the way everybody else is talking," Halloway joined in, "those geezers jumped into that fracas last night against a small army of hired guns and practically saved the whole town. And after they got done throwing lead, they jumped in and helped beat down the big fire that got started."

Peter rolled his eyes. "Oh, for Christ's sake! Do you two believe everything you hear? You never heard of a little thing called exaggeration? You make it sound like McGantry and old Jeth were the only ones shooting back against those cowboys—and that's all they were, by the way, ranch hands with guns, not no army of hired slicks. As far as the fire, the whole town pitched in to fight that, even me and my old man on his crutch. Where the hell were you two?"

Vallen scowled. "Because we didn't have money for no proper hotel room, we were at this shit end of town, bedded down in that empty building yonder with a bottle of hooch we swiped from the saloon and set about making empty, too . . . We never knew about all the excitement until we started hearing the talk this morning."

"Well if you're worried about getting crossways of McGantry and Jeth," Peter said, "then putting yourselves in such a sorry-assed, hungover condition is a hell of a poor way to prepare for it."

"Yeah, yeah," grumbled Halloway. "We don't need no lecture on how to handle our booze, okay? It just would have been nice to have got a clearer picture on who it is we're dealing with."

Peter spread his hands. "Did you think my father would have hired a couple of Sunday school teachers to go after Dar Pierce? Him and his gang are still part of the mix, too, remember. Come to think of it, McGantry and Jeth having some bark on them actually works in our favor, don't you see? The harder the clash and the greater the toll they take on each other if and when they catch up with Pierce's bunch, the better chance it might give you two to slip in and grab the brooch."

Halloway frowned. "I ain't sure I follow that."

"Never mind, it don't matter right now. What matters is that we got ourselves in this damn thing, we got to stick with it." Vallen paused, grimacing. "But what matters most, at this particular moment, is that I got to get a lot more coffee in me before I'm ready to saddle up and go bouncing off on a goddamn horse."

CHAPTER 13

As anticipated, Lone and Jeth easily found the spot where the Pierce gang crossed the river and then were just as easily able to follow their trail as it continued on south. The land remained an undulating, mostly treeless expanse of grass. Since they were moving farther away from the lower reaches of the Sandhills, the soil grew gradually richer, making the grass a little greener and differently textured. They were undoubtedly passing through the grazing grounds of some scattered ranches, though they never spotted any cattle or signs of buildings.

With dusk starting to settle, they came to a tree-stippled slope overlooking what Lone reckoned to be Lodgepole Creek. Under different circumstances, there would have been plenty of light to go on for another couple of hours before making camp. But exhaustion was starting to weigh on the pair and, remembering their agreement about how far to push themselves before finally stopping to rest, it wasn't hard to reach another agreement that this spot satisfied the requirement pretty darn good.

While Lone tended the horses, Jeth got a fire going to cook up some coffee and grub. They'd breakfasted well before leaving Ogallala but had made do for the rest of the day on jerky and biscuits eaten on occasions when they stopped briefly to give the horses a breather and let them drink. Even at that, the chance to climb out of the saddle and stretch their weary bones was more on their minds than eating. Though once prepared, the simple meal of bacon, beans, and more biscuits, washed down by plenty of hot, strong coffee, went down mighty good, too.

"I gotta tell you," declared Jeth afterwards, leaning back against his upturned saddle with a freshly filled, steaming cup of joe cooling on the grass beside him, "I thought I was plumb fed up with bein' plopped on a wagon seat eatin' the dust and watchin' the swayin' rumps of a horse team ploddin' ahead of me . . . But what I forgot was how, years before that, I'd got even more fed up—or near *stove up,* more like—with havin' my bony ol' ass plopped in a saddle. That's what caused me to switch from the cavalry to bein' an army teamster in the first place."

Lone grinned. "Well teamsterin' must not have treated you too bad. You stuck with it even after the army and, unless I got the wrong impression, have been doin' it for Whitlock quite a spell since."

"True enough. But if you'd listened more careful," Jeth said, "you'd've caught where I just said I got fed up with it. Yeah, workin' for Roy has been good. Could even say it became a friendship as much as a job. He always treated me square, the work was steady, the pay was right.

"But a man reaches different points in his life . . . milestones, I think I've heard some folks call 'em . . . where he all of a sudden starts thinkin' about and seein' things a mite different than before. The clock tickin' on how much time a body's got left figures into it, too."

"Hell, Jeth. From everything I can tell, that clock of yours is still tickin' plenty strong." Lone eyed him questionably. "You ain't got some kind of ailment, have you?"

"No, nothing like that. Just the ailment of thinkin' too much maybe. Wonderin'. Regrettin' . . . Not so much regrettin' anything I done, but more some of what I never did." Jeth's coffee had cooled enough for him to take a drink. "That's why I went ahead and cashed in my time with Roy."

"Cashed in? You mean you don't work for him no more? I guess I ain't understandin' something."

"No, I reckon you couldn't. I reckon we never got around to explainin' it all the way." A corner of Jeth's mouth quirked up. "You see, I wasn't travelin' on that train with Roy and Peter on my way to attend the Omaha wedding. That was never gonna be a stop for me. I figured—and still do, eventually—to continue on to Council Bluffs over in Iowa, on the other side of the Missouri River. I got kinfolk, a brother and sister as best I know, in that area. There's some of the regret I spoke of . . . havin' lost all contact with 'em for so many years."

"So you and Whitlock travelin' together was just a matter of headin' in the same general direction for a ways. As far as Omaha for him, farther for you."

"Uh-huh. Wasn't no hard feelin's over me quittin' him. He understood. When it turned out we had cause to be headed in the same general direction, like you say, it only made sense to share the train ride and spend a little more time together as friends."

Lone pursed his lips thoughtfully. "So the money the train robbers took from you—that was your cash-out pay from Whitlock's freight company?"

"Yup. Every cent I had to my name. Over a hundred bucks. Most money I ever collected together in one lump in my life. Ain't that a sorry damn piece of luck?" The remark seemed like it was meant to sound somewhat off-handed, yet at the same time there was an undeniable and understandable trace of bitterness in the old teamster's tone.

"That's a hell of a bite, old friend," Lone said, with absolutely no attempt to hide his bitterness over what he'd just heard. "We catch up with those thievin' skunks, we'll collect more than just Whitlock's shiny thingamabob. And we'll collect with interest."

"Money can be earned back. That brooch of Roy's, though, is a special, one-time thing," Jeth insisted. Then, rolling a bit onto his left side and reaching around to press the flat of his right hand against the small of his back, he added, "But after the aches and bruises I expect to be accumulatin' in places I won't mention, all on account of this saddle-straddlin' I ain't used to, by the time we *do* catch up with those varmints I reckon I'll be in the mood for collectin' payback with plenty of interest, too."

They turned in early and both men fell quickly into deep slumber. Rising with the sun—Jeth's initial movements showing a notable stiffness despite his attempts to hide it—their stated goal for the new day was to push longer and harder in an attempt to substantially close the gap on their quarry. Inasmuch as this would mean more eating from the saddle with only brief stops to benefit the horses, they took time for a good breakfast before starting out; bacon, fresh pan biscuits, and a shared can of peaches. Jeth did the cooking while Lone once again tended the animals— watering them at the creek, graining them, and then making sure all canteens and water bags were filled and ready.

It was while they were squatting beside the dying fire, sipping the last of their coffee before saddling up, when Lone said, "You ever have an epiphany, Jeth?"

The old teamster lifted his brows. "Lord I hope not. Sounds like some sort of fearsome disease."

"No, it ain't that. It's one of those words can be used a few different ways, but I don' think that's one of 'em. Believe I even heard Bible thumpers have a meanin' for it, only that ain't what I'm talkin' about neither."

"How about jumpin' to what you *are* tryin' to say?"

"Way I mean is a sudden hunch or notion about a thing, an idea that pops into your mind so clear it's like it's standin' right in front of you . . . That's what hit me in the middle of the night, Jeth. I had an epiphany. I've been ponderin' on it some more all mornin' before sayin' anything, but now I'm convinced."

"All right. Spill the rest of it and convince me."

"I know where the Pierce gang is headed."

Jeth frowned. "We've had that figured all along, ain't we? Back to Oklahoma, the Injun Territory—back where they came out of."

"Yeah, that's where they're meanin' to end up," Lone allowed. "But I'm talkin' shorter term, where they're headed in between . . . It's got to do with that string of horses they're leadin', the ones they took off the train along with the gun gear and all the rest, all the stuff apart from the money."

"Expect they'll be lookin' to sell that stuff off somewhere, gain themselves some more ready cash."

"Exactly. And I know just the place where they can unload the whole works. Ever hear of a fella named Clevon Jemsil? Most folks call him simply The 'Bino, on account of that's what he is—an albino." When Jeth shook his head, indicating no knowledge of any such person, Lone went on. "He runs a tradin' post a ways into Colorado. Past Julesburg, down nearer a settlement called Yuma. Out in the middle of a lot of empty."

"The middle of a lot of empty don't sound like where a body would set up to attract much business."

"A big chunk of business that The 'Bino does is with folks who tend to like bein' in the wide open and not bein' seen comin' or goin' in their dealings," Lone explained. "Oh, he'll gladly do business with straight-up folks, too. But that's the thing. He buys, sells, trades without carin' or askin' questions."

"Be a mighty attractive place to an outfit like Pierce's with a haul of ill-gotten gains to unload."

"That's what I'm thinkin'."

"How long to get there?"

"We can make it by tonight, I think, if we push hard and nothing goes amiss. We'll still keep an eye on Pierce's actual trail, but I don't have much doubt that's where it'll lead."

"Me neither, not after what you've laid out." Jeth tipped up his cup and drained the last of the coffee from it. "So let's put that epa-ninny thing of yours to work and go pay a visit to Mr. 'Bino."

CHAPTER 14

From a distance, the buildings comprising The 'Bino's trading post looked like a hodgepodge of various bits of debris blown across the rolling prairie by strong winds until they all hit the same snag and then piled together in a weather-battered heap. Up close, it turned out not to be all that different. The main structure appeared to have started life as a basic soddy with some wood beam framing, square in its original layout but now having sprouted three or four ill-fitted additions that made it a shapeless sprawl. Scattered about it was an assortment of small to medium-sized sheds, two rickety corrals, and one precariously leaning barn.

Having made good time through the course of the day, there was still a slice of sun poking above the western horizon as Lone and Jeth reined up at the hitch rail out front of the main building. Fading letters on a lopsidedly hanging sign over the front door read: JEMSIL'S TRADING & SUPPLYS.

Before dismounting, Lone made a gesture toward one of the corrals they could see out back and said to Jeth, "Six horses penned up there. Any of 'em look familiar?"

"Sure do," came the answer. "The other five I

only caught sight of as they were bein' took off the train. But that white gelding with the gray splotch on its right rump is mine, the mount I was bringin' along to ride when I proceeded on from Omaha. The tracks leadin' us all day already told the story, but spottin' my white proves for sure you were right about Pierce's bunch comin' here to unload their booty."

Lone swept another slow scan over the scene, just to make sure, before saying, "Too bad they don't seem to've stuck around to celebrate."

Jeth grunted. "This look like a place *anybody* would stick around any longer than they absolutely had to?"

"Good point," Lone conceded. Then, swinging down from his saddle, he added, "But let's go inside and have a chat with somebody who sticks around and even calls it home—The 'Bino."

"Can't hardly wait. Think he'd object to me carryin' in my shotgun? I mean, nobody thinks twice about hombres packin' iron on their hip, but a body casually swingin' a Greener at his side might strike some as a bit too showy." The gun Jeth was referring to was the same double-barreled blaster he'd taken from the watering station and had used so effectively against the C-Bar raiders. When Whitlock had offered to outfit him with whatever weapons they wanted for this trip, Jeth had opted for a new Henry repeater (not being a particular fan of handguns)

114

but had hung on to the shotgun all the same. It brought him luck, he said.

"I worry about you, the way you've taken such a shine to that piece of stolen merchandise," Lone remarked. "Might become a bad habit."

"I didn't steal this gut shredder, I'm just *borrowin'* it for a while," Jeth argued. "I ever get back up near that waterin' station again, I'll put it back over the door where I found it. In the meantime, it kinda comforts me. Especially goin' in somewhere has the look of this joint."

"Well then, I don't see how The 'Bino can object to a customer just wantin' to feel comfortable," Lone allowed.

A cowbell hanging on a string so that it was made to clatter by the inward swing of the door announced their entrance. Once inside, they made their way down a short, broad hall lined with a stacks of items ranging from piled blankets to articles of clothing to cases of airtights. The hall opened to a low-ceilinged room whose walls were crowded with more of the same, plus a variety of other goods. The air smelled musty and stank of cigar smoke.

In the middle of this room stood two rough-hewn wooden tables with chairs hitched up to them, none occupied. Off to one side there was a raggedly constructed flagstone fireplace. Positioned before it, hunched close as if soaking up heat in spite of the fact no fire was burning, sat an old woman in a rocking chair. She was clad in a shapeless gray dress but, contrastingly, had a bright red head scarf tied over a headful of scraggly, wispy white hair. Her face was a collection of deep wrinkles gathered around two shiny dark eyes peering out from under cotton-ball tufts of brows. From one corner of a thin-lipped mouth hung a black, twisted, crudely fashioned cigar giving off a copious amount of foul-smelling smoke.

Through the curl of smoke rising from the tip of her cigar, the old woman's eyes tracked Lone and Jeth as they entered. She didn't speak, her gaze never faltered, the slow, steady rhythm of her chair rocking back and forth never changed.

Lone held her eyes for a beat or two, then pinched his hat and cut his gaze over to the other side of the room. A serving counter of sorts had been erected there; two planks nailed side by side and stretched across the tops of three wooden barrels. On the back side of this, leaning slightly forward and resting one bony elbow atop the counter, stood a skinny, pale apparition with watery pink eyes, a face the color of bleached flour, and a headful of wispy white hair almost identical to that of the old hag except this unruly growth sprouted from under a jauntily cocked derby hat.

"Gentlemen, gentlemen," greeted Clevon "The

116

'Bino" Jemsil in a surprisingly deep, resonate voice. "Welcome to Jemsil's emporium of . . ." He stopped short, his eyes locking on Lone and narrowing suspiciously. "Wait a minute . . . don't I know you?"

Puffing around her cigar, the old woman called over in a raspy voice, "The lone man ain't ridin' alone today."

"That's it!" The 'Bino made a stabbing motion with one finger. "You're Lone McGantry. But I heard you went over a while back . . . Got gunned down up in Deadwood."

"Not quite," Lone countered. "True enough that I traded lead with some fellas up in Deadwood a while back, but it was those on the other end of the trade who went over. Not me."

"Well, I'll be danged. I shoulda knowed better, you bein' tough as whang leather and all. Onliest reason I half believed it was 'cause you ain't been nowhere around in such a spell."

"Ain't had no call to," Lone said off-handedly.

"Well, sure. Sure, that makes sense. Say, what about that one-legged old mountain man you used to run with sometimes? Come to think of it, I also heard—"

Lone cut him off. "He's dead. There's no more to say on it."

"Okay. Sure, sure."

"Rest of the mountain man followed the leg that went over a long time back," the old woman

117

crowed. "But the lone man made the takers pay, you can bet he did!"

The 'Bino gave her a look. "Auntie Gwen has a way of sometimes knowin' things nobody else seems to. A body can never tell when she's gonna clamp shut like she's got a mouthful of gold teeth, or she's gonna haul off and blab right out."

"I'd sooner call it straight talk than blabbin'," Lone said, "but I came here lookin' for some answers."

"Now wait a minute, Lone. You know I buy and sell a lot of stuff. But you also know I don't sell out nobody to the law."

Lone heaved a sigh. "Clevon, we both know you'd sell Auntie Gwen over there for the right price. Just like we both know I ain't the law."

The 'Bino's eyes slid over to Jeth. "What about him?"

"He's an old friend from my army days. Name's Jeth Howard. He ain't the law neither."

"What I am, though," Jeth spoke up, "is the victim of some lowdown robbin' varmints who I'd damn well like to see the law *sicced on*."

The 'Bino looked edgy. "What's that got to do with me?"

"Nothing . . . 'cept maybe for those six stolen horses out there in your corral, includin' one belongin' to my friend."

"Whoa, whoa," The 'Bino protested. "I paid fair money for those horses. If they was stole, I had no way of knowin'. I can show you a detailed bill of sale."

"A bill of sale ain't nothing but lies put to paper," cackled the old woman.

"Shut up, Auntie!" barked The 'Bino. "Sit there an' mind your own business, elsewise I'll take away your cigars again."

Auntie's cotton puff eyebrows pinched together and she stuck her tongue out at him.

Before anybody could say anything more, a soiled, tattered blanket hanging over a doorway on the back wall was shoved aside and a large, hulking young man crowded through. The new arrival stood at least six inches over six feet tall, had arms as thick as fence posts dangling from shoulders like a pair of beer kegs strapped to the sides of his neck. His torso consisted of a massive chest swelling out and down to a bulging gut, all encased in a pair of faded bib overalls. The expression on his face—a broad, fleshy ball bracketed by bushy reddish sideburns and capped by spiky stubble of the same color—was a look of half-puzzlement, half concern.

"What's goin' on out here?" the young giant asked in a higher-pitched voice than might be expected to come out of such a large frame.

"Clevon's bein' mean to me," accused the old woman, thrusting out her lower lip in an exaggerated little girl's pout which looked all the more ridiculous with the cigar poking out of it.

"Tell Cousin Leroy the truth," The 'Bino was quick to respond. "Tell him how you was interruptin' again when I was tryin' to conduct business."

Cousin Leroy frowned. "Is that right, Ma? Ain't we talked about that before—how you gotta not bother Clevon when he's conductin' business so's he can make the best deals for all our sakes?"

"Stole horses ain't no good deal!" came the reply in a puff of smoke.

Leroy looked around questioningly. "What's that supposed to mean?"

"That's what we was in the middle of discussin'," said The 'Bino. He jerked his chin toward Lone and Jeth. "These gents are claimin' those horses out in the corral that I bought fair and square yesterday are stole animals—taken as part of a train robbery."

Lone jumped on that right away. "Who said anything about a train robbery? Not me or Jeth."

The 'Bino's eyes darted around nervously, knowing he'd slipped up. "Well, I . . . I guess I heard somewhere about a train robbery. Up, uh, up north I believe it was. And I seem to recall there was some horses . . . I—I guess I figured that's what you gents must be referrin' to."

"You know damn well it is," growled Jeth.

"And where you *vaguely* heard about it," said

120

Lone, "was straight from the skunks who done the robbin'—Dar Pierce and his gang!"

Cousin Leroy's eyebrows lifted. "So *that's* who that bunch was."

CHAPTER 15

The 'Bino's attitude changed, turning more belligerent. "All right. So Pierce and his bunch showed up here late yesterday and I did some tradin' with 'em. Bought some stuff, sold 'em a few things. That's what I do. Everybody knows. So are you anglin' to try and reclaim all the horses, or just the one you claim is yours?"

"The one that *is* mine," Jeth insisted. "But we ain't necessarily in the horse wranglin' business today."

"Like I said at the start, we're lookin' for some answers," Lone added.

"What kind of answers?"

"Straight ones. And we're in no mood for anything less."

The 'Bino's eyes narrowed. "That almost sounds like a threat."

"Only if you make it that way."

Scowling, Cousin Leroy said, "Here now, mister. No need to be unfriendly about it. Them other folks was nasty enough, no need for more."

Auntie Gwen suddenly started rocking faster and puffing harder on her cigar. "Nasty red woman . . . So stingy with her shiny pretty."

Lone turned to her, frowning, and said, "Red woman . . . You mean Harriet Bell, the red-haired woman who rides with Pierce?"

"Stingy and mean with her shiny pretty," the old woman repeated, continuing her rapid rocking.

Now it was Jeth who turned to her with a frown. "Stingy with her shiny . . . You mean like a piece of jewelry she had with her?"

"Leave her alone," The 'Bino said brusquely. "You can see she talks out of her head half the time."

"But she ain't now," Cousin Leroy countered. "That red-haired woman *was* mean to Ma. And she did have that piece of jewelry pinned on her. When Ma tried to reach out and touch it, just touch it, she pushed Ma's hand away real hard. If she hadn't been a woman, I'd've done some pushin' back!"

"Yeah," The 'Bino snarled, "and then Dar Pierce would've filled you full of lead for your trouble."

Cousin Leroy scowled. "He mighta *tried*."

"Gettin' back to that brooch, that piece of jewelry—" Jeth got that much out before his words were cut short by the sudden clattering of the cowbell over the front door.

Quickly following this was the sound of tromping boots and then two cowboys came sauntering purposefully into the room. Both were young, twentyish, clad in standard, well-worn wrangler garb with their hats pushed back on their shoulder, hanging from chin straps, exposing wide, eager grins plastered on their sun-burned faces.

"Hey, Jemsil, you bleached-out old skinflint," greeted one of them, the taller and leaner of the two. He had a shock of stringy blond hair dangling down over his forehead and ears that stuck out the sides of his head like a pair of batwing doors swung wide open. A battered old six-gun was strapped around his waist, worn haphazardly in a sagging, equally battered old holster, giving every indication it was carried mainly for shooting snakes and such out on the range, not to present himself as any kind of gunman.

The second cowboy was shorter, stockier, with long, tangled brown hair spilling down over the back of his neck. One ear was left uncovered and had a silver ring plugged through it. He, too, wore an un-showy hogleg on one hip, though his gun belt appeared a bit newer and better maintained.

In response to being hailed by the jug-eared cowpoke, The 'Bino said, "What brings you two around so late in the day? That new Greek cook they hired out at the Lazy H dishin' out such lousy grub you had to run away from supper?"

"Oh, we're skippin' supper right enough," said Jug Ears. "But only because we're anxious to get to some of that special new dessert we hear you're startin' to serve here."

"New dessert?" The 'Bino looked confused. "Not sure what you're talkin' about."

This gave Lone cause to interject, saying, "Whatever it is, you can get to it in a minute. First, you got answers to finish givin' my friend and me." Then, cutting his eyes over to Jug Ears, he explained, "That's the way it works where I come from, son. You walk up on a couple fellas in the middle of a conversation, you hold off and wait your turn. You don't just barge in. It's a little thing called showin' good manners."

For a long moment, Jug Ears simply looked taken aback, his jaw hanging slack. Then he started to turn red, with embarrassment at first it appeared, but then the hue deepening into anger. "Well let me tell you how it goes where I come from, mister," he said, chin jutting out defiantly. "Around here we don't believe in waitin' our turn or takin' no lessons on manners from saddle tramps who come in and out like wind-blown clumps of tumbleweed. So if you know what's good for you, you'd better hold your tongue and step aside. Else, better yet, be on your way."

"Now see here. I don't want no trouble in my place," The 'Bino was quick to say.

"And I won't allow none," added Cousin Leroy, his voice taking on a hardened tone that sounded practiced for just such occasions.

"Where the lone man goes, trouble does, too," Auntie Gwen cackled.

Pointedly, Lone ignored everybody but The 'Bino. Locking his gaze once more on the trader, he said, "It's your call to make, Clevon. It can be over quick and easy, with no trouble, if you answer just two questions. Did Pierce give any specific indication where he was headed when he left here? And did Harriet Bell ride away with that shiny brooch—or did you manage to buy it off her?"

"The mean red woman *took* the shiny pretty!" wailed Auntie Gwen, and then immediately went into another pout.

"There. I don't know what the hell the old crow is cawin' about, but it sounds to me like you got your answer, mister. So now you can leave happy," declared Jug Ears. With that, he turned his back on Lone, slapped his palms down on the counter top and, shoving his face closer to The 'Bino said, "Now we can get to the business of you introducin' me and Rafe—me first, since I won a coin toss between the two of us—to that pretty little Injun filly we hear you've got in a back room needin' saddle broke."

Lone had his right fist balled and partially drawn back while his left hand was reaching to grab Jug Ears by his collar—the former scout's full intent being to spin the cocky young pup around and paste him one—when the words "pretty little Injun filly" stopped him. Later, even after considerable pondering, Lone could never say exactly why that was. Jug Ears could have been referring to any one of dozens of Indian females from anywhere in the vicinity. But something, some instinct caused Lone to think of only one—and the unlikely possibility that Jug Ears might somehow mean her.

"What's this about an Injun filly needin' saddle broke?" he grated.

The 'Bino's eyes shifted at the question and a moment later the trader's mouth was twisting into a lewd smirk. "Why, McGantry you old dog. Never figured you'd show interest in such pursuit."

Jug Ears lifted his hands and slammed his palms back down on the counter, much harder this time. "Goddammit, *I'm* the one showin' interest! Remember? Mr. Gonna-Teach-Everybody-Some-Manners is leavin'. And it looks like I'm gonna have to help him on his way!"

Turning to face Lone, clearly meaning to try and back up his words, Jug Ears didn't get very far. He found Lone waiting and ready—no longer with his fist balled but instead his hand raised, fingers curled claw-like. As soon as Jug Ears got turned, the hand shot forward and clamped on his throat, fingertips gouging in around the Adam's apple, throttling him. Jug Ears' whole body spasmed and his hands flew up to tug frantically on Lone's wrists, trying to break his hold with no success. The cowboy's mouth worked like a fish out of water, only able to make gagging, gasping noises.

"Sonny," Lone said, speaking slowly through tightly gritted teeth, "you had best calm down real quick-like—before I hand you your Adam's apple to take home in a pocket."

Jug Ears' partner, the long-haired wrangler referred to as Rafe, started to make a move to help his friend. He only made it half a step, though, before his way was blocked by the twin barrels of Jeth's shotgun held at waist level and extended across in front of him.

"That's far enough, boy," Jeth said calmly. "Unless your pard does something almighty dumb, he'll be okay. You just stand easy and don't make it worse."

Unfortunately, somebody who *wasn't* willing to just stand easy was big Cousin Leroy. "Alright, that's it! All you troublemakers—out of here!" he bellowed, shoving forward in a bull rush.

Without waiting for the words to have any effect on their own, he immediately swung one of his melon-sized fists to back them up. That amounted to two mistakes on his part. One, the target for his intended punch was Lone; and two, the speed with which the fist came sailing was slow enough for the former scout to have time to partially duck. Lone got his head twisted away and one shoulder hunched up to take most of the glancing blow but, even slightly diminished, the impact was strong enough to send him staggering. He released his hold on Jug Ears' throat and the two of them went stumbling hard into Jeth and Rafe, resulting in a four-man tangle all flailing to stay upright.

Since his punch didn't land as solidly as it was meant to, Leroy was pulled momentarily off balance. But as soon as he got set again, he was ready to continue what he'd set out to do, despite The 'Bino wailing "Stop it! Stop it!" from behind the counter.

And just like Leroy wasn't ready to stop what he'd unloosed, neither was Lone. It flat wasn't in him to take a punch and not retaliate, not as long as he was still conscious. So out of the entanglement with Jeth and the two cowboys he came charging to meet Leroy's renewed advance.

Hardly a small man himself, Lone was keenly aware that here was an instance where his size and strength, and maybe even his core toughness, all stood to be fully tested. Leroy might be slow and somewhat awkward, but his bulk nevertheless packed tremendous power. The full impact from one of his punches or getting caught in the grip of those massive arms could quickly spell the finish for anybody on the receiving end. However, that didn't make an automatic victim of somebody with enough fighting savvy to stay elusive and enough power to deliver some telling strikes in return.

And Lone McGantry never went into a fight planning on being the victim.

The first thing he did was duck another looping roundhouse right that Leroy led with, the crushing fist whooshing through the air above Lone's head as he went in under it and hammered Leroy's sizable gut with short, rapid right-left jabs. A mighty gust of air whistled out of the big man. Dropping lower still, Lone dodged off to his right but, on the way, he whipped his left knee up and inward, driving it against the outside of Leroy's right knee joint and forcing it to bend in a way it was never meant to. Leroy howled in pain and tipped back, flailing, falling against the counter hard enough to nearly topple the barrels supporting it.

Straightening up, Lone moved off a couple feet and then circled back toward his opponent, fists raised. Leroy glared at him menacingly, puffing to try and catch his breath, seeming to be in no hurry to push away from the counter. But when he did, he predictably came once more in a bull rush. This time, though, instead of trying to land another punch he came reaching with both arms, fingers splayed wide, tips curled to grab and tear.

Lone waited until the last second and then ducked again, once more dodging to his right. When Leroy's momentum carried him part way past, Lone uncoiled and twisted into him with a right hook to the hinge of the big man's jaw. The meatiness of his jowl provided a layer of padding but the blow drilled in hard enough so that the crunch of bone giving way could nevertheless be heard.

Leroy's forward momentum was halted and he stood teetering for a moment, puffing hard, bent slightly at the waist with a trickle of blood showing at one corner of his mouth. But he was too damn big to take any chances with; an animal that's only wounded can be the most dangerous kind. Aiming to finish him, Lone didn't waste any time closing in. But he should have used more caution. When he got too close, he was given a jarring reminder of that from Leroy's left elbow whipping back to meet him, its point crashing to the center of Lone's forehead with the force of a sledgehammer. The impact stunned the former scout, buckling his knees and setting off an explosion of brightly colored pinwheels inside his skull. He lurched to the side, grabbing one of the tables in the middle of the room for support and knocking over two of the chairs hitched up to it.

Landing the elbow strike seemed to shake Leroy somewhat out of his daze. Meaning to follow up, he attempted to wheel the rest of the way around so he was once again facing Lone. But the act of doing so meant pushing off on his right leg, the one whose joint Lone had damaged earlier. The pressure that the turning-pushing motion put on the injured joint sent a jolt of pain all up and down Leroy's leg, causing him to falter in finishing the turn. The second or two this cost the young giant and the imbalance it pitched him into, gave Lone all the time he needed to blink away most of the lights popping behind his eyes and shove off the table he'd half-sprawled onto.

This time it was the former scout who threw himself into a bull rush. While Leroy was still struggling to get his feet planted for proper balance, Lone waded in with fists flying. A left hook to the side of the head and an overhand right to the nose and upper lip both landed solidly. When Lone felt the nose cartilage collapse under his knuckles and saw the blood spurt when he drew his fist back, he knew he'd gained an important advantage. A smashed nose blurs a man's vision and clogs his breathing.

But the stubborn brute wasn't ready to go down. Not just yet. The punches had again knocked him back against The 'Bino's counter, once more nearly toppling the barrels. But the barrels managed to stay upright, and so did Leroy. Just barely. He was sagged back against the counter, massive chest rising and falling heavily, blood gouting from his mashed nostrils with each exhalation. Yet the menacing glare from his watery eyes continued to brand Lone and sent a clear message he damn well wasn't done.

Sighing, breathing heavily himself, Lone

leaned over and picked up one of the overturned chairs that had come to rest against the side of his leg. Brandishing the sturdy object in front of him with both hands, he said, "I'm tired of bustin' a gut and splittin' my knuckles on you. You want any more, you big ox, you'll get it with this. And once I start in, I swear I'll keep hammerin' until the chair is nothing but a pile of splinters and your head is a lump of pulp."

"For God's sake, no. Don't beat him no more," The 'Bino pleaded from behind his counter. He reached forward and put a hand on Leroy's shoulder. "Can't you see he's had enough?"

"I can. But does he?" Lone wanted to know.

Speaking calm and soft, minus any of her previous affectations, Auntie Gwen said, "Tell them, son. Let it be done."

Hanging his head, staring down at the floor with the menace finally fading from his eyes, Leroy said, "Okay, Mama . . . I'm sorry I got whupped."

"It's okay, son. You done your best."

With that, still gripping the chair in both fists, Lone cut his gaze over to the pair of cowboys, Jug Ears and Rafe. "How about it, you two pups? You still itchin' for a turn?"

The pair wagged their heads promptly and in unison. Jug Ears said, "N-nossir. No need for any more trouble."

This brought a familiar cackle out of the

old woman in the rocking chair and she said, "Trouble goes where the lone man does. Best stay out'n the way when the two of 'em are on the prowl."

CHAPTER 16

Against all logic or expectation, and yet in keeping with the strange feeling Lone had experienced as soon as he heard Jug Ears' vulgar reference, the "Injun filly" being kept in a back room at The 'Bino's trading post turned out to be none other than Minowi—the Indian wife of Simon Weaver who had fled from the railroad watering station in the wake of killing Tad Clemson.

Following the fight with Cousin Leroy and the abrupt departure of the two cowboys who suddenly decided they needed to get back to the Lazy H for supper after all, Lone had insisted on seeing the girl whose mention had sparked the whole outburst of trouble. What was shown and told to him and Jeth would have riled him plenty, no matter what; but the fact it was Minowi (who Lone had felt an odd connection with right from those first minutes back at the station) made his reaction even fiercer. She was being kept locked in a wooden cage, stripped nearly naked, and restrained additionally by a short length of chain and an iron ankle cuff.

The explanation behind this was that she had been found out on the open prairie, afoot and without provisions, by an old prospector named McFee. In prior times, when there were those who'd pay for such, McFee had been a notorious scalp hunter. His deep-rooted contempt for Indians, seeing anyone with a red skin as only having worth if they were dead or money could somehow be made off them, gave him an idea for a different way to earn something from finding this girl, even if her hair was no longer marketable. So he captured her and brought her to The 'Bino with a proposition that McFee would sell her to the trader who could then not only recoup his investment but make an ongoing profit by offering her sexual services, for a price, to the kind of desperate and lonely customers who were common to his joint. Since The 'Bino was every bit as unscrupulous as McFee and always on the lookout to make some added easy money, the deal had been struck.

But thanks to a wholly unanticipated visit by the likes of Lone, the second part of the deal was never going to get off the ground. When the former scout, barely able to hold his rage in check, demanded the girl be immediately released to him, The 'Bino wailed, "What about the money I paid? The profits I'm never gonna see?"

Lone's icy response had been: "Consider your profit to be the fact I don't burn this shithole to the ground before I leave. And one more whiny peep out of you is all it might take for me to change my mind!"

That had been three hours past.

Now, with those hours and a handful of miles behind them, Lone, Jeth, and Minowi were getting settled into a night camp within a sparse stand of cottonwood trees overlooking a small, spring-fed pond. Full dark had descended. The moon wasn't out yet but a plentiful array of stars in the clear sky overhead were growing steadily brighter.

There had been little opportunity nor any real need for conversation during their ride from the trading post. The same held true, for the short term, as they went about pitching their camp. Each recognized tasks that needed to be done, and each took a share of performing them. While Lone tended the horses (including Jeth's reclaimed white gelding that had served as a mount for Minowi) the others got a fire going and laid out the makings for a meal. Minowi ground beans and filled a pot for coffee, Jeth sliced up several strips of bacon and, while they were starting to fry, unwrapped the morning's leftover biscuits from their protective pocket of oilcloth. He also set out two airtights of canned pears.

By the time Lone finished with the animals and walked over to the fire, everything was nearly ready to dish out. Only a few minutes later, each member of the trio was balancing in front of them a tin plate stacked with bacon, biscuits, and peach slices and had a cup of steaming coffee

137

resting on the grass beside where they sat. On the one hand, Lone was glad to see Minowi eating with gusto; on the other, it angered and saddened him to realize this was a sign she must have been getting by damned sparingly for the past three days.

When the meal was done and final cups of coffee poured, Lone leaned back against his upturned saddle and decided now was a reasonable time for some questions and answers.

Settling his gaze on Minowi, he said, "I know you understand and speak very good English. Better than me or Jeth maybe. So would you mind puttin' those skills to use and fillin' us in on a few things?"

She met his gaze with those deep, dark eyes of hers and held it for a beat before replying, "Of course not. Anything less would be awfully rude of me, would it not? I mean, considering how you seem to keep showing up to aid me when I'm in a time of need."

"Dang. She does speak real fine, don't she?" marveled Jeth.

"That she does," allowed Lone. Then, addressing Minowi again, he said, "Maybe that's a good place to start. My impression was that you only recently became Simon Weaver's wife and before that was livin' on the Sioux reservation up north. No offense, but most Indians fresh off the rez don't speak English nearly as good as you."

"I was taught by missionaries who came to live with our tribe when I was just a little girl," Minowi explained. "My adoptive mother encouraged me to learn. Most others my age resisted, resented anything the White Eyes had to offer. Since most of them resented me, too, that gave me all the more cause to do the opposite out of spite and learn everything I could."

Lone frowned. "You said 'adoptive mother' and that you were resented by others your age?"

Minowi nodded. "Yes. You see, even though I lived with the Sioux from the time I was an infant, I am not of Sioux blood. In the eyes of most, I was a slave claimed in the long ago battle when the Sioux slaughtered a great many of my true people, the Pawnee, and drove them from their Nebraska hunting grounds to eventually be relocated in the Indian Territory."

"The battle of Massacre Canyon," Lone said tonelessly.

"You are familiar with it?" Minowi seemed somewhat surprised.

"I know of it." Lone took a measured sip of his coffee. "Happens there was a past time when I had me a particular interest in the Pawnee. It was because I, too, was orphaned as an infant due to an Indian massacre—only in my case it was a Pawnee war party wipin' out my settler parents. I survived because my folks had time to hide me before the attack. An army patrol found me shortly after. I ended up bein' raised in an army fort, sorta passed around amongst the post wives. That's also how I came by the name Lone. My folks was known to have the last name of McGantry but there was no record of what they meant to call me—so I became 'the lone McGantry' and after a while just plain Lone."

"All the time I've knowed you, I never knew that," said Jeth. "I mean, I reckon I heard about the massacre and all. I just never knew where the Lone came from."

"Well, now you've heard the long and short of it."

All during this exchange, Minowi continued to gaze intently at Lone. Speaking again, she said softly, "So when you mentioned having a particular interest in the Pawnee, you must have meant out of hatred."

Meeting her gaze, Lone replied flatly, "No other word for it. Blind hate. And as soon as I was old enough to start ridin' on army patrols, I didn't waste any time actin' on it. True there was a fair number of veteran Injun-haters in the ranks to encourage me, but I can't lay the blame on them. I was out for blood all on my own . . . And I spilled plenty during those years. Pawnee, Sioux, Cheyenne. Whatever we came up against."

"But don't forget, those red devils . . . er, pardon me, ma'am . . . spilled plenty of blood from our boys, too," declared Jeth.

"Yeah, the prairie ran scarlet." Lone took a drink of coffee. "And in the end what did it amount to? Land changed from red hands to white, lots died in order for that to happen, and old wounds and scars never really healed but in a lot of cases only got covered over by new ones."

It was quiet for a minute. Until Minowi said, "You almost sound like a man whose hatred has burned out in him."

Lone shook his head. "Not really. Only the blind kind. Put those who killed my parents in front of me, I'd want 'em dead at my hands just as bad as ever. But it'd be strictly because of what they did, not because of the color of their skin or their tribe or whatever . . . I guess you could say that part *has* burned out of me. But I can still hate, and do it almighty hard, if given proper cause."

Jeth drained the last of his coffee and then tapped the cup upside down on the heel of his hand, knocking out the leftover grounds. "I don't know about burned out, but I know about *pooped* out. And that's what this ol' mule pusher is," he proclaimed. "So, if you two children promise not to go on the warpath against each other, then I'm gonna roll over, curl up in my bedroll and get some shuteye." As he was pulling up a corner of his blanket, he stopped abruptly and craned his neck to look back at Lone. "You don't reckon we need to post a lookout, do you?"

"For The 'Bino or Cousin Leroy, you mean?" Lone chuffed. "Not likely we got any worry from them. In the first place, I expect they've had their fill of us. In the second, I doubt either of 'em could go a hundred yards in the dark without gettin' lost. Roll on over and go to sleep."

In a matter of seconds it seemed, Jeth began snoring.

After finishing his own coffee and tapping out the cup, Lone said to Minowi, "I guess I interrupted your story and sorta went spinnin' off on mine. But I'd still like to hear the rest of yours."

"Even though you now know I am Pawnee?"

Lone made a face. "Because I might still harbor hard feelin's toward all Pawnee on account of what happened to my folks, is that what you think? Didn't I just cover that? Time was, I admit though ain't particularly proud to say, that would've been the case. But no more blind hate, remember? That is, unless you harbor some toward me for all the Pawnee braves I killed when I did have those feelin's."

Minowi's head moved faintly back and forth. "No. For as long as I can remember, I have saved all my hatred for the Sioux. Yet even then, I could not feel that way toward my adoptive mother, Bright Leaf Woman. Nor, for that matter, her husband Running Wolf, the brave who spared me on the battlefield when other so-called warriors

142

were bashing in the heads of women and children after defeating their men."

"Sounds to me like pretty good cause for a powerful hate."

"I have no direct memory of the battle, of course. But as I grew older, there were those in the tribe—young and old alike—who relished in telling me the details. To them I was just a lowly slave, remember, even though Bright Leaf Woman and, to a lesser degree Running Wolf, treated me mostly like a daughter. The whole reason Running Wolf spared me and took me home, you see, was because his wife had lost two children in the womb and the tribe's medicine man declared her barren. Running Wolf meant for me to ease her grief and sadness . . . And, over the years, I'd like to think I did. She, in turn, sheltered me and spared me from the torment of others as much as she could."

Lone had a pretty good hunch what was coming next.

"When Bright Leaf Woman died," Minowi continued, "those in the tribe who had barely contained their resentment of me for so long, no longer felt any need to hold back. By then Running Wolf had grown old and feeble and, other than wanting to please his wife, had never developed much personal fondness for me anyway. So he was of little or no help to discourage my ill treatment. To attempt running away would have been useless, they would have put every effort into hunting me down just so they could torment me more. My life became increasingly miserable . . . Until Simon Weaver showed up wanting to trade for me and take me as his wife. I did not know him, did not love or even like him, but what I *did* know was that what he was offering had to be better than what I was experiencing. The day I rode away with him was the closest thing to joy I had ever felt in my life."

Lone studied her for a long moment before saying quietly, "I don't know what all lies ahead for you, Minowi. But whatever it is, I sure hope it includes a dose of true joy like you rightfully deserve."

CHAPTER 17

"I half expected her to light out in the middle of the night," Jeth was saying. "She not only stuck around, she was the first one up and busy. Had the fire re-stoked and some coffee already workin' before I ever crawled out of my blankets."

"I know, I was awake and listenin'," Lone told him. "It felt good to stay rolled up a little extra and wait for the first smell of fresh coffee that somebody else was gettin' started."

The two men were having this discussion beside the crackling campfire. The brightening orange-gold glow of an about-to-break-into-sight sun was extending out from the eastern horizon across a cloudless sky. Jeth was squatted down, using a fork to turn strips of bacon in a frying pan resting on a low spiderweb grill straddling the flames. Lone stood over him, cup of just-poured coffee in one hand.

"Then I guess you heard her ask if she had time to go take a bath while I was slappin' together a new batch of pan biscuits. When I tried to warn her the spring water in that pond was likely to be a mite chill, especially so early in the day, she just laughed and said only White Eyes needed hot water and a giant soup bowl to take a bath in." Jeth gave a little chuckle. "I got a kick out of that. And when she smiled and laughed it made her even prettier than I already knew she was. Up until then I don't think I saw her so much as show even a hint of a smile—not back at the waterin' station and not since we took her out of that stinkin' tradin' post."

Lone said, "I doubt she's had much practice smilin', Jeth. Ain't been much in her life to smile about."

"No, I reckon not." Jeth eyed him, looking up from the bacon he continued to poke at. "You and her stay up jawbonin' for a while after I turned in last night, did ya?"

"Yeah. Quite a while."

"She seems to take a kind of shine to you."

Lone's eyebrows lifted. "I don't know about that. She ain't experienced much in the way of decent treatment from very many people along the way, that's all. No need to make more of it."

"She gonna be travelin' with us for a spell?"

"Unless you got a problem with the notion. When she heard we was on the trail of the Pierce gang and we figured they was headed for the Indian Territory, that fit where she wants to get to. So taggin' along with us, at least for a ways— since I explained to her we hope to catch up with those skunks long before they make it to the Nations—seemed better than strikin' off on her own again."

"Goin' to join her real people, the Pawnee, is that it?"

"Uh-huh. Sure as hell not back to the Sioux. That's why she struck out down this way in the first place, not north like everybody expected. Down to where she had the misfortune of lettin' that vermin-infested McFee get his paws on her." Lone lifted his coffee cup to his mouth and scowled over the rim as he took a sip. Lowering it, he said, "One more reason I'd like to cross paths with that varmint again. I tangled with him in the past, off farther west, when his hair-liftin' habits sparked an outbreak of fresh hostilities and stalled a peace treaty with the Arapaho. He got away from me, though, slitherin' off like the reptile he is."

Jeth said, "Easy to understand why Minowi don't want to return to the Sioux rez. But what about her husband, that station fella Weaver? You tell her how she don't *have* to run away nowhere any more—how Ira Clemson ain't no longer a threat to her if she was to go back Ogallala way? Whether she knows it or not, Indian Territory ain't exactly the land of milk and honey for most of the tribes corralled down there. And, from what I've heard, the Pawnee in particular got one of the smaller patches to scratch a livin' out of."

"Yeah, I heard the same. But her mind's made up." Lone paused to cast a brief glance in the direction of the pond before continuing. "The other part of it is that she wants nothing more to do with Weaver, no matter how things might have changed regardin' Clemson."

"Yeah, it didn't take long to see there wasn't a lot of heat in whatever was goin' on between her and the station man. To tell the truth, he had a kind of weasely way about him that was off-puttin' from most any angle."

Lone twisted his mouth sourly. "You don't know the half of it. That sonofabitch is worse than a weasel. Oh, he didn't beat her or nothing like that. Worked her like a dog maybe. But after a while, when he discovered he couldn't exactly hold up his end of things in the bedroom, he blamed it all on her. Worse, the piece of slime then tried to pimp her out. Said maybe she could learn some man-pleasin' skills from other men and earn a little extra cash while she was at it . . . That whole business with Tad Clemson tryin' to have some sport with Minowi the day I rode up? Weaver was in on it, urgin' her to go ahead and give him what he wanted."

Jeth spat out a curse. "You're right, he is lower than a weasel. She ought to go back long enough to stick a knife in his gizzard, too, before she calls it quits . . . And you're also right about that poor child experiencin' precious little in the way of decent treatment in her life. Damned dirty shame!"

• • •

A quarter mile away, Lyle "Big Tooth" Vallen lay on his belly atop a grassy hill with the spyglass he was holding to one eye resting in a notch of the low, rocky spine that ran across the crown of the rise. Hayden Halloway was sprawled beside him, propped up on his elbows.

The initial intent of this bit of reconnoitering had been to check the activity of Lone and Jeth. Where the magnified view was currently focused, however, was not on the two men in the in the campsite but rather on the spring-fed pond several yards beyond where a nude, glisteningly wet Minowi happened to be emerging from her bath.

"Man oh man," Vallen said in a breathy whisper. "I don't know how come those two trail hounds to latch on to something so fine from that ratty-lookin' old tradin' post, but it half makes me want to go back there and see if they got any more like her to be plucked off a shelf. Havin' something like that to tuck in your bedroll with you each night would make this godforsaken trail ride a whole different prospect."

"Give me that glass, let me have another look before she gets all covered up," urged Halloway.

Reluctantly, Vallen handed over the spyglass, saying, "Here. Don't get to pantin' so heavy you get it all fogged up again so's I have to wait for it to clear before I can have another gander!"

Halloway took the glass and hurriedly hitched up to find his own opening in the rocky spine to thrust it through and bring it into suitable focus. No sooner had he done so than he let out a low groan. "Oh, sweet mother . . . That's about as fine a collection of female flesh as I ever did see. And an Injun squaw no less! Every other squaw I can ever remember bumpin' into before this was about as wide as they was tall and had faces looked like somebody stepped on 'em when they was just papooses. Jesus, we get done with this little gallop we hired on for, I'm gonna have to start visitin' more Injun reservations and lookin' more careful at the pickin's to be had."

Vallen grunted. "You go ahead and do that. You try sniffin' around the wrong wigwam, some randy buck also on the prowl will fix it so's you won't have the equipment to do nothing with if you did grab a split tail . . . Besides, if we pull off this job and take back that doo-dad to earn the bonus we been promised, you won't have to go skulkin' around no Injun rez for female flesh. You'll be able to afford the finest money can buy—one of those high-toned fancy gals who knows tricks to turn you inside out and leave you with a smile on your face couldn't be wiped off with anything short of a chair bashed over your head."

"That all sounds good," Halloway allowed. "But it's a maybe thing that's a ways off. At best.

What I'm lookin' at now is right here under our noses."

"Oh, sure. Right under our noses—but with those two ornery old cusses in between. You forgettin' about them?" Vallen made a face. "And if we *did* wade through 'em to go down there so's we could scrub the squaw's back, it would kinda queer the whole bonus-earnin' deal, don't you think? And I mean thinkin' with the brain supposedly between your ears, not the one between your legs."

"Yeah, yeah. You're right," Halloway muttered. Abruptly, he pulled the glass from his eye and shoved it back over to Vallen. "Here, take the damn thing 'fore I work myself up to a heart stroke or some such. Damn. I wish we at least would've took time to get our ashes hauled that last night in Ogallala, maybe the pressure from lookin' at all that prime coppery nekkedness wouldn't be so quick to build up and give a body such a strong tug."

"Just keep in mind that the thing supposed to be tuggin' at us is the job of stickin' tight to these old cusses while they stick tight to the trail of the bank robbers with the Whitlock kid's precious damn jewel." As he said this, Vallen was wasting no time getting the spyglass focused once again on Minowi.

"I just hope they're all they're cracked up to be and know what the hell they're doin'," grumbled

Halloway. "First they take time for a stop at that tradin' post and ride away with a girl for no clear reason. Now, this mornin', they're down there takin' time for bathin' and cookin' up a whole big breakfast . . . While you drag our asses up and out here before first light, without so much as a cold cup of coffee, to make sure they don't get a jump on us. Well it don't appear they're up for much jumpin', leastways not any time soon."

"Yeah, and now that we know that, we can relax long enough to drop back and cook ourselves some coffee. But we had to be sure." Finally lowering the glass because the show was now over by virtue of Minowi having gotten dried off and dressed, Vallen cut a sidelong glance over at his partner and added, with a crooked grin, "Besides, look at the free peep show we would've missed if I hadn't rousted us so we was in position up here to enjoy it."

"Might be a certain amount of pleasure in that," Halloway allowed grudgingly. "But only lookin' at a tasty spread of fried chicken and mashed taters without gettin' close enough to have a bite don't hardly leave you all the way satisfied."

Back across the Nebraska line and still nearly a full day ahead of the pursuit they weren't yet aware of, Dar Pierce and his gang were also in the midst of a breakfast meal before riding on again. While Caldwell, Bandros, and Grissom were busy working on their plates of food, Pierce himself was kneeling before a barefoot Harriet Bell and smearing strong-smelling liniment onto her exposed extremities.

"One 'I told you so' remark from anybody about those boots I tried to squeeze into," she declared loud enough to be heard by all in camp, "I swear I'll make whoever it is pay with a kick where I guarantee you won't like as soon as I get my regular boots back on!"

"You already made that message clear, Harriet. You don't need to keep reminding us," replied Caldwell.

"Besides," Bandros added, "Dar is already making us pay, even though we didn't do any-thing to deserve it, with the terrible smell of that liniment he's using while we're in the middle of eating."

"Maybe so," allowed Grissom. "But not even the dreadful smell of that goop is enough to ruin the taste of this prime beef we came upon. I'm fine with bacon, and those airtights we took off the train have had some mighty tasty contents but"—as he pushed a forkful of what he was talking about into his mouth even as he continued talking—"ain't nothing like fresh, juicy beefsteak to proper fill a person's belly."

"Well don't expect me to just take your word for it," Harriet said, glancing around with a scowl. "There'd better be some left for me when we're finished here."

"Of course there will be, senorita," Bandros promised. "We may be filthy, uncouth outlaws . . . But even we are not *that* un-gentlemanly." And then he laughed.

The source of the food staple under discussion lay about twenty yards away—the slain and half-butchered carcass of a good-sized steer. They'd happened upon the critter the previous evening just before dusk and had promptly shot and carved off some fresh meat for supper and also breakfast.

Harriet spoke again, rolling her eyes. "And as far as the smell of this foot liniment, if you think it stinks over there, you oughta be the one getting it slapped on." Then, frowning directly at Pierce, she asked, "That smell ain't going to stick with me, is it?"

"No, not after I get it worked in good," the gang boss assured her. "But even if it did, apart from punishing everybody else"—here he looked up from his task and returned her frown—"I'll be the one to say it'd serve your dang stubbornness right for not listening to me about those stupid tight boots to begin with."

"Okay, okay. I'll let you get away with that one. But the boots are gone now, thrown down into that gully yonder. Maybe some coyote will come along and try them on for size, see what kind of luck he has with 'em."

"Good," Pierce said. "Since you're being agreeable to that much, might you be willing to listen to another piece of advice?"

Harriet cocked an eyebrow. "Depends. As long as you don't get too carried away. What is it?"

Pierce jerked his chin, indicating the brooch she had pinned on her shirt. "That thing—that thingamabob you've already seen get its original owner shot and then send that old crow back at the trading post into a full conniption. You figure to keep on wearing it?"

"Reckon so. Why shouldn't I?"

"Well, like I said, you've seen the way it draws attention. I can't help thinking that if we find ourselves a nice, fat bank in McCook, the way we're hoping, and we go ahead and pay it a visit . . . Don't you think that shiny brooch contraption bobbing on your chest might continue being quick to draw attention—like maybe a bullet if anybody decides to try and stop us?"

"Hey, that's something to for sure consider," called Grissom around another mouthful of food. "I can tell you from experience how there's been plenty of times, when lead was flying, that I took special care to aim a pill at the shiny badge of some law dog whenever I saw one."

"Si, I have done the same," agreed Bandros.

Harriet looked thoughtful for a moment before saying, "Alright. You convinced me. We find a bank we decide to go after, I'll take my 'shiny pretty' off and put it in my pocket 'til we're done."

"Fair enough," declared Pierce, finished applying the liniment and wiping his hands on his pants. "Now get your socks and proper boots on so you can hobble over for some of that beef and we can get headed out. I figure McCook is another day-and-a-half ride. We get there two days from now, we should have time left in the afternoon to give things a good looking over. We like what we see, we hit it first thing on the third morning from now."

"Sounds good to me. Sounds real good," said Caldwell with a nod.

"Hey, how about cutting a couple more slabs of meat from that cow to take with us for supper tonight?" Grissom asked. "It oughta last long enough to not be spoiled by then, don't you think?"

Pierce shrugged. "Probably. We can judge by the smell, anybody wants to try it."

Bandros emitted a sarcastic laugh. "What the hell. How much can a little food poisoning hurt a pack of poison mean bandidos like us anyway, eh?"

CHAPTER 18

"Yeah, this is the spot. Here's where they made camp last night," said Lone, eyes sweeping back and forth over the area where Minowi, Jeth, and he had reined up and continued to sit their saddles. Cocking his head back to look up at the mid-afternoon position of the sun overhead, he added, "Puts 'em less than a day ahead of us. We gained good ground with our hard push so far today. We keep at it 'til past dusk, we'll tighten it even more."

"Looks like they were obligin' enough to help us by slowin' down for a bit of a feast," noted Jeth, tipping his head toward the carcass of the slain steer off a ways in the grass. It was well marked by the thick, black cloud of loudly buzzing flies that covered it. Further signaling its presence were the buzzards circling above, providing a sign that Lone had noticed from some miles back.

"Like you said, real obligin' of 'em," agreed Lone. "We'll wait and have our feast once we've run the varmints to ground. Barrin' a bad turn of some kind, that oughta be about mid-day tomorrow—in the town of McCook, it's lookin' like."

"What is this McCook?" asked Minowi.

"Place some miles ahead," Lone answered.

157

"When Pierce was at The 'Bino's tradin' post, he showed a lot of interest in it. Asked a lot of questions about the railroad that came in a year or so back, how big the town has grown since and the like."

Jeth said, "We're speculatin' Pierce and his bunch might be thinkin' of pullin' a robbery in the McCook area—a bank most likely, maybe another train—before makin' his final swing for the Nations."

"So that explains why we have been riding east, not yet veering to the south at all," Minowi said thoughtfully.

Lone regarded her. He couldn't get over how she seemed to be growing prettier with damn near each passing hour. Outfitted now in clothing acquired at the trading post, she was clad in a wine red split riding skirt, calf length moccasin boots, and a simple white blouse worn open at the throat and with sleeves rolled up a couple turns on her coppery forearms. Her hair, following this morning's bath, gleamed like black silk in the sunshine, and her eyes had a dark richness all their own.

"I tried to explain to you," Lone reminded her, "that Jeth and me might not be goin' clear down to Injun Territory. Our job is to catch up with Pierce and take back what he stole. If we're able to get that done in McCook, that's as far as we'll be goin'."

Minowi returned his gaze without expression, said nothing.

"If you want to go ahead and start south right away on your own, you're welcome to the horse and saddle," Lone told her, working to keep his tone flat, not let in any hint of the reservation he actually felt toward the idea. "We'll add as much as we can in the way of provisions, too. Certainly more than you had when you lit out from the waterin' station. On the other hand, if you want to stick with us until we find out for sure how things turn out . . . Well, you're sure welcome to do that, too."

"More than welcome," Jeth was quick to add. "If you stick with us a while longer and we're able to get things settled in McCook, might be we can help set you up even better if you insist on still strikin' south."

There was a moment's hesitation before Minowi's lips curved in not only a rare smile, but a beautifully wide one as she said, "You two . . . all of my life I have been made to feel unwelcome. And now I have a plan to leave yet you are saying I am welcome to stay . . . Do you know what a struggle that creates inside of me?"

Lone and Jeth exchanged awkward glances, as if uncertain whether or not they had somehow done something they should feel guilty about.

Minowi's smile only widened. "No, no. Do not misunderstand. It is a wonderful struggle to have." The pair she was addressing still didn't look wholly at ease. Continuing, Minowi said, "While I still want to return to my people, it doesn't have to be immediate. So I am grateful for your invitation, and for now very much want to continue on with you."

"Whew! I'm glad we got that settled," declared Jeth.

"Me, too," said Lone, grinning. "So now that we do, and now that the horses have had a breather, let's get a move on and continue shrinking that gap between us and Pierce's bunch."

The terrain they'd progressed into during the course of the morning had grown steadily more broken and rugged. There were still wide stretches of rolling, empty grassland but included were sharper peaks to many of the hills, an increasing number of rock outcrops, and sudden wash-outs turning in places to deep, twisting small canyons like some giant claw had reached down and made gashes in the land. Clumps of brush and scattered stands of mostly spruce and cottonwood trees had also become more common.

Less than a mile from the camp and its slain steer, as they were skirting around one of these jagged wash-outs, its rim crowded by a heavy growth of brush and spruce, they suddenly found themselves confronted by four horsemen who clearly had been holding in wait for them. The quartet was just as clearly a hardscrabble lot, all of them dressed in frayed, faded clothing with slouch hats pulled low above sun-squinted eyes and ruddy, weathered faces. But there appeared nothing unkempt about the repeating rifles—an equal mix of Henrys and Winchesters—they all held leveled and aimed with casual assurance.

Lone was caught cold, no chance to make a try for the Colt on his hip or the Yellowboy in its saddle scabbard; especially not with Minowi riding right beside him. All he or the others could do was check down their mounts and wait to hear what the four in front of them had in mind.

The apparent leader of the bunch, and also the oldest by about twenty years over the next in line, was the first to speak. "That's right. Just hold steady and careful," he said in a twangy drawl that sounded like it had its roots considerably farther south than just this slice of southern Nebraska. He was a heavyset man well into his fifties, with a scraggly gray goatee, bulbous nose, and close set eyes that somehow made Lone think they peered out at the world with permanent suspicion.

In response to the man's words, Lone said, "We ain't got much choice but to hold steady and careful with four gun muzzles trained on us. What's this all about?"

The second oldest of the group, his nose

too closely copying that of the older man to be anything but a relative, likely a son Lone guessed, gave a snort through the growth on his face. "What's this about, he wants to know, Pap. You reckon he's so stupid he plumb forgot what they done—or does he think we're so stupid we ain't figured it out?"

"Don't matter none, Lud. He owes the same accounting either way," said the old man. Then, without ever taking his eyes off Lone, he spoke out the corner of his mouth to one of the remaining two riders, both of them younger, leaner versions of the one addressed as Lud. "Junior, movin' mighty careful-like and stayin' out our line of fire, you ease up and take the weapons from those two rascals. Wesley, you keep your rifle trained tight along with me and your pa. Either man makes a wrong move, don't hesitate to blast hell out of him—just be careful not to hit your brother."

"Now just a dang—" Jeth started to protest.

But the old man cut him off with a quick, sharp bark. "Best way to keep breathin' for long as you can, mister, is to shut up and hold still!"

Everything went quiet and tense. Junior got down off his horse and cautiously approached Lone and Jeth, began relieving them of their weapons. The old man instructed him to dump them on the ground. When Lud tried to object, his pap cut him short with another bark. "Just for the time bein' is all! Christamighty, boy, you ever see the day Orin Hemper was likely to throw away good shootin' irons?"

Only when Lone and Jeth had been stripped of their guns did Pap Hemper finally divert his eyes from Lone and settle them on Minowi. "You. Squaw gal . . . You speak English?" he said gruffly.

For a fraction of an instant, Minowi looked ready to reply. But then something (a clever instinct, Lone thought as he looked on) caused her to hold her tongue and simply stare timidly in response to the question.

Pap motioned with one hand. "Come here. Come closer."

Minowi nudged her mount forward, stopping again when she was right beside the old man. He canted his head and studied her closely for several beats. Until he said, "You a captive of these devils, ain't you, gal? Bein' bought or held against your will, I'm thinkin'."

"Look at the way she's dressed, Pap," urged Lud. "She don't hardly look raggedy, the way men would keep somebody who was a captive or slave or some such."

"Depends what they was keepin' her *for*," Pap replied stubbornly. "I don't want to say too much in front of the young-uns, but lawless lowlife cusses like this pair ain't got no bottom to their sin. Don't you see? If they're haulin' this gal around to have her on hand in order to satisfy their lust and lewd intentions, wouldn't it figure they'd keep her kinda purty lookin'?"

Lud's brows pinched together. "I reckon. Maybe . . . Guess I never thought of anything like that."

"No, you wouldn't. And I'm proud you didn't grow up with such notions in your head," Pap said earnestly. "I'm sorry to mention 'em now, and I hope you scrub 'em right out again . . . And that goes double for you two young sprouts, you hear?"

Junior and Wesley hung their heads, partly in embarrassment, partly as a sign they understood the message.

Pap brought his focus back to Minowi. "I'm gonna give you a break, gal, and hope the Good Lord smiles a little brighter on you than He did when He let you fall in with such bad hombres as these. You git, you understand? Go back to your people or find somebody somewhere who'll show you some Christian charity and not abuse you no more." Pap swung his arm in a broad, go-away motion. "Git, you hear? Skedaddle on out of here!"

Minowi played her role of looking a bit confused, not understanding his words, for a convincing second or so. Then, reacting to the sweeping motion of his arm and dropping the confused look, she wheeled her mount and

164

galloped away. Watching her go, Pap muttered quietly, "May the Good Lord look after ye, child."

Seizing the moment to perhaps finally get a word in, Lone said, "No matter what you think, that girl's always been free to go whenever she wanted. If anything, we were lookin' after her until we got somewhere safer for her to strike out on her own."

Pap favored him with a sneer of disgust. "Yeah, I can imagine how you was *lookin' after* her."

"Believe what you want, you dirty-minded old mossyhorn," Lone grated. "But what the hell's the idea of waylayin' us at gunpoint in the first place?"

"How else you expect a man to welcome a couple of long-loopin' cattle thieves he finds on his property?" Pap wanted to know.

"Cattle thieves?" Jeth echoed. "What in blazes put a loco idea like that—"

"Take 'em, boys!" Pap shouted, drowning out the rest of what Jeth was trying to say.

Acting so smoothly and swiftly they must have been poised for the command right from the start, Lud and Wesley sent their mounts lunging forward with hard digs of their spurs. At the same time, as the rush of their horses shouldered aside those of Lone and Jeth, caught as much by surprise as their riders, Lud and his son began swinging their rifle barrels in vicious, slashing motions. Lone tried desperately to get a forearm raised in time to block the blow coming at him, but was too late. The heavy gun barrel skimmed across the top of his arm and landed with full, flesh-tearing, bone-cracking force against the side of his head. He felt a brief sensation of fiery pain but then was out cold before tipping from his saddle and spilling to the ground.

CHAPTER 19

The brief jolt of pain he had felt before losing consciousness was instantly present—and with stubborn, grinding intensity—as soon as Lone started coming to. It came in throbbing, hammering waves that filled the inside of his skull and pulsed down through his neck and shoulders. Almost as bad was the flow of water—or was it blood?—pouring over his face, causing him to cough and gasp for breath. And when he tried to raise his hands in order to wipe away the choking liquid, he found that his arms were held fast behind his back, wrists clamped tightly together.

In a moment of panic, Lone's upper body thrashed about and he whipped his face from side to side in an attempt to clear away some of the liquid, at least enough to allow him to breathe and clear his vision in order to see what was happening.

The familiar voice of Pap Hemper, sounding somehow near yet at the same time far away, said, "Enough waste of good water. He's startin' to come 'round, give him the chance to roust himself the rest of the way."

The flow of liquid—water, Pap had called it—stopped. So did Lone's struggles. Able to breathe now, after spitting away excess wetness from around his mouth, he held very still and sucked in deep gulps of air. He came to realize he was sprawled on the ground, turned on his back with his bound arms pinned beneath him. Blinking his eyes open came at a price. Knifing rays of bright sunshine caused the pain in his head to flare hotter and streak with added fierceness down through the rest of him. But it was worth it to finally, gradually be able to appraise his current situation.

A few feet away, Jeth also lay on the ground with his hands bound behind and underneath him. He, too, was spitting water and shaking his head groggily, apparently just coming out of his own bout with getting clubbed unconscious. Standing over the restrained pair, holding the canteens out of which they'd been sloshing water to bring about their revival, were the two young Hempers, Lud Jr. and Wesley. Looking on from a few yards off to one side, still astride their horses, was Pap and the senior Lud.

Straining to lift his head, even though it sent fresh waves of pain through him, Lone swept his gaze in a wide arc that enabled him to quickly determine they were no longer at the same spot where they'd initially been confronted and then struck down. Fresh awareness of a burning sensation all down the left side of his back and its corresponding hip and leg provided a pretty strong sign they had been dragged here—

wherever the hell here was. Its main distinction seemed to be a stand of cottonwood trees rising up behind Pap and Lud. Ironsides and Jeth's black gelding were ground-reined close by. Thankfully, Minowi was nowhere to be seen, showing the sense to stay in the clear and not to come back around to try and help.

Lone let his head drop back again, fighting the urge to groan. He didn't want to give his captors the satisfaction.

"It's good you two are comin' 'round," Pap said. "Only fittin' you're awake to face what you got comin' . . . and to each have the chance to speak up while you can."

"Speakin' up is what we been tryin' to do since you first got the drop on us," Lone told him. "Knockin' a fella cold with a rifle barrel don't exactly help keep the conversation flowin'."

Pap chuckled. "Maybe not. But it sure sets the tone for keepin' things serious, don't it?"

"Before you put our lights out," growled Jeth, "you called us cattle thieves. How the hell can you be serious about an accusation like that?"

"To a small cattle operation like what me and my boys are tryin' to build up," Pap replied, "it don't get much more serious than havin' our stock stole out from under us."

"No right-minded person would argue with that," said Lone. "But we never took any of your stinkin' cattle, or ever even saw none! We're just

169

passin' through—leastways we was until we had the bad luck of runnin' into you and yours."

"So you admit that gettin' caught by us was bad luck," Pap noted.

Lud chuffed. "But not as bad as it's gonna get before it's all over—when you two are left swingin' at the end of a couple ropes!"

"What the hell are you talkin' about swingin' on the end of ropes!" Jeth roared. "The whole lot of you is plumb crazy!"

Pap glared at him. "Is it craziness that accounts for one of our cows layin' dead less than a mile from here—kilt and half-eaten and her remains then left to spoil and get fought over by devil-spawn scavengers? Is that your claim? Even after gettin' caught red-handed whilst clearly lurkin' around to pick off another of our prime beeves?"

Lone finally saw what this was all about. The cow that Pierce and his bunch had killed and left behind half-butchered—the Hempers were convinced he and Jeth were the ones responsible!

"You're makin' a big mistake," Lone tried to tell them. "Yeah, a ways back we ran across the cow you're talkin' about. But we came on it only just a short time ago, and that critter has been dead since late yesterday. If you took time to look, you must've seen the cold ashes of the night camp made by those who actually did what you're accusin' us of—the killin' and cookin' of one of your beeves."

"And if you was able to read trail sign worth spit," Jeth joined in, "you shoulda seen how it was *five* riders—not just three, like us—who made the camp and then lit out early this mornin'."

"It's those same five," Lone added, "we been trackin' since they robbed a train up north four days ago."

"Oh, so now you not only *ain't* cattle thieves, but what you really are is lawmen," Lud said sarcastically. "Is that what you expect us to believe?"

"Nobody said anything about us bein' lawmen," Jeth responded. "But I was on the train got robbed. A good friend of mine was shot, wounded. And both of us had valuables and hard-earned money took . . . When there ain't no close-by official law to handle trouble, then a man sometimes has to see to it hisself."

Pap set his jaw firmly. "Yeah, we know a little something about that. Ain't no close-by law hereabouts neither, so what we're in the middle of right now is handlin' our own trouble."

"What you're also in the middle of," Lone grated, "is a serious matter of not havin' your damn facts straight!"

"You got anything to back up your story?" Pap challenged.

Jeth said, "I done told you—we was *robbed* of everything."

"What about the Injun squaw, Pap?" demanded Lud. "There's proof right there they gotta be lyin'. If they're chasin' after train robbers like they claim, what sense would it make to be draggin' her along?"

Pap's eyes flared. "By the Eternal, you hit it on the head, boy! Don't make no sense at all. Any lowlife who'll lie about one thing can only be counted on to lie right down the line! That settles it . . . Get 'em up on their horses and get 'em over under those branches we got strung. We need to finish this up and get back home 'fore the womenfolk start frettin' about us."

That was all Lud needed to hear. He skimmed off his horse and hurried to join his two sons as they, one by one, dragged first Jeth and then Lone to their feet and then shoved them up into their saddles. Lone resisted with bucks and kicks, getting in at least one good head butt to the skull of one of three (he couldn't tell for sure which) as they jerked and tugged on him. He quickly found out, however, that he was still groggy and saggy-kneed from the initial clubbing he'd suffered. This limited the strength he was able to put into his struggles now and the head butt— along with the general pummeling and additional new punches he was receiving from his captors— didn't help worth a damn. The Hempers weren't overly big, but they were wiry and strong and on top of a numbers advantage they clearly had experience at working together when it came to wrestling unruly livestock against their will.

In the end, dazed and battered and winded, Lone found himself astride Ironsides with a noose being tightened around his neck, the remainder of the rope extending up and over the branch of a tall cottonwood. His head swam. It all seemed like some kind of nightmare illusion yet at the same time bitterly real. He'd never figured to check out any peaceful way, lying on clean sheets with his boots off. Only he'd sure as hell never figured on this either. Not at the end of a rope.

Whimpering or begging for mercy wasn't in his nature. He would have preferred the quickness of a well-placed bullet, but after a life of seldom getting his druthers, he reckoned it was only fitting it would be the same at the end. Glancing over at Jeth, he saw the same kind of stubborn resolve on the weathered face of the old teamster.

"Your last chance," Pap said solemnly. "Any final words? Repentance to your Maker maybe?"

"You don't want to hear any final words I got for the likes of you," Jeth ground out through clenched teeth.

All Lone said was, "Take good care of my horse."

Lud and his boys stepped back out of the way. Pap tipped the muzzle of his Henry skyward, preparing to trigger the shot that would cause the horses to bolt out from under the men in nooses.

Lone's eyes were locked on the old man, wanting him to feel the weight of the stare that his next move would be shutting off forever.

The roar of a gunshot ruptured the moment of tense stillness.

But it didn't come from Pap's rifle. It was a deeper, more resounding *boom!* that came from somewhere in back of Lone. The location registered in the same instant he felt a series of sharp stings bite into the top of his head. He also felt the bite of the noose gnawing into his neck as Ironsides lunged out from under him—though almost immediately the noose went slack again and Lone dropped to the ground. He bent his knees to absorb the shock of landing, went into a choppy shoulder roll. Before he came out of that there was another ear-pounding *boom!* and, in his peripheral vision, he saw Jeth also dropping to the ground as the rope he'd been momentarily dangling from burst apart.

Blue powder smoke rolled out from the bushes clumped around the trunks of the cottonwood trees. Horses shrieked and men cried out in surprise and panic as the Hempers went diving and scrambling for cover.

From the cottonwood bushes, Minowi's voice urged, "Lone! Jeth! Get back here with me—Hurry!"

CHAPTER 20

Bracing on shoulder and hip, his arms still held fast behind him, Lone dug his heels into the dirt and began propelling himself across the ground with hard leg thrusts that shoved him toward the bushes out of which Minowi's voice had called. He could hear the grunts and scraping sounds of Jeth doing the same thing from over where he had dropped.

While they were making these efforts to take advantage of the chaotic but welcome turn in events, their suddenly *ex*-captors were busy with their own frantic reaction. Having no clear idea what just happened except that two shotgun blasts—for that's what the pair of startling *booms* were—had not only disrupted their necktie party but in the process had freed the prisoners by blowing apart their hang ropes, the Hempers found themselves first and foremost needing to find protection against more blasts from the gut shredder.

Since the dense cover around the cottonwoods was already claimed by the shooter, the only choices left for the would-be lynchers were limited to what was available within the mostly open sprawl leading up to the trees—meaning some shallow depressions, a scattering of sage

175

clumps, or a few low, ragged rock outcrops. With their horses having bolted in response to the roar of the shots (including Pap's, whose animal wheeled and fled with such unexpected suddenness that the patriarch was unceremoniously dumped from his saddle), the only thing they could do was scatter and scramble to take up what each deemed to be the most suitable of these positions.

As for Lone, as soon as he got himself pushed fully into the bushes beneath what had almost been his gallows tree, he again felt hands gripping and tugging at him. While there was a firmness and a determination to this action, there was also a degree of gentleness in the touch of the hands and along with it a familiar, soothing scent. *Minowi.*

Twisting his head to look up and around he saw that the Indian girl was indeed leaning over him, her face hovering close to his as she pressed him into a sitting position. He said her name in a hoarse whisper and a moment later felt a sudden relaxation of the pressure squeezing his wrists together. He immediately swung his arms around in front of his chest, shaking off the severed pieces of rope that had bound them, then clenching and unclenching his fists to work the stiffness out of his fingers. As soon as they were loosened, he yanked the dreaded noose from around his neck and flung it off to one side.

"Use that," Minowi said, reaching around him

on the opposite side and stabbing his own Bowie knife into the ground next to his leg, "to go cut Jeth loose. When you return you'll find your guns behind the tree in back of me. I'll make some more noise with this one"—holding up the double-barreled Greener Jeth had been packing around—"but I think they have by now ducked out of its range."

Involuntarily touching his throat, Lone grinned wryly and said, "That's okay, it had all the range it needed for a job that was mighty important to me."

A second later, gripping the Bowie in his fist, he was bellying through the underbrush toward where he had seen and heard Jeth earlier go burrowing for cover. Just as he came within sight of the old teamster there sounded the throaty roar of Minowi discharging another round from her shotgun.

When he saw Lone crawling toward him, Jeth said in a hushed whisper, "What in blazes is goin' on? Who's doin' all that shootin'?"

"Roll over so I can get at your ropes," Lone ordered somewhat breathlessly. Then, as he applied the Bowie blade to the bonds, he explained, "It's Minowi. She circled around and lay in wait. On the way she snatched up our weapons that the old man left tossed on the ground—used your shotgun to blow our hang ropes in two."

"Hot damn!" Jeth exclaimed as he swung his

unrestrained arms. "That gal is as gutsy as she is pretty!"

"You'll get no argument on that outta me," said Lone, twisting around and starting back the way he'd just come. "Follow me. We need to get our hands on the guns she fetched us. We ain't clear of those rope-happy Hempers yet—not by a damn sight."

Jeth fell in behind him without further question and they wormed their way hurriedly toward Minowi. Just before they reached her, she triggered another single-barrel discharge. A fresh cloud of powder smoke went rolling and a spray of leaves and small twigs were carried away within the pattern of the blast.

This time a volley of return fire promptly answered, sending slugs ripping back through the underbrush in the opposite direction. The Hempers were savvy enough, Lone judged, to have identified it was a shotgun opening up on them and therefore had calculated the re-loading time between every two shots as providing them a gap in which they could pop up and safely throw some lead of their own. They were due a big surprise as soon as Lone and Jeth brought some additional firepower into the mix but, in the meantime, while the underbrush made good visible cover, the tangle of leaves and spindly twigs weren't worth much when it came to stopping a bullet.

In recognition of this, Lone called ahead to Minowi, "Drop back! Get a tree trunk between you and that return fire!"

The Indian girl was quick to comprehend and comply. Seconds later, she had shifted back and was slipping in behind the same tree that Lone and Jeth arrived at to claim the guns she'd stashed there for them. A smudge of dirt decorated one cheek and bits of leaves were caught in her glossy hair, but Lone thought she'd never looked lovelier.

Pushing the weapons toward the two men as incoming rounds continued to slice in a blind, crunching sweep through the low leaves and twigs, a few smacking sharply into sturdy cottonwood boles, she said, "I wasn't able to carry everything, so I brought just your gun belt and one of the rifles. I brought the shotgun, too, because it is the only firearm I know how to use. Simon taught me how to load and fire it in case somebody tried to cause trouble at the station when he wasn't around."

Lone grunted. "Whatya know. There's one thing the worthless jackass did that had some smarts behind it."

"I'll take this, if you don't mind," Jeth said, reaching for Lone's Yellowboy. "I'm better with a long gun than a six-shooter, while you seem to be pretty handy with either one."

"Works for me." Lone snatched up the gun

belt with its holstered Colt and began strapping it around his waist. Noting Minowi had broken open the Greener shotgun and was pressing fresh shells into the smoking chambers to replace the spent rounds, he said to her, "You can make some more noise with that if you want, but I think you were right before when you said the varmints out there are mostly beyond its range."

"They are," confirmed Jeth, using a sudden lull in the return fire to peer cautiously out around the tree. "They're hunkered down like prairie dogs out there in that open space—no longer in reach of the scattergun, like you said, but real accommodatin' for this Winnie or your Colt if one of 'em is obligin' enough to poke his ornery damn head up."

"Could be," Lone said, scowling thoughtfully, "we got ourselves a way to encourage their obligin' nature." Cutting his gaze over to Minowi once more, he added, "Which means, on second thought, there might be cause for you to go ahead and empty those barrels again after all."

Both Minowi and Jeth eyed him questioningly. "What are you gettin' at?" Jeth wanted to know.

"They've figured out it's a shotgun firin' on 'em. They don't yet know we're gettin' ready to introduce some backup. So for now," Lone explained, "they're reckonin' they got a half minute or so of re-loadin' time between every pair of shots. In each of those half-minute gaps,

I'm thinkin' they'll believe themselves to be in the clear for poppin' up and pourin' a heavy dose of lead—like they just finished doin'—at where they see the smoke haze from the second discharge."

"Okay. Yeah." Understanding and then a measure of excitement crept into the old teamster's tone. "That's why they stopped shootin' now. They're hunkered down again, expectin' another set of blasts to be comin' their way. And as soon as they get 'em, they'll be primed to send us a receipt."

Lone's eyes turned narrow and flinty. "But in order to do that, they'll have to show themselves. At which point, they'll find out we got more than just a shotgun over here and they ain't the only ones who'll be primed for some additional trigger pullin'."

Minowi snapped shut her re-loaded shotgun. With some flintiness also showing in her bottomless dark eyes, she said, "So I should now go ahead and make some more noise with this. Correct?"

CHAPTER 21

As soon as Lone and Jeth were fanned out to either side and had signaled they were re-positioned with clear lines of fire on the open area out front, Minowi edged forward herself to where she also regained a measure of visibility on the clearing. Enough, at any rate, since she didn't really have much chance of hitting anything. Her goal was strictly to lure the Hempers into revealing themselves once they believed it was safe to attempt a fresh volley of return fire after she'd squeezed off another set of rounds.

The Indian girl didn't waste any time bracing the butt of the Greener against her shoulder and then setting off one barrel followed quickly by the other. Each time she raked the discharges low across the ground where the Hempers were snugged into their meager bits of cover. Clouds of dust were kicked up by the chewed earth and blue powder smoke again rolled from the bushes to mingle with it. Instantly after emptying her second barrel, Minowi dropped low, spun about, and scurried back for the protection of the cottonwood trunk. She'd scarcely made it before the expected bullets sent in response came pouring into the thicket, crashing and crunching as they tore through all around her.

But then Lone and Jeth went to work meeting this rain of lead and doing so with considerably more precision. This was possible due to not only catching the Hempers by surprise but, as hoped, also catching them exposed during their attempt to try and score blindly in the handful of seconds they thought was available to them.

The only shortcoming to the plan was that when Lud revealed himself, Lone and Jeth both viewed him as a main threat and therefore each of them promptly concentrated their aim on him. This succeeded in cutting him down in spray of blood, but at the same time it allowed his two sons (as far as they could tell, and lacking any sign of Pap) to duck back out of sight unharmed. Eliminating Lud still had significance, but failing to accomplish more was nevertheless lamentable. Rejoining Minowi when the shooting once again fell into a lull, Lone was quick to voice this regret.

"Damn it all, we should've had it planned out better. We should've decided our targets ahead of time and we might have took down at least one more of those varmints," Lone grumbled.

"Yeah, and if wishes was fishes we'd all have something to fry," countered Jeth. "Your plan was a good one. We didn't have a lot of time to fine tune it, that's all. But gettin' rid of that damn Lud is a good step, no matter how you slice it."

"What I can't figure," said Lone, still brooding,

"is what became of the old man. I didn't spot him at all, did you? If he'd've poked up his shaggy old head, I'm pretty sure one of us would have found time to send some lead his way, don't you reckon?"

"No doubt about it," Jeth agreed.

"His horse threw him when I first fired to break your hang ropes," Minowi said. "I saw him go down, but never saw him get back up. Maybe he was injured by the fall."

"We should be so lucky," muttered Lone.

A moment later, as if the words were prophetic, a tentative voice called from the open area out front. "Hello, you in the trees! Can you hear me?"

The voice wasn't familiar. It didn't belong to Pap, and it sure as hell wasn't coming from the ventilated carcass of Lud. It had to be one of his boys.

After a quick exchange of looks with Jeth and Minowi, Lone called back, "Yeah, we hear you. What's on your mind?"

There was a hesitation. Then, breaking slightly, the voice responded, "We're in a bad way out here . . . You done k-kilt our pa. And Grandpap is hurt from gettin' pitched off his horse. B-busted up inside, seems like . . . Me and my brother, we got no fight left in us 'thout them. We need to get Grandpap somewhere he can be looked after so's he don't—don't go over like Pa has already done."

Lone again exchanged looks with Jeth and Minowi. Then he called, "Those sound like some tough breaks. But you can't expect much sympathy out of somebody you had lynch nooses on just a few minutes ago . . . What is it you're wantin' from us?"

Another hesitation. "We're sorry about that hangin' business. We truly are. But me and Wes, our way has always been to go along with whatever Pa and Grandpap laid out for us . . . We don't blame you for fightin' back the way you done, even if . . . Is there any way you'd be willin' to just ride on like you was wantin' to do before, and . . . and leave us to salvage what we can here?"

"Has the smell of a trap, you ask me," whispered Jeth. "That old rascal Pap, if he's hurt at all, could be layin' out there like a wounded griz—waitin' to catch us with our guard relaxed."

"That may be true. But it could also be," said Minowi, "the boy is sincere in what he's saying. We know for sure he and his brother are out there with their dead father. Is it so hard to believe they would be willing to do whatever it takes to try and keep their grandfather—no matter how evil he seems to us—from the same fate?"

"The fate I can't help thinkin' about," replied Lone, one hand lifting as if by its own volition to the noose abrasions on his throat, "is the one that was in store for me and Jeth. And those two *boys*—who looked pretty damn full grown to me, no matter whose say-so they claim to be actin' on—was right there in the thick of it."

A long, tense silence gripped the scene.

Until the voice, apparently belonging to Lud Jr., called again. "We're beggin' you. Grandpap's breathin' is gettin' awful ragged. Like I said, I think he's busted up on the inside, maybe some ribs stove in."

The voice of the other brother, Wes, chimed in. "Please, mister. We'll throw out our guns, do anything you say . . . Just give us a chance to try and help him. He's an old man and he's hurtin' bad."

Lone grimaced. Once more sweeping his gaze over Jeth and Minowi, lingering for an extra beat on the way her eyes were looking back at him, he said, "Hell. What choice do we have? If they're tellin' the truth, we can't just mow 'em down in cold blood—not even the old buzzard, if he's busted up like they say."

"Your call," Jeth allowed. "But however you go about it, use a powerful amount of caution. That's all I'll add."

Heaving a ragged sigh, Lone turned again toward the clearing and called out. "All right, let's see 'em. Throw your weapons out. Everything you got. I expect at least four rifles, plus any handguns, knives, the whole works."

His command was promptly met. The four

186

repeating rifles—two Henrys and two Winchesters, exactly as Lone remembered—were pitched into plain sight; followed by two knives and one short-barreled revolver.

"That's it. All we got," Lud Jr. stated. "We don't none of us pack gun belts."

"Okay. Now you two," Lone told them. "Stand up, walk forward slow, arms raised high. Walk past the guns, I'll tell you when to stop."

Nothing happened.

After several beats, Wesley's voice asked meekly, "You ain't gonna just gun us down, are you? If you are, go ahead and tell us . . . So we can say goodbye to Grandpap and speak a word to our Maker before goin' over."

"As long as you do like you're told and there ain't no shenanigans to any of this," Lone said, "nobody's gonna get gunned down."

Slowly, the brothers rose up and began walking forward. They suddenly appeared much younger than Lone remembered. Their foreheads were puckered with fear and grief and the layer of dust covering their hollow cheeks was streaked with tears.

They stopped when Lone told them to. Then he added, "You know we got a shotgun in here, along with some other guns. You're close enough now for the shotgun to do the job all on its own, but there's also a Winchester Yellowboy trained on you. I'm gonna walk out and check on your grandfather. Anybody makes a move that looks wrong in the slightest way—you, him, whatever—you'll get blown half in two and the old man will go next. We all clear on that?"

His answer came in the form of a couple mute nods.

Given that, Lone emerged from the bushes with his Colt held down at his side. He walked silently past the brothers and proceeded to the shallow depression where Pap lay. He could hear raspy, irregular breathing as he approached, before ever coming in sight of the old man. He found him lying on his back, hugging his ribs, gazing up with glassy eyes. His bared teeth were outlined in blood.

His gaze bored into Lone. "Go ahead and kill me if you've a mind to. Be a blessin', save me some pain . . . I got busted ribs stabbin' into something deep inside, ain't gonna make it anyhow . . . But if there's an ounce of decency in you, go easy on Wes and Junior. They're good boys, just doin' what was asked of 'em by their elders."

"I know," Lone grated. "That's why I won't go back on my promise to 'em not to kill you . . . I'll take my satisfaction knowin' you're gonna go over slow and miserable. My only regret is that I can't afford to stick around and enjoy watchin'."

CHAPTER 22

The encounter with the Hempers had cost precious time and had stalled their closure on the Pierce gang. Despite this and also contrary to his earlier statement about pushing hard until after dusk, Lone called a halt for night camp when there was still plenty of light left in the sky. He recognized that what they'd just gone through had taken a toll both emotionally and physically and it would be wise to help try and offset that by taking a couple extra hours to recuperate.

The sun had already dropped close to the western horizon by the time they rode away from where the shootout occurred. Ironsides had come back around not long after the gunfire stopped and Lone had ridden him to round up Jeth's gelding and a couple of the Hempers' horses. While he was doing that, Lud Jr. and Wesley had begun cutting branches to make drag litters for their injured grandfather and the body of their father. That's how Lone and the others left them, tending to their dead and wounded. They also left them the short-barreled pistol for protection against scavengers or other varmints until they got back to wherever their ranch house was. The remaining rifles and knives—along with the rest of their own temporarily abandoned weapons—Lone's group took with them.

Although they covered only a few miles before stopping again, it had felt necessary to remove themselves at least some distance from the specter of death and the frayed remains of the meant-to-be hang ropes still dangling from the tree limbs.

They made their camp on the shoulder of a shallow, grassy bowl with a jagged spine of weather-worn rocks along the north rim and a clump of spindly trees on the opposite slope. A small pool of run-off water lay at the base of the rock spine. It proved somewhat bitter to human taste, though would have sufficed under more desperate circumstances. The horses didn't seem to mind, however, so Lone watered them from it and also drew from it to top off one of the water bags for slaking the animals' thirst later on the trail.

Before taking their supper meal, while there was still some light other than what the campfire would provide after darkness set in, Minowi insisted on ministering to the various scrapes and cuts Lone and Jeth had sustained. She did so by crushing some particular stems she selected from the surrounding grass and making a paste-like salve. This she spread liberally on the noose abrasions around their throats and also to the bruising and scratches on their backs and shoulders left by being dragged across the ground from where they were knocked unconscious to where the nooses were intended to be put to use.

That left a final piece of business that Minowi brought up hesitantly and with a decidedly sheepish look on her face. "Judging by the blood tracks running down the back of each of your necks," she said, "you have a few additional wounds I should have a look at. Unfortunately, I fear it was I who caused them."

Jeth looked puzzled. "Huh?"

But Lone, remembering the stings to the top of his head that he'd felt just before his hang rope snapped, was quicker to understand what she was talking about. "The pattern of those shotgun blasts you cut our hang ropes with," he said. "Couldn't hardly help but for some of the pellets to skim the top of our noggins."

"I was afraid that might happen so I aimed as high up on the ropes as I dared," Minowi explained. "But at the same time I had to center the blast low enough to make sure it caused a break."

"Thunderation," exclaimed Jeth, sweeping off his hat and clapping a hand to the top of his head. "I been feelin' some pricklies up here, but I thought it was from gettin' poked by crawlin' around in all that bramble. With my hat knocked off back then, wasn't like the layer of hair left on this old dome is thick enough to offer much protection."

"Reckon my pelt is still fairly thick, but it

didn't seem to've made much difference," said Lone. "Though what I also reckon is that a few pellet bites is a mighty fair trade over gettin' my neck stretched."

Putting his hat back on, Jeth said, "Amen to that."

The sheepish look returning, Minowi replied, "I'm just glad to hear you're not holding it against me."

"Hold it *against* you?" Lone and Jeth echoed in near perfect unison.

"Good Lord, gal, you saved our lives," Lone declared. "You think skinnin' us up some holds any kind of candle to that? The only thing we feel toward you—and we ain't took time to begin sayin' it proper—is bein' grateful."

"Goes double for me," said Jeth.

"Don't forget I wasn't without owing some gratitude of my own," Minowi reminded them. "But regardless of any of that, I still should try digging out those shot pellets. If they are not too deep, they eventually ought to work out on their own. But in the meantime they may scab over and cause a lot of itching and discomfort when you start sweating under your hats." Here she paused and her mouth slowly curved into a sly, teasing smile. "That is, of course, unless you find even more discomfort in the thought of having a redskin poke at your scalps with the point of a knife."

This display of humor, so rare and unexpected considering the source, was at first met with blank silence. Then, all at once, the three of them burst into a prolonged stretch of full-throated, tension-breaking, eye-watering laughter that was about the best recuperative medicine anybody could ask for.

"They're doin' *what?*" Lyle Vallen grumbled irritably.

"You heard me. They're down there laughin' their fool heads off," replied Hayden Halloway. "The girl got done patchin' up the scrapes to the men's necks and hides, all serious-like. Then they palavered for a minute, still lookin' serious— until they all of a sudden went into a fit of laughter, holdin' their sides and carryin' on like somebody told the funniest joke in the world. If I didn't know better on account of how we been watchin' 'em the whole while, I might think they was actin' peculiar enough to have been puffin' peyote or some such."

This exchange was taking place atop a grassy ridge about four hundred yards to the north of where Lone, Jeth, and Minowi had made camp. The ridge was high enough to look down into their shallow bowl. Halloway was on his stomach, holding a spyglass to one eye with the working end of the instrument extended out through an opening in the high grass. Vallen was stretched out beside him, rolled onto one hip and propped on an elbow.

"In case you ain't noticed," Vallen grunted in response to his partner's observation, "that bunch don't need much help when it comes to actin' peculiar. Startin' with those two hombres headin' out to run down a whole outlaw gang strictly on their own."

"What does that make us then? We're on the trail of them *and* the outlaw gang."

"We're only aimin' to pick the bones afterward. That's different."

"If you say so." Halloway lowered the spyglass and rubbed his eye with the heel of one hand. "Wasn't long ago we was lookin' at maybe havin' bones to pick a mite early and then bein' out of a job altogether, when that pack of ranchers trotted out those hang ropes. It was down to lettin' the outlaw chasers swing or risk tippin' our hand— not to mention riskin' our own necks—if we'd've rode in to break up the necktie party. Lucky you spotted that Injun gal slinkin' around in those bushes and we held off to give her a chance."

"Lucky for us, even luckier for those two she blasted free," said Vallen. Then, in what could only be described as an admiring tone, he added, "Damn, ain't that gal something? Lookin' so fine and havin' all that spunk to boot. A fella was to find hisself with a woman like her at his side, he'd have reason to strike out in the world and reach to grab it right by the throat!"

Halloway clearly didn't see things the same. "Maybe . . . Then again, with a spitfire like her, that spunk could turn on a fella, too. Say or do something she took bad enough wrong, you might sit down to supper some evenin' and get the back of your head stove in by a fryin' pan or such like. Hell, in her case, maybe both barrels of a Greener."

Vallen rolled his eyes. "Jesus Christ, Harlan. Talk about pickin' the bones of something . . . You done had all the romance picked clean of yours, you know that? You only see women as bein' good for one thing. Not that that ain't a real fine thing, mind you. But don't you ever see a time when you're gonna want more?"

"More women, you mean?" Halloway blinked. "Yeah, I always want more. Remember what you said about how the bonus from this job is gonna afford us some top dollar fancy gals? I sure got me a wantin' for that."

Vallen started to say something, but then changed his mind. Instead, with an exasperated sigh, he merely replied, "Come on, let's drop back and see to our own camp. It's been a long day and I fully expect that bunch down yonder will be done laughin' and ready to try makin' up lost time by gettin' another early start in the morning . . ."

CHAPTER 23

Harriet Bell planted her fists on her hips and proclaimed defiantly, "To hell with that notion! If you think you're going to stop me from going into town and having myself a decent meal and a hot bath, mister, you have got another think coming!"

The target of these words, Dar Pierce, stood square in front of the feisty redhead and sort of leaned into the verbal onslaught like one might lean against a strong wind. He was also getting blistered by a double-barreled glare from her flashing green eyes.

"Now doggone it, gal, you need to be reasonable," he barked back. "I ain't out to deprive you of the things you want without good reason. You ought to know better than that."

"What I know," Harriet insisted, "is that I've shared your bedroll and been part of this gang since the beginning. In that time, I've always held up my end when it came to hard riding and straight shooting, and nobody can say otherwise. It's damn seldom I ever asked for any kind of special consideration on account of being a woman."

"Nobody's saying you did. And that's got nothing to do with what I'm asking now," Pierce told her.

"Well, it's got to do with what *I'm* asking for," said Harriet. "Maybe you galoots don't mind taking your meals around smoky campfires all the time or smelling no different from the horses you ride. But *I* do! At least once in a while I like to remind myself that I'm still a woman . . . no matter if it means anything to you mangy critters or not."

Pierce scowled. "The only critter in this bunch who'd better be taking any notice of that is me. The rest know what I'd do to 'em if I even *thought* they had a wrong urge in their dirty minds." Here he paused to rake his scowl over the other three gang members, each of who found somewhere else to look in order to make sure Pierce didn't see anything in their eyes he might not like.

This discussion, for lack of a better word, was taking place in a patch of shade on the banks of the Republican River about two miles outside of McCook. The group had stopped to get out from under a boiling mid-day sun long enough to water and rest their horses, and to finalize plans for a reconnoiter of the town in advance of returning to rob one of its banks if the situation looked right. Pierce's stated intent for just himself and only one other man to go in for the look-see was what had resulted in the strong objection from Harriet.

Softening his gaze now, the gang leader cut it back to Harriet, saying, "Blast it, you know you're plenty enough woman for me. The only one I need or want. And I reckon I said wrong a minute ago when I claimed this ain't got nothing to do with that, with you being a woman. It's got to do with the *particular* woman you are— the flame-haired, gun-totin' hellion who rides in the thick of the Pierce Gang. I'm afraid that you being part of the team who goes in to scout the town and its bank setup ahead of time might cause you to be recognized. Don't you see?"

"Why would that leave out any of the rest of you then?" Harriet challenged. "If word about us has reached down this far and put the law dogs hereabouts on alert, your mugs are plastered all over Wanted posters same as mine. I'd say that makes an equal risk of somebody recognizing *whoever* goes in on the scout."

"Now you're being just plain stubborn," Pierce declared, his scowl returning. "You've seen the sketches on those posters. They could fit a hundred different scruffy-looking hombres. If only a couple of us go in for a quiet look-see, no reason anybody'd look twice at us. You, on the other hand—the red hair, the trail garb, showing up on horseback . . . Come on. You can't deny that would be a lot more apt to draw attention."

Harriet's eyes narrowed into a scowl of her own, but for the first time she didn't have a quick comeback.

From where he squatted with his back against

a tree trunk, Paul Caldwell removed the half-smoked cigarette from his mouth and spoke into the strained silence. "If this ain't too much of a private fight, would you two be willing to listen to a suggestion from an outsider?"

Pierce eyed him. "Long as you take a suggestion in return and choose your words careful-like."

Before continuing, Caldwell took an unhurried drag off his cigarette and expelled a jet of smoke. Then: "If you recall, just a short ways back we passed a small farm down off in a little hollow. Didn't look like much, but what it did have was a buckboard parked out front. Occurs to me that if we was to drop back there and pay that farmer a visit, we no doubt could 'persuade' him to lend that rig to you and Harriet . . . Anybody besides me see the possibilities that could open up?"

Harriet's scowl was suddenly gone and her eyes shone with eagerness. "I sure do! Believe it or not, I've got a dress in my possibles pack. Me in a proper dress and riding on the seat of a buckboard alongside you, Dar . . . Wouldn't that be enough to remove your worries about drawing undue attention?"

It took Pierce a minute to come around but in the end he had to admit it wasn't a half bad idea. It would accomplish the task of reconnoitering the town and at the same time allow Harriet her chance to participate while minimizing the concern about her being recognized.

As soon as the gang boss showed signs of agreeing, others spoke up to help nudge him along. "Having that farm house to hole up in while you're in town," said Grissom, "would be a welcome break from the trail for the rest of us, too. Bound to be more comfortable, especially if things look right for following the plan to wait out the night and then hit a bank in the morning. And figuring the farmer's likely got a wife to do some cooking, we could help pass the time with some good vittles while we're there."

Pierce cocked an eyebrow. "Goldy, if you put as much thought into planning ways for us to make money as you do fretting about your next meal, you'd be running this outfit and we'd all be rich as kings."

"Suits me okay the way you run things, Dar." Grissom shrugged. "Besides, even kings gotta eat."

"Si, and even kings need also to concern themselves with other matters," said Bandros, smiling slyly. "While your thoughts run toward how good the farmer's wife might cook—me, I wonder if she might be good looking and have additional talents to explore. Better yet, I wonder if the farmer might have a pretty young daughter."

Harriet rolled her eyes. "I would tell you you're disgusting, but you'd probably take it as a compliment. Grissom may have a one track mind when it comes to food, but your mind runs on a single track toward something else."

Bandros spread his hands. "As the saying goes, man cannot live by bread alone."

"No, and jobs don't get done by just taking about doing 'em," Pierce said gruffly. "If we're gonna drop back to that farm and expect to have time to make it into town in order to look things over while the businesses are still open, then we'd better get after it . . . Mount up, let's get a move on."

CHAPTER 24

At the same time the Pierce gang was altering its plans to incorporate "borrowing" a buckboard for the reconnoiter into McCook, Lone, Jeth, and Minowi were taking a break of their own some twenty-odd miles behind. They had risen before the first glimmer of the sun now hammering down from its noon peak and pushed hard all morning to try and make up for the time they'd lost due to yesterday's encounter with the Hempers. The terrain they covered had grown steadily more rugged, marked by steeper and more frequent hills, sudden gullies, and deeper, sharper washouts. The latter were often several yards across at their widest, essentially small canyons, with bare, furrowed sides bleached almost white in contrast to the green of the high grass and brush that ran along their rims, often masking the existence of the openings until one was practically on top of them.

Lone had called their halt on a relatively flat expanse just off the raggedly pointed mouth to one such fissure. Gazing out and down into this twisting gash in the earth while they gave their mounts a breather and waited for them to cool some before allowing them to drink, Jeth commented, "I speculate this likely was a popular huntin' ground back in the days when buffs ran thick hereabouts. Any number of these open gaps woulda worked as jumps for a herd of woolies."

In decades past, when a seemingly endless supply of bison roamed for as far as the eye could see in any direction, a favorite hunting technique of many Plains Indian tribes had been the practice of *buffalo jumping*—or *pishkun* in the native tongue, translating to *deep blood kettle*—This called for large numbers of the animals to be stampeded and driven over a sharp cliff—or *jump*—where they would fall either to their deaths or to crippled conditions that left them immobile until the hunters went among them and finished the killing. Processing camps would then be set up nearby where the women, children, and elderly of the tribe would gather to help participate in rendering the slain beasts into not only meat, but clothing, blankets, and a wide variety of other tools and utensils that would be of benefit to all for months and sometimes years to come.

Responding to Jeth's speculation, Lone said, "Not much doubt you're right. Conditions around here are too good to think otherwise, leastways up until us Whites joined in to butcher the buffs damn near out of existence. Matter of fact, something I should have thought of before," and here he cast a sidelong glance over at Minowi, "is that on up ahead, not too far this side of McCook, we'll be passing mighty close to Massacre Canyon. Dispute over these huntin' grounds while there was some woolies still left on 'em is what caused the final battle between the Sioux and Pawnee that ended up with the Pawnee chased off for good."

Lone continued to watch Minowi closely as he related this. Her expression remained impassive but he expected a good deal was going on behind those dark eyes.

She revealed as much a moment later when she spoke in a quiet voice, saying, "Massacre Canyon. It is there where my life began and then ended. I do not count the time with the Sioux or with Simon Weaver as part of *my* life—it was a life structured *for* me by others."

"Only now you've reclaimed it—your life and your future," Lone pointed out. "In a way, you might say it's kinda fitting how we're returnin' to the place where it all went bad for you. A body could look at it as exactly the right spot to start over, a sort of jumpin' off point for a fresh new start."

"Dang. That was downright inspirin'. Almost poetic," said Jeth.

"But *are* we returning to the battle site? How close will we truly pass?" Minowi asked.

Lone's brow puckered. "I can't rightly say for certain. I heard the story about what happened there and I passed through the general area a time or two in the past. But I was never at the actual site, leastways not as far I know. You see how the land rises and tumbles all through here, and since the battle was near twenty years ago there'd be no sign left to mark it plain. I might be able to get pretty close but—"

Minowi cut him short, saying, "If you got us close, I think I would be able to tell. I believe I could *feel* it . . . My soul is there."

The emotion and conviction behind this statement left both Lone and Jeth temporarily at a loss for how to respond. Until Lone finally said, "I never knew you had such a hankerin' to go back."

"Nor did I," Minowi replied. "In fact, any previous thought of returning to that bloody place more likely would have been repulsive. But now, suddenly, it seems to be calling me. Signaling that I *need* to return . . . Maybe, as you suggest, as a first step to starting my life over."

Again Lone and Jeth were slow to respond.

This time it was Minowi herself who broke the awkward silence, saying, "Of course, such a detour under the circumstances cannot be. It would be selfish of me to expect your pursuit of the Pierce gang be delayed in order to search for something that may not even be recognizable."

Jeth scrunched up his face. "Now doggone it, just a minute ago you said you'd know the place if we got anywhere close."

"I said I believed I would, yes. But—"

Not letting her finish, Jeth turned to Lone and said, "By my reckonin', we ain't gonna reach McCook until this evenin', maybe after full dark. You agree?"

"About then, yeah," Lone allowed.

"So it ain't likely we're gonna ride in and bump into Pierce's bunch right off easy-like," Jeth continued. "They won't have got there much ahead of us and if they're plannin' on robbin' something before they move on, it's gonna take 'em a little time to slink around and size things up, don't you reckon?"

"Sounds reasonable."

"Okay. That means tomorrow, soonest, before they're apt to try anything," Jeth said. "So what else that means, it seems to me, is that we could afford a couple or so hours to swing a little wide once we get closer and see if we can't find this here Massacre Canyon. We could still make it into McCook either late tonight or first thing in the morning so's to be on hand if and when Pierce's bunch show their mangy selves."

Lone felt slightly amused and not the least bit offput by the crusty old teamster's willingness to accommodate something that so obviously held deep meaning for Minowi. His own inclinations had been the same, so he in fact was glad Jeth had made the pitch ahead of him.

Minowi tried declining the offer, but the

excitement that had flared in her eyes as Jeth spoke told the truth about her feelings. Her attempted objection only lasted a couple words before it was Lone who cut her short this time, saying, "Okay, we'll give it a try. Like I said, I'm thinkin' it's fairly close to McCook anyway, and I expect I can take us pretty near to the spot. So let's get these horses watered then go see what we can find."

As it turned out, it was close to dusk but not very far off the course of the trail they'd been following when they located the fateful battle site. Massacre Canyon.

As the afternoon wore on, a stiff breeze had swept in from the northwest. The cooling effect of this was welcome, but less so the sooty-looking clouds it dragged along with it. As was usually the case, farmers and ranchers in the area would probably be happy to get some rain out of such an overcast; but not so for riders traveling out in the open.

When they came in sight of the canyon—a deep, twisting slash in an expanse of otherwise mostly bare, blunted hills, its rims on either side choked by dense brush and fir trees interspersed with a few stubborn cottonwoods—there was an immediate *feel* about it that was experienced by more than just Minowi. For a moment, the breeze seemed to lift somewhat and slanting rays of sunlight, cutting through the sooty clouds, shone down on the scene as if to highlight it before the three riders.

Lone and Jeth checked down their horses and remained in their saddles. Minowi rode slowly forward another dozen or so yards. Dismounting, she stood for a time gazing out on the canyon, her hands hanging loosely at her sides. Sinking to her knees, she wrapped her arms over her breasts and hung her head. She remained like that for several minutes. The wind picked up again, stronger and more chill than before, causing her long silken hair to trail out to one side while the rest of her stayed perfectly still.

Lone and Jeth sat patiently waiting, watching in silence.

When she was ready, Minowi rose, turned and walked her horse back to them. Gazing up into their faces, the expression on hers appeared somber yet very much at peace. "As much or more than all else you have done to help me," she said in a sincere, somewhat husky tone, "I am grateful for allowing me this moment."

"Mighty small bit of bother on our part," Lone told her. "All the less so if it was meaningful to you."

"And the look on your face says it was. So that makes it plenty worthwhile," said Jeth.

"This is an evil place," Minowi stated, both her expression and tone growing increasingly more somber. "Or, more accurately, it is a place where great evil was done. Many women and children, accompanying the Pawnee hunters to help process the buffalo they killed, were mercilessly slain by the attacking Sioux. They were slaughtered in the most savage way, some even set on fire.

"When members of the Sioux tribe in which I was raised would talk of the battle to taunt me, before Bright Leaf Woman chased them away, they did not tell these details of course, but spoke only of the Sioux warriors' great bravery and skill. I learned the truth one night when I overheard Bright Leaf Woman and Running Wolf arguing because she accused him of not sticking up for me the way she did. In his anger he reminded her that he had stuck up for me in the greatest way possible by saving me from the kind of vicious treatment he went on to describe happening to others."

Frowning, Lone said, "Do you really think it's a good idea for you to be draggin' that through your mind again—re-livin' it all over when you're on the brink of movin' past it?"

A wan smile passed across Minowi's lips. "Surely you must know one cannot control certain thoughts that rush in. It's not that I *wanted* to re-live the horror of what happened here . . . And yet, somehow, I think it was important that I did." She paused for a moment, as if debating whether or not to say more. Then: "When I was kneeling out there, I could hear the wailing of many voices. My true mother and father might have been among them. Not surprisingly, they were lamenting their suffering and loss . . . And yet, at the same time, they seemed to be urging me to go forward, to continue on. To put the past behind, no matter how dreadful, and to embrace being alive—to live *for* those whose lives had been cut short."

"Whatever you heard," said Lone, "it sounds to me like there was a good dose of wisdom in the message."

Another brief smile came and went from Minowi's face before she replied, "I'd like to believe that my parents' voices *were* among those I heard. That, from beyond, they were guiding and encouraging me."

"Then go ahead and believe it," Lone told her. "There's nothing stopping you."

"But if you're finished here and you don't mind too much," spoke up Jeth, "how about also figurin' there's nothing stoppin' us from movin' on now. Whether it's only the cold wind or all the talk about voices from beyond, I'm gettin' the shivers just plunked here in this saddle. If we're fairly close to McCook, then we still got a chance to make it in before it gets too dark or before those clouds decide to start spittin' rain. What do you say?"

CHAPTER 25

"I just can't shake the feeling, Walt. In fact, the more I think about it the more I'm convinced there's something wrong out at the Keough place!"

Walter Kent, the town marshal of McCook, studied the agitated citizen pacing back and forth in front of his desk. The man—Boyd Langly by name, blacksmith by trade—was normally a level-headed, non-excitable type. The fact that something had him so worked up told Kent it was something he probably needed to pay attention to.

"Alright. Just calm down and take it easy for a minute," the marshal said. He was a tall, beefy specimen with a broad face and a high forehead capped by sparse butter-yellow hair. He had sad blue eyes, a blunt nose, and a wide mouth that could spread easily into a warm, friendly grin or, if provoked, take on a menacing twist. At the moment it was somewhere in between, curved downward in a frown as he continued, "Now tell me again, what is it you found so bothersome about that couple and the buckboard they were driving, the one you think belongs to Tom Keough?"

Langly stopped pacing. "That's just it—I don't

think it was Tom Keough's buckboard, I *know* it was. And that means there's something fishy about how come those two are riding around in it."

"You said they claimed Tom let 'em borrow it."

Langly scowled. As befitting his trade, he was muscular in build, only average height but with sloping shoulders and thick forearms generally on display, as they were now, by the sleeves of his shirt being rolled up past the elbows. Having halted his pacing, he continued to show his agitation by the way he stood clenching and unclenching his fists as he said, "Yeah, I almost swallowed that 'borrowing' line of guff. I did, in fact, for too long. But it was the lie they told along with it—when the truth finally smacked me in the head after I had time to think about it— that tripped 'em up for certain."

"You mean the lie about the gal half of the couple being Mary Keough's cousin from back east?"

"That's the one. Mary never made any secret about how she came west on the Orphan Train when she was only twelve years old. So why didn't lunk-headed me remember that right off when the red-haired hussy was looking me square in the face and lying her pretty head off? How can a girl without a family all of a sudden have a cousin show up years later for a visit?"

"She can't. Not no way I know of." Kent sat

up straighter in his chair and planted his forearms on the desktop. "You're right, the whole business smells damned fishy."

Before either man could say any more, the front door to the marshal's office opened and a short, wiry, middle-aged man wearing a deputy marshal's badge entered.

Kent eyed him expectantly. "Well? What did you find out, Curly?"

Curly Hutchison thumbed back the front brim of his hat and said, "They was seen rolling out of town about half an hour ago. While they was here, far as I can tell, they never used their names nowhere."

"Any idea where-all they stopped?"

"Uh-huh. Made the rounds pretty good in the couple hours they stuck around. Started out with a stop at Della's dress shop where the gal made a purchase. Then they went to Mel Henry's barber shop. The man got a haircut and shave, the gal bought herself a long soak in that big copper tub Mel has in the back room. Came out all dolled up in the new dress she bought at Della's."

"They was coming out of the barber shop when I ran into 'em," said Langly. "I noticed the buckboard parked out front and went over to have a look because I recognized it. I'd just put new steel rims on the front wheels only a couple weeks back, see, and wanted to check how they was holding up. The couple came out while I was

213

having my look and the fella right away got all huffy about what I was up to. Wanted to know why I was 'nosing around' their rig. So I barked back and asked what they was doing with the Keough wagon. Before things got too heated, the woman stepped in and told the lie about her being Mary's cousin and the rest. Which is how we left it—until I got my noodle working a little later on and came here to talk to you, Walt."

"What's that all about?" Curly wanted to know.

Kent gave him a quick rundown of the concerns Langly had presented. After hearing them, Curly made it unanimous in agreeing something smelled fishy.

"So that much is settled," the marshal said. "But what else did you find out about what that pair did while they were in town?"

"From the barber shop," Curly related, "they stopped at the Cattleman's Bank to cash down a large bill and then took in a leisurely meal at the Topp Diner. After that they strolled around a bit, doing some window shopping, and finally made another stop, this time at the Doctrow Bank to cash down another big bill before heading out."

Langly's brows pinched together and his eyes darted back and forth between the two lawmen. "Say, it sounds like you fellas had some suspicions about that pair even before I showed up."

Half of Kent's mouth lifted in a lopsided grin.

"Not that we don't appreciate helpful tips from alert citizens, Boyd, but we like to think that we sometimes pay attention to goings on around town all by ourselves."

"Well, a-course you do. I never meant to say otherwise," sputtered the blacksmith.

"No, I know you didn't," Kent assured him. "But the main takeaway, when you add all the pieces together, is that the fishy smell gets stronger and stronger." He held up one hand, fingers folded down, and began lifting them one at a time as he counted off: "We start with the redhead's lie about being Mary's cousin when we know Mary had no family. Number two, even if her and the man *were* visiting the Keoughs and borrowed their buckboard for some legitimate reason, why would they come all the way into town to pay for a shave and a bath when they could get both for free at the Keough farm? And number three, why make stops at two different banks to cash large bills instead of just doing it once and getting it over with?"

Curly had the answer. "Because they needed to see the operation inside each bank—to size 'em up."

"Size 'em up for what?" said Langly, looking puzzled. Then, a moment later, he got it. "To *rob them,* you mean?"

Marshal Kent slapped his palms down on the desktop. "That's the way it scalds out. To hit one of 'em at least, the one that looked most suitable. Plus, I all of a sudden got a gut-souring hunch who those two might have been."

So saying, the marshal pulled out a side drawer of his desk and withdrew from it a stack of papers revealed to be Wanted circulars issued against various lawbreakers. He separated one from near the top and skimmed it across the desk for Curly to have a look at, saying, "Remember when that came in a couple weeks back?"

"The Dar Pierce gang," Curly read aloud. "Including Pierce's girlfriend, the red-haired spitfire Harriet Bell."

Langly's face scrunched up, trying to remember. "Dar Pierce. That name sounds familiar, but I can't quite . . ."

"His bunch never operated anywhere around these parts. At least not before," Kent said. "They first made a name for themselves down in the wild country, the Oklahoma Indian Territory. Then, a couple years back, they swung up into the Dakotas where competition wasn't so fierce. They raised hell up there pretty successfully until a federal posse finally flushed 'em out of their hideout in the badlands. That's when that most recent Wanted notice got issued, warning they were on the run and thought to be headed south, likely back to the Nations."

Curly grunted. "Our sorry luck if they decided to pay us a visit on the way. This description of

Pierce,"—tapping the piece of paper—"could fit the fella who showed up today, though also plenty of others. The red-haired gal maybe being Harriet Bell is a closer fit but, still, that hardly makes her the only redhead around."

Ruffling the rest of the paper stack, Kent said, "There's some older dodgers in here that've got pictures of the different gang members. But they're only sketches so who knows how accurate they are or who-all is still even riding with 'em. Not worth the bother of digging through."

Curly eyed his boss. "So how much bother *are* we gonna go to? We gonna go on sharp watch and wait to see if they come back . . . Or you got something else in mind?"

"The clincher," Kent replied, "is that business with the Keough buckboard. Whether the gang comes back to make a try on one of our banks or gives us a pass because they didn't like what they saw is something we *maybe* could wait out. But if they're in the meantime holed up out at the Keough farm the way I fear they are, and putting that poor family through grief I hate to even think about . . . that's something we damn well can't wait on."

"I was hoping you'd say that," said Curly.

"Me, too," agreed Langly.

"Good to hear, Boyd. That makes you the first volunteer for the posse we're going to put together." Kent stood up behind the desk and locked his gaze on Curly, saying, "If I ain't mistaken, there are a half dozen or so riders from the Slash M over at the Thirsty Dog saloon. They're a pretty rough bunch, go round up any that ain't too drunk and tell 'em we need a posse and need it pronto.

"Grab anybody else you can think of, I'll go interrupt a few suppers, too. I'd like to ride out with at least ten men. We'll meet back here in twenty minutes. I'll provide a rifle and cartridges to any who ain't got their own, but tell everybody to gear up for some foul weather on account of that sky out there looks like it's gonna sooner or later kick down a storm . . . Come on, let's get moving."

CHAPTER 26

"There's something odd here," Lone said, squatted down and carefully scanning the ground ahead and to either side.

"Odd how?" questioned Jeth, who remained mounted close by. "It's the same bunch, ain't it?"

"Oh, it's them alright," Lone answered. "They stopped here, no doubt to water their animals at the river. Milled for a spell, 'long about the middle of the day I judge. But when they lit out again, they didn't continue on toward town— they turned back and angled off a bit to the north."

"What would make 'em do that?"

"Don't know. That's the odd part."

"Is there anything in that direction that might be of interest to them?" asked Minowi, also still mounted.

"Nothing I know of." Lone frowned. "Bein' this close to town where there's stores for tradin' and such, I expect some farms or ranches are scattered not too far off. That's all I can think of."

Jeth said, "You figure they might be lookin' for a place to hole up tonight—maybe a barn or some such, to get out of the storm that's comin'—and wait 'til tomorrow to go on into town?"

"Could be something like that." Lone straightened up. "Only thing I know for sure is that I never caught anything I was chasin' by not goin' the same as their tracks. So while we still got some light and before the rain hits and starts washin' out their sign altogether, we'd better stick with it and try to find out what caused 'em to cut back."

They hadn't gone far before they came to a broad, shallow hollow in the middle of which they could see the house and outbuildings of a small farm. There were lights glowing in the windows of the house but no sign of activity anywhere on the outside. A buckboard with a horse still hitched to it was parked in front.

Lone, Jeth, and Minowi reined up on the shoulder of the hollow and gazed down on the scene from their saddles. In that moment, rain began to fall. Small, cold droplets at first but wind-whipped to give them a chilling sting against exposed flesh. Luckily, sensing the inevitability of the cloud cover opening up, the three riders had earlier taken time to don rain slickers dug from their saddlebags. Lone had even unearthed a spare hat, crumpled and misshapen due to being stuffed in his possibles pack, that he gave to Minowi to wear. On anybody else it would have looked droopy and a little silly; on her it did nothing to detract from her natural loveliness.

"I ain't no tracker on your level," Jeth said to Lone, "but even I can make out the trail of five riders leadin' down there. Only I don't see no sign of 'em leadin' out nor do I see any horses except that nag hitched to the buckboard."

"I make it the same," Lone agreed. "I also make it the buckboard only recently rolled in. And I see a couple plow horses in that fenced area out behind the house. Must mean the gang's mounts are in the barn."

"So where are the riders?" asked Minowi.

Lone's mouth pulled into a grimace. "For the sake of the people who live down there, I hope they're hidin' in the barn, too . . . But I got a sorry hunch that ain't the case."

"I still can't figure why Pierce and his bunch doubled back here," said Jeth. "You reckon maybe they know these folks—maybe some shirttail relatives to one of the gang or something like that—who are willingly givin' 'em a place to stop over?"

"Possible, I suppose. But it seems mighty slim." Lone hitched his collar up tighter against the rain stinging the back of his neck. "If they're in the house like I suspect, odds are they forced their way in."

"So how we gonna play it?"

"We'll start with the barn," Lone said. "We'll swing wide, ride down, find a way inside. Once we make sure the gang's horses are there—

meanin' their riders have got to be in the house—we'll plan what to do next."

"Sounds good," Jeth grunted. "I plan better when I ain't got rain blowin' in my ears."

It only took a handful of minutes for them to make their way down the slope and cut in on the back side of the barn. The rain continued to fall steadily, the wind continued to whip it in gusting sheets.

Tying their horses on a fence rail, they moved across the far end of the barn until they came to a crookedly hanging door. The rain slapping against the weathered structure did a good job of masking any noise they made getting the door open on its creaking rusty hinges. Keeping in mind that, no matter how slim the chance, there *might* be some gang members inside, Lone silently motioned for Jeth and Minowi to hold off while he drew his Colt and went in alone.

Given that the last light of dusk had nearly faded, spurred by the murkiness of the cloud cover and now the rain, the inside of the barn was dark as hell. Lone paused for nearly a full minute before his eyes finally adjusted enough to the inner gloom to be able to make out some shadowy shapes surrounding him. Thin strips of pale gray seeping in through cracks between the boards of the barn walls aided him, as did his senses of smell and hearing. He could smell horses. And cows. He could hear the scuff of their hooves, their nervous snorts and lowing, and was able to vaguely discern their lumpy outlines milling about in the center bay of the building. Overriding all was the sporadic groans of the building bending under the wind gusts and muted beat of the rain splattering on the roof.

Signaling for Jeth and Minowi to come on in, Lone waited until they were huddled close around him before whispering, "Looks like the horses are here alright. They're minglin' with two or three cows off toward one side. Must be some feed bunks along that wall."

"No sign of Pierce's bunch?" said Jeth.

"Wouldn't have motioned you in if there was," Lone told him tersely. "So now we've got to think about dealin' with 'em bein' in the house. If they got the farm family in there with 'em, it kinda matters as to what we can or can't do."

"If they took over the house, you reckon they'd even bother leavin' whoever's in there alive?"

Lone ground his teeth. "Hard to say. In the long run, probably not. But until we know for sure, we gotta figure it as a possibility. Means we can't just haul off and blast our way in for fear of innocents gettin' caught in a crossfire."

"So what does that leave?"

"For starters, it leaves takin' advantage of the rain and the dark. Under cover of that, I should be able to work my way up close to the house without much trouble. From there I oughta have a chance to peek in and get a clearer idea what the situation is."

"Okay. Yeah, that sounds good. Like you said, for starters. At least we'll know one way or the other."

"But first," said Lone, "we'll take care of another matter. These horses—while we got the chance, we're gonna turn 'em loose and scatter 'em. That way, just in case something goes sideways, Pierce's gang won't have 'em handy to try a getaway."

"Say, that's a good idea, too," muttered Jeth in a hushed voice. "Makes me glad I'm workin' at your side and not stacked up against you—you got a dang sneaky mind."

"Not sneaky, just smart," Minowi said firmly. "His thinking is what will make us succeed and keep us safe until this is finished."

Such unexpected praise made Lone feel pleased and proud, but at the same time a little awkward. He was glad for the poor visibility that enveloped them because he might even have blushed a little. Before he could respond in any way, a sudden loud noise—an amplified metallic screech, coming from the front end of the barn— cut sharply through the gloom and the sounds of the wind and rain and caused the three intruders to drop low into a pool of deeper shadows.

CHAPTER 27

Craning his neck to peer cautiously around a corner of the wooden storage bin built flush to the wall at one side of the doorway he and the others had entered through, Lone scanned toward the front of the barn to try and determine what had caused the sudden loud screech. What he saw was one of two double doors at that end sliding open. The tall, wide slab was suspended from a set of metal casters rolling on an overhead track, an apparent lack of proper lubrication causing the turning wheels to groan and squeal mournfully.

Coming through the opening created when the door had been shoved back sufficiently, their shapes silhouetted against the slightly better lighting outside, was a man leading a horse. The animal, Lone guessed, must be the one that had been hitched to the buckboard in front of the house. The man, a specimen of average height and build as best could be discerned given the sugarloaf sombrero perched on his head and the long, fringed poncho draped over his shoulders, was swinging a hooded lantern in one hand, throwing splashes of gold-yellow illumination beside and ahead of himself.

As he walked, the man was muttering a string of words Lone couldn't make out. After a minute he realized the words were being spoken in Spanish. It was a lingo Lone didn't understand very well, but he was able to catch enough to figure out the hombre was lamenting about being the one selected to go out in the rain and put away the damn horse.

Once said horse was led far enough into the barn, the man stopped and hung his lantern on a nail jutting out of a support beam bracing the elevated platform to a narrow hayloft that ran for some distance along that side of the bay. In the illumination now cast by the secured lantern, the man began removing the bridle and harness from the horse. He continued to mutter his lamentations as he worked.

By now, Jeth and Minowi had crowded in tight behind Lone and positioned themselves so they also could see what was going on. As they watched, the man in the sombrero finished stripping the horse and then swatted it on the rump to send it trotting over with the others by the feed bunks. That done, he hung the harnessing gear on a rail and took down the lantern. Instead of leaving to go back to the house, however, he walked a ways farther into the barn and stopped at the next support beam where the lantern he carried revealed for the first time two men who were lashed to the base of the post.

Minowi gave a quick intake of breath at the sight but the sounds of the rain on the roof and the wind gusting in through the still open door easily offset it.

Holding the lantern over the captives and looking down at them, the man in the sombrero now spoke English with only a slight Spanish accent. In any language, his tone was unmistakably taunting. "See how fortunate you are, amigos, to remain warm and dry while I, Jorge Bandros, am forced to venture out in the storm because of a stupid horse? You should be grateful for such kind treatment." And then he threw back his head and laughed.

Looking on, Lone realized the man who called himself Bandros was drunk. He also could see, in the illumination thrown by the lantern he held, that the men tied to the support beam appeared to have been pretty badly roughed up. They were propped in sitting positions—legs splayed out in front, backs to the post—with their wrists tied behind and then a length of thick rope wrapped around them several times, securing them to the post. Their clothes were torn and streaked with dirt as if they'd been rolling around on the ground. And while their heads were hanging forward, chins on chests, Lone could see enough of their faces to make out blood-stained rags tied around their mouths as gags and splotches of bruising on their cheeks.

Between continued snorts of taunting laughter, Bandros said, "I will tell you someone who *is* grateful for the treatment they are receiving, Senor Dumb-Ass Farmer—that is your wife and daughter. Too bad for the rain and wind or maybe, even clear out here, you could hear their moans of great pleasure from the way I and my compadres are treating them."

Here Bandros paused to throw his head back for another prolonged bout of braying laughter. When he caught his breath, he went on, "It must be that you spend so much time in the fields and tending your stupid livestock, Senor Dumb-Ass Farmer, that you are too tired to give proper attention in the bed at night, no? It must be so, because your wife is most eager for the attention we now are giving her that she has clearly been lacking." The Mexican paused as if expecting some kind of reaction. When he didn't get one, he grunted as if in disgust and went on. "Ah, and then there is the fine, supple young daughter . . . Caramba! The fires we have awakened in that lovely and so very willing—"

The rest of Bandros' taunt was cut short by the nearest captive suddenly straining against his bounds, emitting a muffled roar of rage through his bloody gag, and kicking viciously at his tormentor's legs. But Bandros had been smart enough to position himself just out of reach and now stood laughing more gleefully than ever.

When the captive gave up struggling and Bandros once again caught his breath, he wagged his head in an admonishing way and said, "You are not a grateful man at all, Senor Dumb-Ass Farmer. At another time I may have decided to remain and punish you for your unfriendly outburst . . . Instead, I shall save my energy and take it back to the house where it can be spent on those who *do* know how to show gratitude." With that, now chuckling to himself rather than grumbling as he'd been doing on the way in, he took his lantern and departed, closing the screeching door behind him.

The inside of the barn was again cast in near darkness. The only sounds were that of the rain and wind, the shuffling of the animals . . . and the wretched sobbing of one of the captives, presumably the one who had kicked out at Bandros.

"Well now we know the situation inside the house," Jeth whispered.

"And an ugly one it is," Minowi added bitterly.

"But at least they're alive," said Lone. "Wait a minute for our eyes to adjust again, then we'll go help those men tied to the post. They obviously could use it, and we can use any additional information they might be able to give."

"Well this is the shits," grumbled Hayden Halloway. "Everybody else is somewhere dry with a roof over their heads while we're stuck out here in the damn cold rain."

"You think I like it any better than you do? I'm just as wet and cold as you are," Vallen responded. "But, like you said, for right now it's what we're stuck with—leastways until we figure out what the hell's goin' on."

"What's goin' on, near as I can tell, is that these we're followin' are actin' goofier by the hour. I'm beginnin' to wonder if they *did* smoke a batch of loco weed somewhere along the way and we just missed seein' 'em do it. First they have that laughin' fit at their camp last night after near gettin' hung, then they swing wide a little while ago to stare out at that empty canyon off to the south, then they go for a ways before cuttin' back here to hole up for the night in that old barn instead of goin' on into the town. You tellin' me those are the actions of somebody ain't got their brains clouded?"

"I ain't tellin' you nothing," snapped Vallen. "I ain't sayin' on account of it don't make sense to me neither. The only guess I can make is that our boys and that squaw they're draggin' along with 'em didn't come here simply for the sake of spendin' the night but rather the trail they're followin' must have led 'em here."

"You mean the Pierce gang came here first?"

"Like I said, it's a guess."

"But what reason would Pierce have for comin' here?"

"Goddamnit, I don't know. I'm just gropin' for

230

an explanation how we ended up here. If you got something better to offer, go ahead and spit it out."

Halloway passed a hand across his face, wiping away the rain. "You don't have to bite my head off. I'm just askin' questions as a way to try and help think this through."

"Well it ain't workin'. I can't think good with you yammerin' in my ear."

The two men were sitting their horses on the shoulder of the hollow in which the Keough farm was located. They'd reined up in a clump of scrawny birch trees about twenty yards to one side of where Lone, Jeth, and Minowi had paused a half hour earlier to look down on the same scene.

Taking some of the edge off his voice, Vallen spoke again, saying, "Look, us snarlin' at each other for sure ain't gonna help. The only thing I can say for certain is that those three horses tied to the fence rail at the ass end of the barn down there belong to who *we* been followin'. The fact they're tied that way seems to say the riders are wantin' to stay clear of the house and went into the barn for a closer look-see without showin' themselves. So who would they not want to be seen by? Pierce's bunch seems most likely. And seein's how there's so many lights burnin' in the house and we can see the shadows of quite a few bodies movin' back and forth inside—a hell of a lot more than just the hombre who came out and put away the horse a minute ago—then those shadows *could* belong to the gang. Their mounts must already be in the barn. That's all I can speculate. As to *why* the gang came here or what the hell is due next . . . Man, I do not know."

After considering for a moment, Halloway said, "Sounds like you got it speculated pretty fine from what we got to work with. No way of knowin' more until somebody makes the next move."

"Yeah," Vallen said sourly. "And the only way we can be sure not to miss what the next move might be is to stick tight and keep a close watch."

Halloway groaned. "I guess you're right . . . But man oh man, that's *really* the shits!"

CHAPTER 28

"Don't be alarmed and don't try to call out," Lone whispered as he slipped silently up on the two bound men. Their heads lifted, faces turning to his voice, and even in the murkiness he could see the gleam of their widened eyes. "I mean you no harm, me and my friends are here to help," the former scout added. "Now I'm gonna cut your ropes and get those gags off, so hold still 'cause I can't see worth a damn in this dark."

The captives did as he said, pressing back tight against the post and holding very still. Lone's razor-edged Bowie made short work of their restraints and the severed ropes fell loose around them. As soon as the gag was removed from his mouth, the man who'd tried to kick Bandros said in a hoarse whisper, "Who are you?"

"We'll get to that in a minute," Lone told him. "First, let's get you somewhere a little more out of the way in case that hombre or somebody else comes back in. Can you stand okay?"

"Damn right I can stand," the man declared. "But I ain't going no place out of the way—I got to get to the house! I don't know if you heard or not, but my wife and daughter are in there and those dirty—"

"I heard everything," Lone cut him off. "But

if you go chargin' straight for the house all reckless-like, the only thing you'll accomplish is gettin' yourself killed—and maybe your wife and daughter, too!"

"But you heard what that scurvy bastard said," the man argued, shoving to his feet and lurching unsteadily so that he had to grab the post to balance himself. "You heard what him and the others are—"

This time it was the other captive who cut him off. "We *all* heard, Pa! It sickens me, too. But I also saw what else that pack of skunks is capable of. Look at you, you *can't* hardly stand. They beat us half to death the first time—you think they'll hesitate one eye blink to finish the job if you go at 'em in a bull rush?"

In the dimness, Lone could make out that this second speaker, the son of the first, was tall and leanly muscled, appearing not more than a couple years past twenty. His father was that many years older, equally tall, bulkier in build. Both had heads covered by pelts of thick, rust-colored hair, the father's reaching down into mutton chop sideburns.

With his father continuing to lean unsteadily against the post, the son pleaded, "This man has already helped us a lot, Pa. He says he wants to help more. We ought to at least hear what he has to say . . . for the sake of Ma and Sis, too."

The father emitted a single shuddering sob from

deep in his chest. Then he pushed away from the post and instead stepped forward to be steadied by the reaching arms of his son.

Lone led them slowly across the barn bay to the area beside the storage bin where Jeth and Minowi were waiting. "Sit down, rest a minute," Lone directed the pair. "I don't know how well you can see, but these are my friends Jeth and Minowi. I'm McGantry. Here"—holding out the canteen of water Jeth had gone and fetched from his horse while Lone was cutting loose the captives—"drink some of this, not too fast."

After he and his father had each taken a turn with the canteen, the young man said, "There's a lantern hanging a ways farther down this wall. I can go get it. If somebody's got a match, we could have some light. They'll never spot it from the house, not way back in here."

"That would be good," Lone told him.

The lad slipped away. He also moved a bit stiffly from the beating he'd received.

After he took another sip of water, the father spoke, his voice now a little steadier and less hoarse. "We're the Keoughs. I'm Tom, that's my boy Ben. My wife Mary and daughter Sara are . . . in the house." His voice broke somewhat at the last.

"Just stay steady. Have another sip of water," Jeth advised him.

When Ben returned with the lantern, Jeth

235

snapped a match and they set the wick to a soft glow. In this improved illumination, the cuts and bruises shown on the faces of the two Keoughs were further evidence of the harsh treatment they'd endured. But, partly due to being caked with dirt, at least none of the visible lacerations appeared to be still bleeding.

After everybody's eyes re-adjusted and they had the chance for a good look at one another, Tom Keough said, "Not to sound like I don't appreciate it, but can I ask why you folks are here?"

Lone grinned crookedly. "Reckon that's a fair question. The short answer is that we're a sort of unofficial posse on the trail of the murderin', train-robbin' varmints now inside your house. In case they didn't introduce themselves, they're the Dar Pierce gang. A few days back they robbed a train up in our neck of the woods, near Ogallala. We started trackin' 'em shortly after that and this is where the trail led us."

"But why our place? What made 'em come here?" Ben asked.

"Was hopin' you might have some idea on that," Lone said. "We had it down to runnin' about a half day behind. Was figurin' they was headed for McCook, maybe to do some robbin', and we'd catch up there. But then they veered off and came to a halt here for reasons that ain't clear."

"But they *did* go into town. Leastways two of 'em did," spoke up Tom Keough. "The man who acted like the leader and the woman they have with 'em—some red-haired she-devil he called Harriet—took our buckboard in while the others waited here. After they jumped me and Ben and stomped hell out of us, they left us laying out front on the ground for a while, thinking we were out cold."

"I was," Ben remarked.

"I was, too, mostly," said his father. "But I drifted in and out some before they dragged us in here and tied us to that damn post . . . I heard 'em make Sara point out which of our horses was for pulling the buckboard and . . . and I caught enough of their talk to hear that the man and woman was going to use it to go to town."

"They say why? For what purpose?"

Keough shook his head. "No . . . Nothing I can remember."

"When we first rode up, it looked to me like that buckboard rig had rolled in not very long ahead of us," said Lone. "That would fit with the Mexican unhitchin' the pull horse and bringin' it in just a few minutes ago. So how long does it take to go back and forth to town?"

"Forty, forty-five minutes," answered Ben.

Lone twisted his mouth in thought. "That says Pierce and Harriet spent a couple or so hours in McCook . . . But it still don't say why."

Minowi broke her silence and said matter-of-factly, "To examine the town for the robbery you suspect they mean to commit." All eyes swung to her and there was a long moment of expectant silence before she added, "Isn't that what you thought they would do? What did Jeth call it— 'sizing things up' before going ahead with the robbery?"

"Hey now. That could be it," exclaimed Jeth.

"It sure could," Lone agreed. "It makes as much sense as anything. Those federal marshals who chased Pierce's bunch out of Dakota sent out paper on 'em, warnin' they was headed south back toward Injun Territory. Knowin' that, Pierce would want to be cagey about showin' up in any sizable town for fear of bein' recognized."

Jeth nodded. "Him and Harriet in a buckboard would make a pretty good cover. Let 'em give things a good lookin' over without drawin' attention—until they're ready to hit with the rest of the gang."

"Which, if they go through with it, would likely mean first thing tomorrow," Lone summed up.

Tom Keough suddenly grew agitated. "Now hold on. If anybody thinks for one minute I'm going to leave my wife and daughter in there all night with those filthy—"

"Knock it off," Lone growled. "Nobody's sayin' anything of the kind. We're just tryin' to piece some things together, that's all. But no matter how it shapes up, the one fact that don't change is that if you try bargin' in like a damn fool, it's more apt to cost lives than save any. Get that through your head!"

Keough sank back, his breathing suddenly quick and ragged.

Lone cut his gaze from the man to his son, then back again. "Listen. I know this is hard. Bitter hard. But what's done is done. Your women are still alive. If we can keep 'em that way, then they'll have a chance to heal. That won't be easy, neither, but ain't it better than seein' 'em dead?"

Keough hung his head and kept breathing raggedly, half sobbing.

Ben met Lone's eyes and said, "What have you got in mind, mister?"

CHAPTER 29

Tom Keough had finally snapped out of it and was sitting up straight, listening intently along with the others, as Lone laid out a plan.

He started with, "You willin' to trade your barn for your wife and daughter, Keough?"

Tom's answer was simply a hard, flat stare.

Lone nodded. "All right, then that's the key. First we'll clear the cows and horses out the back, like we was plannin' on doin' anyway. Might want to tie our own horses a ways farther out, too. On them we've got some spare rifles we happen to have come in possession of recently. Can you two shoot?"

"I'm a fair shot," Keough answered. "Ben here is sharp as a tack. He bags wild game for our dinner table real regular."

"Either of you ever shoot a man?"

"I fought in the tail end of the war," Keough replied. "I surely shot *at* some fellas in a few skirmishes. In all the smoke and confusion, though, I was never certain if I scored any hits or not. But I damn well *can* shoot a man if I need to."

His expression grim, Ben's answer was, "No, I never shot a man. But I don't count the swine wallowing in our house as rightly deserving to be

240

called men. Them I can put a bullet in with no hesitation at all."

"That's the talk," Jeth said approvingly.

"Okay," Lone continued. "Then, after we've scattered the animals and put rifles in the hands of you two, we'll spread plenty of hay and straw all across the front. Stuff that will take fire quick and burn bright. Something they're sure to notice from the house. Thinkin' their horses are still in here, the gang is bound to come a-runnin'. With any luck they'll figure it was caused by the drunk Mexican bein' sloppy with his lantern when he came out so they might not even be overly suspicious."

"Only we'll quick give 'em reason to see they shoulda been," Jeth said with a nasty chuckle.

"That's the idea," Lone affirmed. "You and me will go out ahead of time and take up positions on either side at the front of the house. That will put 'em in our crossfire as soon as they show. Keough, you and Ben set the fire once we're in place. Feel free to come out and join the shootin' when you're ready, just find some cover to fire from and be sure not to backlight yourselves against the flames."

"What about the girl?" Keough asked, tipping his head to indicate Minowi.

"I will be with Lone," Minowi answered for herself.

Lone grinned. "That's right. Her and a certain

shotgun she happens to be right handy with."

Then Ben had a question. "What if one of the gang stays in the house . . . with Ma and Sis?"

Lone's grin faded. "We'll have to play that hand if and when it's dealt, son. With their horses at risk, I gotta believe everybody in the gang is gonna be powerful anxious to try and save 'em. If any one of 'em does lag back, seems most likely it would be the woman, Harriet. Not that she should be taken lightly. But if we cut down the rest like we're settin' up for, she's gotta see that'll leave her in a mighty hard place."

"Can I make a suggestion?" Ben said.

"Have at it."

"It don't need two people to set the fire here. Pa can handle that. What if I went out with you three and I circled around to the back of the house? I know the grounds well enough to move quick an' quiet, even in the dark. And I know how to get in the house quiet, too. That way, if they do leave somebody inside, I'd be there to help keep Ma and Sis safe."

"That ain't a half bad idea," said Jeth.

"No, it's not. It's a good one," agreed Keough. "But I should be the one to go. It could be more dangerous, working in that close."

Ben gave his father a stern look. "No offense, Pa, but you ain't moving spry enough. You're breathing too ragged. I think you got some cracked ribs from the stomping you took. If

242

there's need for quickness when things start to break, you'd be in trouble—and that might also affect Ma an' Sis."

Keough held his son's eyes for a long count, not responding.

Lone spoke, saying quietly, "The boy's right, Keough."

Keogh's eyes dropped. "Yeah, I know he is . . . But he ain't a boy no more. He's a man."

"No argument on that. Your idea is solid, Ben. We'll go with it."

"One more thing," said Ben. "If they leave somebody inside and it's the woman . . . Was there need, I wouldn't hesitate putting a bullet in her neither. Even though she's a woman, she's just as bad as the rest."

"Again. No argument."

"Hey. Wake up," said Vallen, jabbing an elbow into his partner's ribs.

Halloway straightened up from his slouched position. "I am awake," he grumbled. "I'm too damn wet and miserable to sleep."

"Well your snorin' sure told a different story. But never mind that. Hand me the spyglass from over on the other side of you."

The pair were hunkered in the stand of scrawny birch trees with a short length of canvas tarp draped over their heads, weighted down on the ends by chunks of rock to help hold it in place.

As a shield against the rain, it was better than nothing; but not by much.

"I don't know how much this will help," Vallen said, taking the glass Halloway handed him, "but there's something goin' on down there and I'm tryin' to make out what it is."

Frowning, leaning forward to peer down into the hollow without sticking his head too far out from under the tarp, Halloway said, "Yeah, I see it. Lot of motion there in back of the barn. What is it?"

"A handful of horses comin' out . . . and a couple milk cows. Some fellas hoorahin' 'em along. All the way out through an open gate— scatterin' 'em into the night."

"What sense does that make?"

Vallen lowered the spyglass and wiped its rain-dotted lens on his shirt sleeve. "Ain't sure about the cows, but it looked to be five or six horses in the mix. That would fit with the number of gang members there's supposed to be. And that would then fit with our reckonin' from before about our two boys trackin' the gang here and the gang bein' in the house after puttin' their horses in the barn."

"So the trackers are scatterin' the gang's get-away mounts."

"Looks like. And if that's what they're up to, then it can only mean they're figurin' to have it out with the gang sometime soon and are wantin' to cut down the chances for any to give 'em the slip."

"Hot damn," Halloway said excitedly. "You really think it's all gonna come to a head right here before much longer?"

"That's the way it feels to me," allowed Vallen. "They might wait 'til daybreak to set it in motion. But whenever it comes, I'm bettin' that right down there in that farmer's hollow is where we're gonna have the chance to do our bone pickin' when they're done."

"Hot damn," Halloway said again.

"Best get our rifles and hoglegs ready," Vallen suggested. "Wipe 'em down good and take extra care to keep 'em dry from here on. Soon enough, I'm thinkin', we'll have cause to heat 'em up some . . ."

CHAPTER 30

Branching off from the road out of town that passed near the Keough farm was a lesser worn trail leading down into the hollow where the farm lay. At the point where this branch-off occurred, nine riders clad in sodden ponchos or drenched rain slickers reined up. Each man was marked by a bright yellow bandanna tied around his left bicep.

Wheeling around to face the others, Marshal Walt Kent spoke loud enough to be heard over the wind and rain, saying, "Okay, men. I gave you the lowdown in town, but I'm going to go over it quick one more time. Most of you know Tom Keough and his family. Good people. We have reason to suspect they may be under threat from an outlaw gang known to be headed this general way from up in Dakota. We're going in to find out for sure. If it's as we fear, things could turn hot in a hurry."

The marshal paused to let that much sink in before continuing. "If it comes to shooting, we need to take care not to gun down each other in the dark and rain. That's why the yellow bandannas. But we also have to watch out for the Keough family, God willing they're still alive. For the sake of that, when we get in a little closer the main bunch of us will hold back while two men—that'll be you Curly, and take Ned Brimmer with you—slip in careful-like and give things a good looking over as to what we'll be faced with.

"Once we know that, we'll figure how to proceed. The main thing is to watch and wait for any signals from me. If it comes to gunplay, don't be trigger happy or reckless. I appreciate every one of you coming along on this, I ain't looking to save one batch of folks by trading some others."

"We all know the score, Marshal," said one of the posse members.

"That's right. We'll follow your signal, just like you say," added another.

Kent gave a satisfied nod. Then he reined his horse back around and led off once again toward the hollow.

Inside the barn, everything was ready. Piles of loose straw and hay were strewn all along the front of the barn and soaked with coal oil from two additional lanterns Ben had produced. He and his father were armed with Henry rifles that Jeth had brought in from the horses. Jeth was carrying his own Henry; Lone his Yellowboy and Colt; Minowi gripping the Greener shotgun.

"Looks like we're ready," said Lone as they all huddled at the front door. He ran his gaze across the faces of the others. "If this works, it's gonna go fast and bloody once it busts loose. They're vermin, but I shouldn't have to remind anybody that they're also snake mean and dangerous. Don't give 'em no more chance than you would a rattler. Hell, not as much.

"Jeth, you'll take a position on this near side of the house. Minowi and me will go with Ben to the back, he can get us that far the quickest. Then, while he slips inside, we'll work our way on around to a spot on the far side. Give us about five minutes, Keough. That should be enough because it'll still take a little longer for the fire to burn bright enough for those in the house to notice. When you come out and take up you own spot, remember not to backlight yourself against the flames."

Lone paused, waiting to see if anybody had anything else to say. When no one did, he shoved the sliding door open far enough to allow passage through and Ben led the way out.

The rain was bracing, like a face slap from a cold, wet cloth. The four of them leaned into it and moved forward at a half-trot, Ben still leading the way. When he felt the time was right, Jeth dropped off. Lone and Minowi continued on with Ben, swinging wide and then curving in toward the back end of the house. The structure provided a good bearing but at the same time its many lighted windows had to be avoided staring at in order to keep the darkness from seeming that much blacker in contrast.

At the rear of the house they halted. From inside, faintly, they could hear raucous laughter.

With their heads leaned close together, Ben whispered, "Go on around to the other side, stay close. You'll see a well housing up about level with the front of the house. That would make good cover for you to drop in behind."

"Got it," said Lone.

Another outburst of bawdy laughter could be heard from within.

Lone put a hand on Ben's shoulder. "When you get in there, no matter what you see or hear, you're gonna have to hold back until the time is right. That might require the most strength you'll ever have to show in your life."

"I understand. I know what's at stake," Ben replied gravely.

Lone gave the shoulder a final pat and then he and Minowi moved off.

Around the far side of the house they made their way, staying just outside the splash of light thrown from the glowing windows. They spotted the piled stones of the well housing with no trouble and soon were slipped in behind it.

As soon as they were in place, Minowi said softly, soberly, "That young man. He is taking a great burden on his shoulders."

"I know," Lone told her. "But he's got the

shoulders to carry it. If I didn't believe that, I wouldn't have agreed to his idea."

They were quiet for a minute. More muted laughter drifted out from the house.

Then, leaning out from behind the piled stones, Minowi said, "Look."

Also leaning out, following her gaze, Lone saw the first flames visibly licking up in the barn windows and through the sliding door they had left cracked open.

Wiping rain from his face, he said, "Won't be long now."

Ben Keough eased open the rear door of the house an inch at a time to minimize the low creak he knew the door's hinges always made. Having removed his boots outside so they wouldn't clump on the bare wood floor, he entered into the mud room. When his wet socks squished with his first steps, an abundance of caution made him take them off, too.

The inner door leading from the mud room to the pantry opened soundlessly and Ben passed through the same. He paused. He was breathing hard. Not from exertion, but from excitement, anticipation. He willed himself to calm down, to slow his breathing. He squeezed the Henry rifle in his hands tighter, telling himself he needed to stay as steady as the cold, damp steel.

The doorway from the pantry to the kitchen

was covered by a split, flower-patterned curtain. Beyond that, he could plainly hear more laughter and some talk from deeper in the house—somebody boasting about a bank in McCook and how rich it was going to make all of them.

Ben parted the curtain with the barrel of his Henry and stepped through. All the familiar smells of his mother's kitchen wrapped around him and for a moment it almost seemed like everything was normal and all the rest—the ugly things that had already taken place and the bloodshed getting ready to be unleashed—were some kind of crazy nightmare. But then one of the men up ahead issued another guttural laugh and the harsh reality of the situation came slamming back.

A moment later, Ben was struck by an even harsher reminder of how things stood.

Here at the back of the kitchen, as it had been in the mud room and pantry, everything was in darkness. But ahead, through the dining room and into the parlor, three or four brightly burning lanterns were bathing everything in full illumination. One lantern sat on the dining room table, the others were out in the parlor. All the people present in the house also appeared to be in the parlor.

Ben's line of sight, combined with the fact the doorway from the kitchen into the parlor was set off-center, only allowed him to see part of the sitting room. It was enough. It was too much.

Seated in his father's favorite easy chair was the taunting Mexican who had led the horse out to the barn a short time ago. Sitting on his lap was Sara, Ben's sister. She was naked from the waist up. Her head hung down, long hair trailing to conceal her face. The Mexican's sombrero was pushed off his head, suspended by its chin strap onto his shoulders. In his left hand he held a nearly empty bottle of whiskey; his right arm was draped over Sara's shoulder, that hand insolently cupping and squeezing her bared breast.

Ben felt a rush of equal parts revulsion and rage. He gripped the Henry rifle harder still, until his hand threatened to cramp. By great force of will held himself in check. He remembered Lone's words.

The only other of the room's occupants he could see were the red-haired woman and the man Lone had identified as Dar Pierce, the leader of the gang. They were sitting side by side on a couch. Ben thanked God he was unable to see his mother; if she was being treated in a similar way as Sara, he didn't know if he'd be able to hold back.

Pierce was the one doing the talking about the town bank. He, too, had a bottle of whiskey in one hand and the woman beside him was taking occasional sips. She was outfitted far differently than the dusty trail garb Ben had first seen her

252

in, now clad in a nice dress with her hair pinned up and a shiny brooch pinned in front. But Ben refused to appreciate anything good about her appearance. He looked past Sara and focused a hateful glare at the woman—to him nothing but a vile creature who sat by smiling and laughing while another female, an innocent barely beyond childhood, was mauled and humiliated right before her eyes.

In that moment, Ben hated Harriet Bell more than he ever had anything or anyone in his life. Except for the Mexican. He wanted to see both of them dead before this night was over. He expected he wouldn't get a chance at the Mexican. But the woman . . . if there'd been even the tiniest doubt he could put a bullet in her, it was long gone. In fact, he now *ached* for the opportunity.

But, above all, he had to do his part to save Ma and Sis. Once again, Ben remembered Lone's words: *"Your women are still alive. If we can keep 'em that way, then they'll have a chance to heal."*

CHAPTER 31

The trail branching off the town road and leading back to the Keough farm dropped into the hollow on a slightly lesser grade than the steeper shoulders to the west. Before feeding into the clearing where the house and outbuildings sat, it passed between two fairly thick stands of birch and fir trees. Just back from this opening, Marshal Kent again signaled his posse to a halt.

"Okay, Curly," he said. "You and Ned ride in a ways farther. Then dismount and work your way up to the house on foot in order to see if you can tell—"

But he never got the rest out.

A couple of the posse men had reined their horses a bit off to one side of the knot gathering in behind the marshal—far enough wide to see through the gap in the trees for a full view of the farm buildings. What that included was the wall of fire now raging inside the barn, flames churning wildly, reaching out the windows and the open door, billowing clouds of smoke pouring skyward.

"Holy shit! The barn's ablaze!" one of the men shouted, cutting off the instructions Kent had been issuing.

"Fire! A big one—the whole thing's gonna go!" the other man wailed.

Fire was one of the most dreaded and panic-inducing words on the frontier. Whole towns were known to be flattened before a bad enough outbreak could be brought under control. Individual houses or buildings, especially barns, were almost always a lost cause. Even rainfall, unless it was a major downpour, seldom helped until after significant inside damage was done. This awareness, this fear, was so deeply ingrained in the minds of many of the posse members that shouts of the word "fire" instantly propelled them beyond any other thought.

"We've got to at least try to save the livestock!" somebody shouted, and that was the final nail.

Three more men spurred after the first two and all of them went tearing off toward the barn, aiming to sweep past the house on the way. The night rang with cries of "Keough! Tom Keough! Your barn's afire!" and "Hurry, man! Come a-runnin'!"

Kent hollered after the fleeing men in a futile attempt to call them back. But it was no use. They were gone, and so was any hope of determining the Keoughs suspected plight with any degree of stealth. All that was left was to charge in, too, and hope like hell more than just the barn might be salvaged.

"Come on, men. Follow me," the marshal told those remaining with him. "Stay sharp and watch yourselves!"

• • •

Lone and Minowi, crouched in back of the piled stones of the well housing, were caught totally off guard by the shouts and the sound of pounding hooves rising up suddenly from behind them. They had been focused intently on the front of the Keough house and the burning barn beyond—poised in the belief that any second now somebody in the house would *have* to take notice of the blaze. Turning, they saw the first dark shapes of the riders streaking out of the trees, hurling their warnings ahead.

"What the . . ." Lone muttered in bewilderment.

At the same instant, the front door of the house flew open and four men came boiling out, all brandishing pistols. They, too, had heard the shouts and now saw the approaching riders—*and* the blazing barn.

"The barn! Our horses!" one of the outlaws shouted.

"Never mind the damn horses—We're under attack!" bellowed another.

Even as he said this, he was raising his arm and extending the hogleg he fisted. As the first of the riders drew even with the front of the house, still bent on getting to the barn and barely glancing over at the men outside the doorway, the pistol roared and spat a bullet that knocked the man out of his saddle.

The next riders coming behind the one who just

256

bit the dust were momentarily stunned by what they saw, too much so to try taking evasive action or even begin checking down their mounts before the rest of the men outside the doorway started throwing lead, too.

"Cut 'em down!" hollered the man who'd taken the first shot. "There's more coming, we may need to grab some of their horses to hightail it outta here!"

Lone had no way of knowing who the incoming riders were but the yellow bandannas fluttering on their arms—a common practice among posse members or vigilantes heading out in a group, anticipating trouble during which they may need to quickly identify one another—were enough to mark them as a force arriving to confront the Pierce gang. If true, that put them on his side. The fact the gang was starting to open up on the riders only reinforced this. But whatever the case, the overriding fact was that Pierce's bunch— though by means other than the plan Lone had put in motion—were now flushed and exposed. No way the former scout could *not* take advantage of that!

All of this ran through his mind in a flash. But at the same time he also recognized that if he opened fire he stood the risk of drawing return lead from both sides. It was a risk he was willing to take for himself, but not one he wanted to subject Minowi to.

"Flatten yourself to the ground and stay down!" he told her.

By now more riders were thundering into the farm clearing and shots from both horseback and the front of the house were filling the air in a cadence almost as rapid as the sound of the hoofbeats. Hot lead sizzled through cold raindrops.

Two more riders pitched from their saddles.

Lone saw one of the gang members jerk his leg back and stagger as he took a bullet to the thigh. But he quickly righted himself to a half crouch and raised his pistol to continue shooting.

Bracing his Yellowboy on the piled stones, Lone stroked the trigger and felt the buck against his shoulder. The gang member nearest to his position flung up both arms, sagged at the knees, then toppled out away from the house and onto the muddy ground.

"We got to get back in the house!" one of the remaining three shouted.

"No!" countered another, the man who by now Lone reckoned to be Pierce himself. "We'll be trapped for sure. Our only chance is to make it to some of those horses . . . Harriet, get out here!"

Inside the house, Ben Keough was crouched at the rear of the kitchen, just back from the circle of illumination thrown by the lantern on the table. When he heard the shouts and then the sound of pounding horses coming from outside, it jolted him. Enough time had passed so that, like Lone and Minowi, he was poised and growing somewhat anxious thinking that surely one of the varmints in his parlor *ought* to be noticing the barn blaze pretty soon. The cries of "Fire!" and the sound of horses galloping up outside came out of the blue and made no sense.

But it quickly proved to serve the same purpose as far as rousting the four outlaws out of the house in order to see what was going on. They all jumped to it so fast, guns drawn, they nearly trampled each other getting through the front door.

The only one left inside, as expected (and as *hoped* for, by Ben) was Harriet Bell. She also drew a gun from somewhere in the folds of her dress and at first stood just back from the open door, looking out, as gunfire began splitting apart the night.

Ben felt the strong tug of wanting to drill her right there. But two things stayed his trigger finger. First, the idea of shooting someone in the back, even someone like the red-haired witch, repelled him. Second, and more important, was the fact his sister was partly in the line of fire.

When the Mexican jumped up to go outside, he had spilled Sara from his lap and dumped her unceremoniously to the floor. She was sprawled there still, her upper body pushed part way up on

259

one arm. Her back was to Ben but he could see that her head continued to hang forward, her hair spilling down limply. Her bare shoulders were shaking with soft sobs . . . And directly on the other side of her stood Harriet Bell looking out the door.

Under different circumstances, it was a shot Ben would have taken with confidence. But the slim, slim chance that Sara might unexpectedly raise her head . . . No, he couldn't do it. Wouldn't do it. Especially when neither Sara nor his mother appeared to be in any immediate danger beyond the harm they'd already suffered.

But, abruptly, Harriet threatened to change that.

Turning, swinging her gun around with her, she addressed Sara in a snarl, saying, "Shut up, you mewling little pup! Get over there with your mother, where I can keep an eye on both of you."

Sara rose shakily and started toward the side of the room out of Ben's sight. Her slinking movements were like those of a whipped pup.

Rage welled up in Ben. There was nothing to stop him now.

Waving her gun some more, Harriet said to the unseen half of the room, "Best keep her quiet, Mommy, or I'll do it permanent-like!"

Then she turned back and took a step toward the doorway.

Ben straightened up and brought the Henry to his shoulder. But in his eagerness, he bumped against a chair hitched up to the table and caused its legs to scuff loudly on the bare wood floor.

Harriet, as skilled and dangerous with a gun as any member of her gang, reacted instantly. She wheeled around and thrust her gun in the direction of the scuffing sound. She and Ben pulled their triggers simultaneously. The house shook with the explosive reports.

Ben saw Harriet slam back against the edge of the doorway, a bright crimson splotch appearing just above the shiny brooch pinned to the front of her dress. But the satisfaction Ben usually felt when he saw that his shot had scored a hit was missing. Instead, in its place, was a feeling of fiery pain blossoming outward from his ribs on the right side. He also realized he'd been jerked hard into a half turn and a wave of dizziness was washing over him along with the sensation of falling.

The last thing he was aware of before the floor came rushing up to meet him was a gruff voice calling from outside, "Harriet, get out here!"

CHAPTER 32

"He's startin' to come around," said Lone. "Stand back a little, give him some air."

Lone, Marshal Kent, and Tom and Mary Keough stood gathered around the couch where Ben had been carried to. Across the room, Minowi sat with Sara Keough who was now covered by a hastily grabbed old faded work shirt. Jeth was outside, helping some of the posse men load bodies into Keough's buckboard for the return trip to town.

The barn was still burning, though by now the roof had collapsed so it was only a heap of blazing, smoking fallen rafters and a few upright beams. The rain had stopped abruptly and the overcast sky was starting to clear up. Every now and then, slices of moon would peek through the separating dark clouds.

On the couch, Ben's eyes opened and he blinked several times in a somewhat dazed manner. Once the eyes were open for good, they began searching, looking around, sweeping across the faces hovering over him.

Then his gaze locked on his mother and Ben said hoarsely, "Ma."

Mary reached down and took one of his hands in hers. "I'm right here, dear. Everything's okay now . . . We're all going to be okay."

"Wh-what happened?"

"You took a bullet crease to the side, probably cracked a rib," Lone told him. "When you fell, appears you hit your head and knocked yourself out for a spell. Half hour or so."

"What else? I—I don't hear any shooting."

"Shootin's all over with. For now."

When Ben tried to sit up, his father put a hand on his shoulder and said, "Take it easy, son. You've been through a lot, no need to rush things."

The weight of his father's hand and the sharp pain that had lanced through him when he tried to move convinced Ben to stay put. He dropped his head back on the soft couch cushions. But then a thought struck him. "Sara! Where's Sara?" he wanted to know.

"She's okay, too," his mother assured him, squeezing his hand. "She's right across the room. A little worse for wear, but fighting to pull herself together."

"She's going to make it. We all are," said Tom Keough. His voice was firm, yet at the same time it sounded vaguely like he was trying to convince himself as much as the others.

Speaking for the first time, Marshal Kent said, "In case you're wondering, Ben, that red-haired wildcat who shot you also took some lead in return."

"I know. I—I'm glad I didn't miss," Ben replied.

Kent twisted his mouth sourly. "Trouble is, it didn't put her down. Worse yet, her and two others got away. In all the chaos—the shooting and the rain and dark, and half my doggone posse panicked by the fire—those three grabbed a couple horses from men they'd shot out of the saddle and then squirted clean out through our ranks."

"They didn't make it all that clean," argued Lone in a bitter tone. "One of the others was wounded, too, and the woman was doubled up on his horse. That makes three people, two of 'em shot-up, lightin' out on two horses. I don't see that as puttin' 'em in particularly good shape."

"Maybe not," Kent allowed. "But it still leaves them on the run, not captured. Or killed, like the two they left behind."

"Runnin' critters can be chased—and caught," Lone insisted.

Kent eyed him. "That what you mean to do?"

"I didn't track 'em this far to turn away now."

The marshal gave it a beat then said, "Guess I figured that's how you'd feel. Can't say I'm sorry to hear you say so. Things were different, I'd be going after 'em with you. Hell, I'm already out of my jurisdiction, what difference would another handful of miles make? But I've got three dead men and two wounded ones. I owe it to them and

264

their families to take 'em back to town and do some explaining and consoling."

Lone gave a faint nod. "Sometimes that's the worst part of a job like yours."

"When do you figure on heading out?" asked Keough.

"Quick as possible. No reason to hold off now that things are mostly settled here."

"I want to go with you," Tom and Ben said in near perfect unison.

"I understand the want," Lone said, cocking an eyebrow. "But, to put it plain, neither of you are in good enough shape for it. We're gonna have to move fast and light, and conditions out there ain't very pleasant. Besides, your women need you here. They got healin' to do, same as you. Best you stay tight together to get through it."

Father and son averted their eyes, knowing he was right and hating it. Mary's gaze was grateful.

"I know for certain there are considerable rewards out for the Pierce gang as a whole," said Kent. "I expect there are some for 'em individually as well. Means there's likely money to be owed for the two dead ones, once I'm able to identify 'em."

"Bounty money ain't what we set out for," Lone replied. "Though what got left behind here in the house is from the train robbery up north so is partly owed Jeth and his ex-boss."

"I can't hand that over right now, not until a

blasted bunch of paperwork is done and I get a court order," the marshal explained. "But I'll be sure to keep track of it and have it ready as soon as I can."

Lone nodded. "Fair enough. As far as any money due for the two dead ones . . ." he paused for a moment, cut a glance over at the Keoughs then back to Kent ". . . I'll trust you to split it up between the Keoughs and the widows of the posse men you lost."

"That's mighty generous."

"Like I said, we never set out for bounty money."

Now it was the marshal who gave a short nod. Then: "Your man Jeth has been telling the men in my posse that you're the trackingest sonofagun west of the Missouri River."

Lone shrugged. "There's plenty who'd agree with the sonofagun part. And worse. As for the trackin', I've known better. Then again," he showed the hint of a crooked grin, "if I do say so myself, I've also known a passel who ain't."

"You mentioned how unpleasant the conditions out there are. You really think you'll be able to pick up sign in the dark, especially after all that rain?"

"*After* the rain—that's the key," Lone said. "The rain quit right after those polecats lit out. The moon's breakin' through and the ground is soft, it'll hold tracks plain enough with nothing fresh comin' down to blur 'em . . . Plus, there'll be blood."

"Sure enough," said Vallen, from the shoulder of the hollow and peering once again through the spyglass held to his eye. "They're gettin' ready to saddle up and head out. Must be figurin' to go after the ones who got away."

"Aw, man," Halloway groaned. "Ain't there no let-up in those trackin' damn fools? Wouldn't you think they'd at least rest a spell and wait 'til daybreak?"

"Probably the way I'd do it," Vallen admitted. "And damn sure the way you would. That's what you're beefin' about now, knowin' that if they're on the move again then we're gonna have to be, too."

"Damn right I got a beef about that," grumbled Halloway. "I'm cold and wet from my ass both ways and plumb tuckered out. We ain't had a decent night's sleep since we started, always havin' to keep one eye open even when we do stop, for fear of missin' when they up and take off again."

"That's the job we took on," Vallen reminded him. "You think I wouldn't like to sack out in a bed and sleep until I could wake when it suited me? I want to believe that day's comin', but it ain't here yet. I was figurin' things was gonna come to a head right down there at that pissant little farm in the middle of nowhere, and we would've been that much closer to havin' this over with. But it didn't work out that way."

"Yeah," Halloway said bitterly. "Whoever the hell those other riders who showed up were, they sure kicked a fat gob of manure in the buttermilk."

"You can say that again. After the shootin' died down, as they was goin' in and out of the lighted doorway to the house, I spotted badges on a couple of 'em. That and the bandannas on their arms says to me they was a posse from somewhere who must have got wind the Pierce gang was in their neck of the woods and came lookin' to make a name for themselves."

Halloway grunted. "What they got instead was shot to hell and about half of 'em now stacked like cordwood in the bed of that buckboard to be took back wherever they came from."

"The town of McCook, I expect. But that don't really matter. What matters where we're concerned is that what's left of the Pierce gang is now once more runnin' ahead of the trackers who've been on 'em all along. Bein' how they're so eager to take out again, it can only mean that the brooch—the main thing to them as well as us—must not have been left behind in the house and so has to still be with the getaways." Vallen heaved a sigh. "And since there ain't no let-up in those damn trackers, as you rightly said before,

268

we can't afford to let up neither . . . Come on, let's get to our horses and try to figure out how the hell we're gonna keep up with 'em in the dark."

CHAPTER 33

"Can't stop . . . Gotta keep moving," rasped Dar Pierce.

He sat his saddle, hunched forward in pain, with Harriet pressed tight against his back, her arms wrapped around his middle. They were halted on the banks of the Republican River. Paul Caldwell sat his mount beside them, reaching over to grip the bridle of their horse, steadying it more than Pierce's weak hold on the reins was able to. The river was swollen and running fast from the rain, but inasmuch as it had been low to begin with from the dry summer, it still appeared fordable.

"We've *got* to stop pretty damn soon," argued Caldwell. "You're both bleeding too bad not to. We don't take time to deal with that, the blood loss will take care of stopping you on its own. Neither of you will be able to stay on that horse."

"I've been shot before. I can last as long as this bag of bones can," insisted Pierce. "At least get us across the river." Harriet clung to him, said nothing.

Caldwell remained still, holding his mount and Pierce's motionless. He studied the fast moving water, scanning the opposite bank and then looking both downstream and up. The overcast sky had by now broken up into increasingly scattered splotches of clouds with enough moon- and starlight showing through to provide fairly decent visibility.

"Damn it, what are you waiting for? Get going!" demanded Pierce. He seemed barely able to hold his head up.

Caldwell nodded. "Okay. We're gonna go. But we ain't gonna cross, not just yet. We're gonna go up upstream a ways first."

"Upstream! Against the current? Are you nuts?"

"Maybe. But you're gonna have to trust me. The river don't run that deep through here," Caldwell explained, "plus that rain wasn't as hard as the wind made it seem. We can fight the current and move away from where our tracks lead in by going the least likely direction anybody following us would expect. That will buy us valuable time if they show up searching for where we came out."

"I still say it sounds crazy," Pierce objected. "Who the hell is gonna try following us before daybreak, anyway?"

"I don't know. But who the hell figured we were gonna get cornered at that nowhere shit-box of a farm a little while ago?" Caldwell countered stubbornly. "You're gonna have to go along with me on this. I'll take the reins and control the horses, all you got to do is hang on tight."

A moment later they were out in the water, turned into the current. The horses balked some at first, but under Caldwell's steady hand and sharp commands they soon enough straightened up and found adequate footing to proceed as directed. Gradually, he angled them over closer to the opposite bank where, in shallower water, they had better footing and so slogged on stronger still. Clutching the saddle horn fiercely, Pierce weaved from side to side a bit, but for the most part appeared secure in his saddle. With her arms wrapped tightly about him, Harriet was, too.

Caldwell pushed them along at a steady pace. At least a half mile, he reckoned. More. The land on either side was mostly low and grassy but occasionally there would be a higher embankment, now and then a few trees. The horses were holding up well, as were Pierce and Harriet. Caldwell might have pushed on even farther if he hadn't spotted the flat-bottomed fisherman's skiff pulled up on the bank and purposely turned upside down to protect the inside from foul weather. It was well up from the water, just short of a cluster of fir and cottonwood trees.

Caldwell swung the horses in, steered them to the edge of the trees. He dismounted, tied off the horses, helped Pierce and Harriet down. He settled them on the pine needle-strewn ground with their backs resting against a cottonwood tree. Told them to sit tight while he took care of some things.

With effort, Caldwell dragged the skiff farther up on the bank where he turned it up on one side and propped the end against a tree trunk to hold it that way. Inside there was a paddle, a folded blanket, and a small lantern, all good and dry. Caldwell kicked out the two wooden boards that were wedged inside the hull for seats, making the area now a tilted-up concave space serviceable as a cramped shelter. After spreading the blanket across its bottom, he brought Pierce and Harriet over and sat them on it.

Next Caldwell rummaged through the saddlebags of the confiscated horse he'd been riding. The other horse had no saddlebags at all, Caldwell reckoning it for the mount of some townsman who seldom ventured out very far. The animal he'd grabbed he guessed probably belonged to a wrangler who had the bad luck of happening to be in town when the posse got formed. There was also a leather-wrapped bedroll behind the saddle, but the blankets were too soaked to be of any use. Nevertheless, he had some luck unearthing a tin of matches, a half-full whiskey flask, a couple tattered dime novels, and a wadded up old flannel shirt. These he took back to the makeshift shelter, announcing, "We're gonna have things a site more comfortable in no time."

He handed the whiskey flask to the wounded

273

pair, telling them to each take a slug but not drink it all. Then he went to work breaking up the paddle and the seat boards and placing them in a pile close to the front of the shelter. After ripping and stuffing the dime novels into the pile, he doused the whole works with some coal oil from the lantern and struck a match to it.

As flames began licking up, Pierce said, "You sure it's smart to risk a fire? Could be seen from quite a ways off."

"A minute ago you said we didn't have to worry about anybody following us until daybreak," Caldwell reminded him. "Besides, I got this skiff propped in a way that will block the fire from being seen back the way we just came. Right now it's important for you two to soak up some drying heat. Here,"—holding out the flannel shirt—"spread this over yourselves the best you can to help a bit more."

Pierce took the shirt and wrapped it around Harriet, who was shivering and clearly in a lot of pain.

"That fire ain't gonna last long, and I'll be hard pressed to find any more dry fuel to feed it," said Caldwell. "So now, while I've got the light from it, I ought to take a look at your wounds and see what I can do to stop the bleeding."

Harriet rolled her pain-dulled eyes up at him and, speaking for the first time since they rode away from the farm, said, "What are you waiting for, then? You don't have to worry about hurting me—can't hurt much worse than I already do."

So, after receiving permission from Harriet to remove her petticoat and then lighting the lantern and setting it close for extra light to work by, Caldwell applied his limited skills to treating the wounds. Harriet's was the worst. The bullet was still in there and the bones and cartilage of the shoulder joint were pretty badly messed up. Caldwell first doused the wound good with splashes of whiskey (momentarily disproving Harriet's claim that she couldn't hurt any worse). Then he pressed a strip of torn petticoat folded into a thick pad directly over the damaged area and packed it in place with a handful of river mud to seal it. This he tied tight with more strips of torn petticoat.

Pierce had two wounds, but the bullets had passed all the way through in both cases. One was a deep gash to the outside of his left thigh; the other a punch through the edge of his gut, just above the hip bone on that same side. "You're gonna have to learn to lean a bit more to the right when you're in a shooting stance," Caldwell advised him wryly. To which Pierce replied with a grimace, "I hope your doctoring is better than your idea of a joke."

Other than the pain and the possibility of some minor muscle damage, the thigh wound didn't seem overly serious; it wasn't even bleeding too badly. The stomach wound was a different matter. Blood was seeping steadily from both the entrance and exit holes and there was no way of knowing what might have been torn on the inside. In all cases, all Caldwell could do was try to stanch the bleeding. He did so by following pretty much the same procedure he had with Harriet. Whiskey to disinfect, bandages and river mud to seal the openings, tight wrapping to hold everything in place.

The fire was nearly burnt out by the time Caldwell had done all he could. He was sore and exhausted in his own right, but he knew they needed to push on.

When he said as much, Pierce asked, "Where? You got any ideas?"

"Near as I can tell, by the glimpses of the moon and stars I can get through the clouds," Caldwell replied, "we're headed more or less southwest. Angling across the route we came in on. Remember all those gullies and twisty canyons we maneuvered around? The broken land you spoke of when you first talked about coming this way?"

Pierce's expression seemed to brighten somewhat. "Yeah. Yeah, I do remember."

"Well, I reckon by daybreak we oughta be in amongst them again. I'm thinking we can pick a good deep one, burrow in, and just lay low for a spell. Again, like you said back then. Hole up and heal up. I'll have to scrounge for some kind of food but, other than that, we can stick it out for days. Maybe a week if we have to."

Pierce's eyes narrowed. "Yeah. And if the bloodhounds sniff us out again, this time we'll be ready for 'em. We'll pick not only a good hiding spot, but also one where we can make a stand if we have to. We'll hold those bastards off until Hell freezes over!"

Caldwell's expression showed nothing but weariness. "Sure. If it comes to that. But first we need to get there. So I know it's gonna hurt like hell to crawl back up on that nag again, but we have to keep moving. Come on, I'll give you a hand."

CHAPTER 34

Lone scowled down at the rapidly flowing Republican and swore. "Damn. I forgot we'd be runnin' into this rascal again."

Reined up beside him, Minowi said, "Is it so bad we won't be able to cross?"

"No, that ain't the problem. We can make it over okay," Lone told her. "The thing of it is, those we're after will likely go in but not cross straight over. They're more apt to drift a ways and then try to find a spot where they can slip out and hide it so's we'll have trouble pickin' up their sign again."

"Might even come back out on this same side," said Jeth from where he sat his saddle to Lone's left. "I've seen that trick tried a time or two."

"You think they're truly that clever?" asked Minowi.

Lone made a face. "Pierce's bunch has been dodgin' posses and bounty hunters goin' on four years over half a dozen different states. They didn't last this long by not bein' plenty savvy."

"So how you want to play it?" Jeth wanted to know.

Lone pointed. "I'll go across and we'll start workin' our way downstream. You stay on this side just in case, like you said, they tried something extra tricky. These banks are soft and muddy from the rain. If we stay sharp, I think it'll be mighty hard for 'em to have hid where they left the water."

"What if they went upstream?" questioned Minowi.

"Not very likely." Lone shook his head. "With two wounded riders on one of the horses, fightin' that current would be mighty tough on 'em. I think our surest bet is downstream. If we don't have no luck after a reasonable stretch, we'll have to back up and try the other way."

In the end, that was unfortunately what it turned out they had to do. For an hour they worked their way downstream—Jeth scouring the bank on the near side, Lone and Minowi on the other. When Lone made the frustrated decision to turn back they were able to return more quickly to where they'd begun but it was still more than another hour before they finally reached the overturned skiff where Caldwell, Pierce, and Harriet had quit the river. The cold ashes of the fire was there, along with the empty whiskey flask and a few bloody bandage remnants.

"Appears they took time to do some patchin' while they was stopped here," Lone said frowning. "Damn! If I'd've made the right call on which way to try pickin' up their sign again we could have closed a lot tighter on 'em. Now we're farther behind than when we started."

"Quit beatin' yourself up," Jeth told him. "You made the sensible call and you know it. So it didn't pan out. That don't mean we've lost em, not by a damn sight. Sun'll be pokin' up in another hour or so. With better light we'll be able to track easier and we'll gain again. They might be patched up some, but by the look of these bloody rags they ain't gonna be movin' very doggone fast."

Lone heaved a ragged sigh. "Yeah, reckon you're right. We'll get 'em in the end, that's the main thing."

Jeth eyed him. "Something else I'm right about is sayin' we need to take a breather. I want to catch those varmints as bad as you do. But we been pushin' hard for a lot of hours with barely any rest and no decent vittles. Time we stopped at least until that sun breaks. Do us wonders to just stretch out some, cook a pot of coffee and put a little grub in our bellies. When we do catch up with those three, we don't want to be as wore down as they are, do we?"

Lone's first inclination was to resist. But then, taking time to appreciate the exhaustion showing on the faces of both Jeth and Minowi and grudgingly admitting to his own bone tiredness, he gave in to the wisdom of the suggestion.

Sighing again, he said, "Okay. But only 'til sunup. Break out the gear, I'll bust some dry wood out of this skiff and get a fire going."

• • •

Two hundred yards away, belly down on a grassy hillock, Vallen and Halloway were once again monitoring the activity of Lone's group. Vallen had the spyglass to his eye. Halloway was stretched out beside him, wet, miserable, and, as usual, complaining.

"They're doing *what?*" he asked in a strained whisper.

"You heard me. They're buildin' a fire and looks like bringin' out the fixin's to cook some coffee."

Halloway groaned. "I'll be a sonofabitch. They couldn't have stayed at the farm and did that? Had some coffee, took a bite to eat. They had to tromp straightaway out here in the dark and wet, then sniff to hell and gone up and down the riverbank—and *now* they're gonna stop and take a break?"

"Pipe down," Vallen warned him. "Sound travels out here on the flat, they might hear you."

"You know what? I'm nearin' the point where I don't much care. I'm so sick of chasin' after those three and their crazy ways, I'm ready to shoot holes in the whole lot. To hell with that Whitlock pup and his reward for the shiny doodad, too. There's got to be easier ways to make money than this. If I don't come out of this dead from pew-monia, I'll be so wore to a frazzle that the most high-toned fancy lady in the West couldn't stir my blood."

Vallen grunted. "That'll be the day. Besides, if you're in such a yank to gun it out with those trackers, why didn't you do it when they all of a sudden doubled back down river and most near bumped into us followin' on their heels? Looked to me like you damn near shat yourself at the thought of facin' 'em."

"That's 'cause they caught us by surprise, that's all. What's more, the goofy bastards hadn't yet stopped and started cookin' coffee right under our noses." Halloway made a face. "I suppose it ain't even worth askin' . . . But is there any way we could maybe slip back a ways and cook up a quick pot of our own?"

Vallen lowered the spyglass and gave him a look. "You're kiddin', right? Take our eyes off 'em, after all this, and give 'em the chance to do a slip-away of their own? Ain't happenin'."

"Yeah, yeah. That's what I figured." Halloway spit away a blade of wet grass clinging to his lip. "I'll stick it out a while longer. But I'm warnin' you, if the wind shifts and I get too strong a whiff of that fresh coffee, there might not be no holdin' me back. And don't try tellin' me about all the coffee and fancy women I'll be able to have when we get the reward money . . . that shit's wearin' powerful thin."

CHAPTER 35

Caldwell pointed. "There. That one appears good and deep and looks like it stretches back quite a ways. Plus there's a lot of bramble and some trees for cover. It's the best we've seen yet. I think we ought to give it a try."

Sagging in his saddle, Harriet pressed to his back, Pierce nodded in agreement. "I think you're right. Looks like most everything we wanted."

The trio sat their horses atop a long, gradual slope with mostly bare, blunted hills rolling off to either side. But directly ahead, at the bottom of the slope, a long, twisty canyon was slashed deep into the earth, extending away from their perspective. It was the pale gray, half-light of early dawn. The air was cool and crisp with only a lingering hint of dampness. The sun hadn't broken above the eastern horizon yet, but brightening, pinkish gold fingers were reaching steadily higher in that direction.

"Okay. I'll take the reins and lead out," Caldwell said. "Hang on tight and, when we get down in there, watch out you don't get swatted by any low branches."

They proceeded in that manner. Caldwell picked his way carefully into the canyon. The passage was quite narrow at first, the bottom strewn with rocky rubble, the walls not very high and choked with bramble and pine growth. It quickly deepened and widened out, however. The floor became a mix of grass and gravel, the sides much higher and steeper. Most of the thicker brush and overhanging tree branches started to be above their heads, along the rims on either side.

At one point, Caldwell said back over his shoulder, "With any luck, we might come to a washout or a notch on one of these sides that we can sort of tuck ourselves into for a while."

Not much later, a little over an eighth of a mile in, they came to something even better. On the right side was a large scooped-out section of the wall, what might be called a shallow cavern, recessed nearly ten feet and as high to its dome-like ceiling.

"Looks like home away from home to me," declared Pierce as Caldwell brought the horses to a halt.

"I second the motion," murmured Harriet, her cheek pressed to Pierce's shoulder.

"Guess I'll make it unanimous," said Caldwell. Swinging down from his saddle, he added, "You two sit tight for a minute longer, give me a chance to dress the place up a bit."

Wasting no time, he took the blanket they'd found in the skiff back at the river and spread it on the floor of the cavern. Over this he also spread the two blankets from the bedroll that had been on his horse—having had the foresight before leaving the river to unroll them and drape each over the rumps of the horses so they had the chance to dry while traveling.

Once he'd helped Pierce and Harriet off their horse and had them settled on the blankets, he took time to examine their wounds. "I know they probably still hurt like hell," he reported, "but the good news is that I don't see any leakage through any of the outer bandaging I put on. So it appears the bleeding is stopped and now with you both holding mostly still for a while, it hopefully will stay that way."

"You did a good job on us, Caldwell," said Pierce. "I'm mighty obliged."

"Here, take this." Caldwell held out the nearly empty whiskey flask. "Ain't much left, but split what's there and maybe it will oblige easing your pain some. In the meantime, I'm going to saddle strip the horses and make sure they don't go nowhere. Then, if you'll spare me a few inches of that blanket, I'm gonna stretch out for a while myself. I'm bushed."

"By all means. You earned it," said Pierce.

"And, like Dar said, we're awfully grateful," Harriet added.

Lone, Jeth, and Minowi were on the move with the sun. The riverside respite, complete with sugar-laden cups of coffee, a shared can of sliced peaches, and some beef jerky, had proven every bit as refreshing as hoped for. Lone easily picked up the trail of their quarry leading away from the river and they set out following it at a strong pace.

It wasn't long before they found themselves entering the stretch of broken land, with its numerous gullies and canyons, they had passed through previously. And it wasn't long after that that Lone got a hunch about what might come next.

"I got a feelin'," he said to the others, "these polecats are aimin' to go to ground."

"Meaning?" questioned Minowi.

"Meanin' they're gonna stop runnin' and find a spot where they can lay low for a while. Do some healin' and plannin'. Hopin' for that ruckus back at the Keough farm to die down some, along with the searchin' for 'em, before they start on the move again."

"Couldn't staying in one spot also present risk?" Minowi said.

"Could," Jeth allowed. "But less so maybe than runnin' out in the open, slowed by their wounds. If they find themselves a good enough hidey hole down in one of these brushy canyons and are careful about pokin' their mangy heads out, they might could ride it out for several days. You gotta remember, an average town posse made up of clerks and barflies and such ain't likely to have the trackin' skills of Lone, probably not even me."

"And that's what those three are most apt to expect," said Lone, continuing to mull the notion in his head. "Marshal Kent's suspicion was raised by the pair's visit to his town. That's what Pierce will probably figure out. He had no way of knowin' we was even in the mix at that shootout. But what he *does* know is that his bunch shot hell out of those that did show up. Without us in the picture, he'd have every right to count on nobody even startin' out after 'em again 'til this mornin'."

Jeth grinned. "Puts us in position to throw a nice little surprise party, don't it?"

"Their tracks will tell the tale," Lone said. "If they lead into one of those canyons, we'll know all this speculatin' amounts to something."

Jeth's grin faded. "Oh, yeah . . . Then'll come the part where we have to go in after 'em."

CHAPTER 36

Caldwell had dozed off and slept longer than he meant to. When he woke it was with a start. He sat up and was somewhat surprised to find Pierce also awake and sitting up. The gang leader was smoking a cigarette and looking at him, like that's what he had been doing for some time. On the other side of him, Harriet was asleep and breathing evenly.

"What's the matter?" Caldwell wanted to know.

Pierce gave a faint shake of his head. "Nothing. Just thinking about things. Wondering about some others."

Caldwell gave it a beat before asking, "How do your wounds feel?"

"They hurt. No worse, no better. Nothing I can't take."

Caldwell looked around, listened. Everything was quiet. The sun was growing brighter in the sky, but down here in the shade of the cavern and the thick growth along the canyon rims it was shadowy and cool.

"You know what does hurt?" Pierce said abruptly, exhaling a cloud of smoke. Not waiting for an answer, he went on. "The sorry goddamn shape we're in, that's what. Like I said, I been thinking. Going over some things. Yesterday about this time we were flying high, had some stash left over from that railroad job and were planning to hit a McCook bank then ride back to the Territory with bulging pockets.

"You know what we got now? First off, we ain't riding no damn where because we're shot up and short one horse. Not to mention two good men. What's more, we ain't got a lick of money because we left it all in a bag back at that damn farm house. And the McCook bank job sure as hell ain't happening any time soon, is it?"

"We've been down on our luck before," said Caldwell, hearing the lameness in the words as soon as they were out of his mouth.

Pierce chuffed. "This is more than down on our luck, pal. This is rock bottom. The only spoils we can claim from all our jobs is that stupid hunk of jewelry, a brooch she calls it, pinned to Harriet's dress under that flannel shirt you found. Ain't that a hoot? The damn thing probably ain't worth a round of drinks in a cheap saloon." He took another drag of his cigarette. "I did some more tallying, too, while you were asleep. Weapon-wise we got three six-guns and that hideaway pea shooter you keep tucked behind your belt. I loaded all the hoglegs, full wheels, eighteen rounds. Didn't mess with your derringer. In your cartridge belt and mine we got a total of eleven more rounds for the revolvers . . . So much for

289

my big talk of holding off anybody who comes after us 'til Hell freezes over."

"The idea is that nobody finds us here so we don't have to worry about having to hold 'em off," Caldwell said. "In a little while, I figure on doing some scouting. See what's on the other end of this canyon. Got to be a ranch or a farm somewhere close. That ought to provide me a chance at finding some food for us—a couple chickens, maybe a young calf or lamb. I can check out any available horseflesh, too, to give us another mount when we're ready to go on the move again."

Pierce ground out his cigarette stub and eyed Caldwell through its final curl of smoke. "Uh-huh. And now there's the part I been wondering about."

Caldwell met his gaze. "Wondering?"

"About you. Why you're sticking with me and Harriet the way you are, the way we're slowing you down. Was you to have rode off and left us at any point since we got clear of that posse at the farm, you could have been well down into Kansas by now. Why didn't you?"

Caldwell's brows bunched tight together. "What kind of question is that? We're part of the same outfit, ain't we? We been through good times and through hellfire together. Alright, maybe we ain't exactly on equal footing, you being the boss and all. But we been running together going on, what,

290

about six years now. Right? You think some kind of bond, some sense of loyalty, don't form in all that time? If it didn't, I would have lit out long ago. But when the bond and the loyalty is there, then it holds tightest at the toughest times."

Pierce's expression became a puzzled scowl. "But having been with me so long, you know the rule I've always followed about not letting one man bog down the whole crew. You've seen twice—with Hendershott and then Gilby—when they were shot up too bad to keep up and I left 'em behind."

"Hendershott and Gilby were never gonna make it anyway," Caldwell argued. "They were dead weight who just hadn't died yet. That was different. You and Harriet are hurt, yeah, but you ain't ready to die. Not unless you give up."

"Nobody's talking about giving up!"

"Then quit sounding like it, damn it. You don't give up, I won't give up on you."

Neither of them said any more for several beats, just sat eyeing one another speculatively. Until Harriet spoke from where she lay, saying, "That's better. Keep the growling to a minimum, you two. This girl needs her rest."

They gave it another beat before Pierce said, in a quieter tone now, "Maybe I been reading you wrong all this time, Caldwell. I always knew you was smart, good with a gun, kept a cool head and was a good man for a fella to have at his side in a tight. Yet, at the same time, I could never quite shake the feeling that you had a kind of chip on your shoulder, that you resented me being the leader of the gang. The way you always asked questions and sometimes made suggestions, like you was trying to second guess me."

Caldwell wagged his head. "The only reason I asked questions and made suggestions was to help our outfit, help think things through as thoroughly as possible. I never coveted your leadership role. Like I said, if it bothered me to ride behind you, I would have lit out a long time ago."

"I'll be sure to keep that in mind. And I mean that for if we make it through this and you want to stick together back down in the Territory."

"Sounds okay to me," Caldwell said. "Only let's figure it as *when* we make it through this."

Pierce wasn't big on grinning, but he now managed a lopsided one. "See what I mean? Right away being contrary again."

Caldwell put a finger to his lips. "No growling, remember. Harriet needs her rest."

CHAPTER 37

Lone abruptly reined Ironsides to a halt.

Pulling up beside him, Jeth said, "What's the matter? Something wrong?"

Lone tipped his head forward, indicating the direction of the trail they were following. "Don't you see where we're headed?"

Checking down her mount on the other side of Lone, Minowi said solemnly, "I do . . . Massacre Canyon."

Jeth's eyebrows lifted. "Holy cats. I reckon I wasn't payin' close enough attention."

"No way of knowin' whether or not Pierce aimed for it on purpose," Lone said with a frown. "But it's about the longest and deepest of the canyons we passed on the way through these parts before. Be a good spot for what we think he's got in mind."

"Yeah, it would," Jeth agreed. "Those three could lose themselves right proper down in that twisty cut."

Lone looked over at Minowi. "Bother you if we have to go in there?"

She gave a firm shake of her head. "No. If that is where they are, then that is where we need to go . . . I said before it is an evil place where evil things were done. The ground there has been

293

whetted, it will always be thirsty for more blood. We must take care it does not drink ours."

Jeth's forehead puckered. "Damn, girl. You got a way of givin' me shivers the way you talk about that place."

"Perhaps it is you," Minowi replied, "who are too bothered to go in after those we pursue?"

"That'll be the day," the old teamster harrumphed.

"Actually," Lone told both of them, "none of us are goin' in. Leastways not straight on and not right away." When they turned to him with questioning looks, he said, "That little episode back at the river taught us how crafty these three can be. Remember? Doin' what they're expected to do or even what it *looks* like they're doin', ain't necessarily how it plays out."

"Care to spit that out a little plainer? Their doggone tracks do lead into the canyon, don't they?"

"That they do," Lone allowed. "But it don't guarantee those who made 'em mean to *stay* in the canyon, to hole up like we're figurin'. Could be they plow on through and leave anybody who might come along on their trail wastin' time goin' slow and careful-like, keepin' an eye out for 'em when they're already long gone. Or maybe they do pick a spot somewhere down in there—only not to just hole up, but to do it in a way that gives 'em an ambush point. A *reason* for anybody comin' after 'em to be damn careful."

"But what other choice does that leave us?" Minowi wanted to know.

Lone raised one hand and cut a semi-circle in the air. "We circle high around to the other end of the canyon. That way we'll be able to tell if they've already passed through. They have, we'll take up the trail again and keep after 'em. If not, *then* we head into the canyon—only from the direction they'll be least expectin'."

Jeth spread his hands. "See? Like I said before . . . Sneaky-minded."

"No. Smart," Minowi once again corrected him.

Lone chuffed. "I'd say that remains to be seen. Let's go find out."

They split up. Lone and Minowi worked their way along the rim on one side of the canyon; Jeth along the opposite side. This allowed them to move at a good pace while at the same time providing views down into the canyon (when permitted by the trees and foliage) from two different angles on the chance they might catch a glimpse of their quarry.

As they proceeded, a flinty-eyed Minowi whispered to Lone, "This is how the 'brave' Sioux warriors conducted much of their slaughter against my people all those years ago. When the Pawnee chiefs sent the women and children down into the canyon to hide, the Sioux took up positions on the sides and rained arrows and bullets down on them. What is the White Man's expression—like shooting fish in a barrel? The canyon drank plenty of blood that day. Pawnee blood."

"Reckon that's the way it goes too much of the time," Lone replied softly. "Whether it's red man fightin' red man, or white against white, or white against red . . . The ground laps up the blood, but as it's spillin' nobody ever seems to notice how it's all the same color."

Not long after, they reached the far end of the canyon. Jeth rejoined them there. The sun was well up into the sky by that point and the morning was warming rapidly.

Dismounting and making a quick but thorough examination of the ground thereabouts revealed no indication their quarry had exited the canyon.

"Looks like we're comin' down to it," Lone stated, his jaw set tight. "They're in there. Ours for the takin' . . . All we gotta do is go in and flush 'em."

"Sure. That's all," said Jeth.

Lone looked at Minowi. "I suppose there ain't no sense in me askin' you to hold back here with the horses?"

"You suppose correctly," came the answer.

Jeth gave it a try, too, saying, "Dang it, gal. You just got out from under a whole lifetime of ill treatment. You got the dream of returnin' to your people. Why risk that for something that ain't rightly even no fight of yourn?"

Minowi's eyes blazed momentarily, but then quickly cooled. "I will not take offense to that because I know you say it out of caring for me. So I say back to you: We have been through much together leading up to this, we shall remain together until it is finished." To emphasize the matter was settled, she reached up and pulled the Greener down from her saddle boot, broke it open to check the loads, then snapped it sharply shut again.

Lone and Jeth exchanged looks, a faintly bemused expression playing across the former scout's face.

"Looks like," he said, turning to reach for the Yellowboy in his own saddle scabbard, "it'll be the three of us goin' in."

CHAPTER 38

All things considered, Paul Caldwell felt a measure of optimism. Things weren't great by any means, but at least there was hope he and Pierce and Harriet still had a chance to make it out of this mess. He'd successfully stanched their bleeding, that was a big step. And Dar was so far showing no signs of internal injury. The damage to Harriet's shoulder, unfortunately, was doubtlessly going to leave her with some impairment. She was tough, though, and thankfully still alive. Too bad the same couldn't be said for Bandros and Grissom; but they well knew that was always the card waiting to possibly be turned up when you rode on the wrong side of the law.

Thoughts of the law, specifically in the form of the posse that had surprised the gang at the Keough farm, made Caldwell grimace. It remained unclear what had sicced those law dog bastards on them and, while there hadn't been much opportunity to discuss it, Caldwell's own conclusion was that the reconnoiter by Dar and Harriet into McCook had somehow been the trigger. Not to lay blame, after all he'd been the one who proposed the disguise they used. Nevertheless, some sharp-eyed so-and-so had evidently seen through it.

If that was truly the case, if it was a town posse and not another pack of federal marshals like the ones who'd rooted them out of the Dakota Badlands, then it improved the odds for him, Pierce, and Harriet to make it the rest of the way clear. No bunch of clerks and store owners led by a soft-bellied town marshal was as likely to track them to where they were now burrowed in. Not after the rain and the fire and especially the way they'd shot hell out of so many of those who'd made the initial try.

All the more reason for some guarded optimism, Caldwell told himself.

These thoughts and more were rolling through his head as he heeled his horse leisurely down the length of the canyon, having left his comrades behind to heal and rest while he ventured out on the scout he'd told Pierce he had in mind. Dodging any kind of pursuit was only part of succeeding in their full escape. In order to supplement the healing of Pierce and Harriet—not to mention for the sake of just plain surviving—Caldwell was going to have to find some sources for food, nourishment. Plus, ever mindful of the lead still in Harriet's shoulder and the potential for infection it presented, he badly, badly needed to try and find some kind of medicine, even if just more whiskey, to keep treating it.

Harriet . . . She, as was often the case under

most any circumstance, played a prominent role in his thoughts. While what he'd told Pierce about his sense of loyalty to the overall gang was mostly true, what else was true—what he never dared admit out loud—was that his feelings for Harriet was the thing above all else that had made Caldwell stick for all this time. And it sure as hell wouldn't let him abandon her now, even if him riding straight out of this canyon and continuing on alone was practically a guarantee of him making a clean escape.

Though he never breathed a word to her or allowed it to show in any way, he had fallen hard for her right from the first and the feeling had never waned. How many times had he fantasized about her and Dar having a falling out and finally providing him the chance to make his move? Hell, he'd even thought about—but never *wished* for, not exactly—what would happen if Dar ever caught a fatal bullet and . . .

Caldwell's reverie was abruptly broken when he rounded a slight twist in the passage and found himself facing a man standing in the center of the canyon floor directly ahead. The gent was tall and broad-shouldered, with a squarish, weathered face and a generally rugged look about him. The look of somebody not to be trifled with, especially not given the Colt riding on his hip and the Yellowboy repeater held leveled at his waist.

Caldwell checked down his horse and fought

valiantly to also hold himself in check, not wheel around in panic or make a try for his own gun. With that Winchester leveled on him, he had zero chance. No, he told himself—mind racing—the only way was to stay cool and try a bluff in the hope maybe this character was more of a yokel than he looked like and could be lulled into lowering his guard.

Flashing a nervous grin (which came easy enough), Caldwell said, "Whoa, mister. The way you're swinging that hardware, somebody could get hurt. I sure wouldn't want it to be me."

In response, Lone just eyed him coldly. Said nothing for a long beat. If there was the slimmest whisker of a doubt this jasper was one of the Pierce gang, it was erased by the smears of blood on his sleeve and shirtfront. There was no evidence of the man being wounded himself so, recalling the bloody remnants of bandages back at the riverside camp, Lone knew he was looking at the fleeing skunk who had patched up the other two.

When he finally spoke, Lone said, "Always struck me curious how pieces of crud like you, who make careers out of causin' other folks hurt, are so queasy when it comes your turn to be on the receivin' end."

Caldwell gritted his teeth. This wasn't looking good. Yet he was determined to keep trying to sell his act. "I don't know what you're talking about, friend. You seem to have me confused with somebody else. The only harm I'm causing anybody is to myself and this poor old nag I'm riding on account of how I've gone and got us so lost we're—"

"Knock it off!" Lone barked. He made a thrust with the Yellowboy's muzzle. "Let go those reins and spread your hands out high and wide. Make one wrong twitch, I'll blow you halfway back the way you just came."

After a single tick of hesitation, Caldwell did as he was told. Hard to argue with a Winchester aimed square at you.

"So far so good," Lone grated. "Now, real slow an' careful, lower one hand and unbuckle your gun belt. Let it drop to the ground."

Once again Caldwell did as directed. All the while his eyes stayed locked with Lone's.

The gun belt buckle came unclasped and the weight of the Colt holstered on one side caused the rig to pull away and then go slipping off and drop to the ground. The faint flick of Lone's eyes, drawn by this, was what Caldwell had been hoping for. In a smooth, well-practiced move that had worked in his favor at least three times in the past, the hand already lowered to his waist suddenly darted in behind the beltline of his pants and jerked free the .44 caliber, two-shot over-under derringer snugged there.

The hand raised in a blur and Caldwell's

arm started to extend, reaching to aim the little hideaway at Lone.

But the former scout's distraction had been only minimal. His Yellowboy spoke first, spitting lead in a tongue of flame.

Caldwell's nose disappeared, driven through and the back of his skull. His head snapped back and the rest of him was driven into a kind of floppy somersault off the rear end of his horse. The death spasm of his hand triggered one barrel of the derringer, burying a slug harmlessly into the wall of the canyon.

Continuing to hold his Yellowboy at the ready and remaining in the slight crouch he'd dropped into, Lone's gaze searched beyond the fallen man, scouring the canyon from side to side. When he sensed Jeth and Minowi starting to emerge from their concealment behind him, he snapped over his shoulder, "Stay put! No way of knowin' how close the other two are."

He let another half minute go by before he finally relaxed and motioned for Jeth and Minowi to go ahead and come out. When they were standing beside him, he said, "Well, there's one tricky bastard we won't have to spend time chasin' no more."

"If you'd've let me and Minowi stand where he could have seen us, too," Jeth pointed out, "he wouldn't have been moved to even try that trick."

"But if the other two had been hangin' back close, hidin' themselves like I had you do, we'd all three have been sittin' ducks for 'em," Lone countered.

"So where are the other two?" Minowi asked. "Why were they not traveling with this one?"

"Maybe they're dead," Jeth suggested. "Or too shot-up to continue on."

"Could be," Lone allowed. "Could also be they're just holed up back a ways, restin' and healin' like we thought they might do, and this one was simply out to do some scoutin'. If burrowin' in for a while was their plan, somebody'd have to go out to find some food and the like."

"True enough," said Jeth. Then, scrunching up his face, he added, "Comes back down to the same thing . . . Onliest way for us to for sure find out the story on the other two is to finish goin' on in. But now, since they're bound to have heard this shootin'—less'n they *are* dead—they'll know we're comin'."

Lone frowned in thought. "That bein' the case, the surest way to play it is to go at 'em from both ends of the canyon. Wounded and with only one horse, it seems to me they'd be more likely to hold and make a fight of it rather than try to run. No way of knowin' for certain, though. But either way, was you to drop back, grab your horse and

304

ride around to come in from the front end, Jeth, we'd have 'em boxed in good."

"Sounds like a good plan," the old teamster was quick to respond. "Consider me on my way."

CHAPTER 39

"Maybe he spotted a jack rabbit or antelope and decided to bag us some fresh meat," Harriet suggested in a hopeful tone.

A grim-faced Dar Pierce shook his head. "There were two shots close together. In the first place, I can't see Caldwell taking the chance of drawing attention to us this close and in the middle of the day. Not if he had any choice. And if he was bagging fresh meat, it wouldn't take him two shots."

Harriet's expression clouded. "So he must have run into trouble of some kind."

"Wish I could think of some other explanation. But I can't."

"That posse?"

"I wouldn't have thought it possible. But again . . ."

Pierce let his words trail off and the two of them went quiet for a minute, just listening. Until Pierce spoke again, saying, "I told Caldwell I'd never give up. And I won't. But if he ran into a posse out there and ended up on the short end, that runs our chips mighty low, gal."

Harriet put a hand on his arm. "Living the outlaw life, you knew the day might come. You once told me how the house always wins in the end."

"Yeah. For me, I accepted it right from the start. But I never meant to drag you that far."

"You never dragged me anywhere I didn't want to go," Harriet told him.

Pierce gazed deep into her eyes, his brow puckering deeply. "You're a hell of a woman, Harriet Jane Plunkett. I always aimed to someday take you away from the riding and shooting and chasing and settle you into an easy life with fine things about you. Hell, I probably never even told you in proper words how I felt . . . the way I . . ."

She put a finger to his lips. "You told me enough. More than that, you *showed* me. You showed me the wildest, most exciting time I could ever ask for. Like I said, you never took me anywhere I didn't want to go—and did I ever for one second indicate to you that I *wanted* a settled-down life with fancy things about me?"

"No, I guess you never did," Pierce admitted with a wry grin. Then, reaching out to tap the brooch still pinned to the front of her dress, he said, "But you've sure shown a fondness for this bit of fanciness."

"Yes, and you let me have it." Harriet smiled. "And, just yesterday, you saw to it I got my hot bath, a nice restaurant meal, and this pretty new dress . . . Which I fear has become a bit bloodied and worse for wear."

Pierce started to reply but stopped short when their horse, tied and grazing just outside the cavern, lifted its head suddenly and cocked its ears back, obviously sensing something.

"I got a hunch," said Pierce, "we're about to find out what Caldwell ran into."

"Good. I'm all for getting it over with."

Pierce regarded her intently. "We go easy—or hard?"

"We both know where going easy will lead. The gallows," said Harriet. She raised her six-gun. "I'd rather take it this way."

Pierce leaned over and kissed her. "I'll say again, you're a hell of a woman, Harriet Jane Plunkett."

Then, rising painfully, he stepped out to untie the horse and tug it closer into the cavern. Once he had it positioned the way he wanted, he reached down to pull the knife from his boot then swept it suddenly up and across in a throat-slashing stroke that killed the animal and caused it to drop and serve as a breastwork for him and Harriet to fight behind.

Lone and Minowi heard the dying shriek of the slain horse and stopped walking.

"What was that?" whispered Minowi. "It sounded like an animal in pain."

"Not for long, I'm thinkin'," Lone replied grimly.

"What do you mean?"

"You'll see soon enough. Stay a step or so

behind me, we'll continue movin' on quiet-like. Keep that scattergun ready."

Skimming as close as the bramble and uneven rock face of the wall would allow, they edged cautiously forward. Lone brushed the hat back off his head, let it hang down over his shoulders by the chin thong.

At an outward bulge of the wall, they halted and Lone bent down low to peer carefully around the bulge. He caught a glimpse of the shallow cavern, the horse carcass sprawled across its mouth, and two murky faces in the shadowy recess. He also glimpsed the flash of a gun muzzle discharging and jerked his head back just as the bullet it sent sizzling his way spanged off the rock swell three inches above where his face had been.

Seconds later, while the boom of the shot was still rolling down the canyon, a man's voice called out, "Did you get a good look, you nosy bastard? Poke you head out again and I'll help you out—by putting a third eye smack in the middle of your forehead!"

Lone pressed back against his side of the rock bulge and grinned a wolf's grin. "Thanks for the generous offer, but I'll get by with what I got," he called in return. "If you can't shoot no better than that, though, you're the one who needs some extra help."

"I can shoot good enough with what I got to blast your sorry hide and a dozen more just like you. Same as I've done plenty of times in the past," came Pierce's reply.

Lone gave it back just as thick. "That's mighty big talk. If there was any truth to it, it'd serve as good practice seein's how a dozen deputies is what's closin' on you right now—half a dozen here with me, that many more comin' from the other end of the canyon."

"Leave it to a filthy law dog to try and replace guts with pathetic lies. You never had a dozen deputies at that farm to begin with, and we blew away more than half of 'em!"

"Don't know what farm you're talkin' about," Lone claimed. Then, laying it on thicker still, he added, "I'm a federal marshal from up north. We been on your tail since you hit that train outside of Ogallala. You hadn't been stupid enough to take time out to pull that, we might've lost track of you for good!"

This time there was no quick response.

Lone winked at Minowi and whispered, "Now I got 'em rattled a bit more, ponderin' how much truth there might be to the rest of what I claimed."

But the silence from the cavern didn't last long. "I can hear you squeaking out there like cockroaches," Pierce called. "You got a posse of men with you—or just a bunch of bugs?"

Lone ground his teeth. Then, motioning for Minowi to hand him the shotgun, he decided to do some talking with more than just words.

Laying down his Yellowboy, he took the Greener and eased out once more to the curved edge of the rock bulge. One-handing the gut shredder, he reached around suddenly, triggered both barrels at the cavern, then ducked back.

Knowing the distance was too great for the loads to have any telling impact, Lone reckoned it was still close enough for the spray of pellets to do some stinging and startling. And from the howling reaction it got, he quickly knew he'd been right.

"You sonofabitch!" Pierce bellowed, at the same time firing a pair of rounds in blind fury, the slugs doing nothing but chipping splatters of rock off the edge of the bulge. He might have fired more if Lone and Minowi hadn't heard a female voice shouting, "Stop it! You're doing nothing but wasting bullets!"

Lone didn't miss the chance to do some further needling. "How about that? That seem like the work of bugs? And, by the way, your shootin' still ain't worth shit—especially if you don't have any bullets to spare!"

"It only takes one, damn you," Pierce roared back, clearly still fuming. "Show a big enough piece of yourself for half a second and you'll find out!"

Leveling his voice some, Lone replied, "The trouble with that, for you, is that there's a lot more than just me out here. So you want to go out in a blaze of glory. What about the woman? You bound and determined to take her with you?"

This time it was Harriet who called out. "I speak for myself, law dog! If you're the one who's bound and determined to save this poor little damsel in distress, come ahead and try—see what it gets your dumb ass!" There followed the mocking laughter of both man and woman.

Lone leaned back against the canyon wall and looked over at Minowi. "I tried. You heard me. It's like the Keough kid said, she's as bad as the rest."

Minowi met his gaze with a flat return stare. "I thought you'd figured that out long ago."

Lone grimaced. "It's time to get this over with."

"Shouldn't we wait for Jeth to come in from the other way?"

"Lookin' past that cavern they got themselves tucked into," Lone said, "I don't see where he'll have any better angle than we do. Even a chance he'll expose himself tryin'. No, I think our best bet is right over there." With those finishing words, he pointed to indicate a good-sized boulder close to the opposite side of the canyon. At some past point, it had evidently broken away from higher up and tumbled down.

Lone added, "There's enough room for me to fit in behind it. It'd give me cover and at the same time give me almost a perfect angle on those two."

"But how will you get over there?" Minowi frowned in disapproval. "It's too far, they will cut you down trying to make it across."

"Not if you give 'em something else to worry about for a few seconds," Lone said, handing the Greener back to her. "You pull the same stunt I did a minute ago. It'll make 'em duck down in reaction. When they pop up again, I'll be behind that boulder ready to pick 'em off."

Minowi took the shotgun, for the first time with a trace of reluctance. Her gaze probed Lone's face. "It sounds very daring. Reckless."

Lone showed her a crooked grin. "Not me. I'm too smart. Remember?"

"If this fails," Minowi said, breaking open the Greener and starting to push in fresh shells, "it will disappoint me to have been so wrong."

"Good. That gives me two reasons not to fail— keepin' my hide, and not disappointin' you."

Considering the close quarters behind the boulder and the relatively short distance from there to the cavern, Lone decided to leave the Yellowboy behind and go with just his Colt. Drawing the hogleg, dropping into a half crouch, getting poised and ready, Lone glanced up at Minowi and nodded for her to go ahead.

Keeping his focus from that point strictly on the boulder, his first target, it seemed like an awful long time before the double roar finally sounded and propelled him into motion. Lunging forward, staying in the half crouch, Lone raced across the canyon floor and went into a diving roll that took him skidding in behind the boulder. Twisting around and shoving up onto his knees, Colt all the while gripped in his fist, he looked across the top of the boulder and through the dust and rolling cloud of powder smoke from the Greener and laid eyes on Dar Pierce and Harriet Bell for the first time in his life. And for the last time in theirs.

Having reflexively ducked away from the shotgun blast, like Lone had counted on, the pair were in the act of rising up again, wild-eyed in anger heightened by catching a glimpse of Lone's bolt across the width of the canyon. They began immediately trying to pinpoint where he'd ended up, guns thrusting out over the horse carcass and opening fire randomly.

But there was nothing random about Lone's return fire. Clenching his teeth, extending his Colt across the top of the boulder, he triggered four rapid but carefully aimed shots and it was all over. The murky faces fell away deeper into the shadows of the cavern, never to rise again.

CHAPTER 40

In the wake of the resounding gunfire that filled it only minutes earlier, the canyon had become almost eerily quiet.

Standing next to Lone outside the shallow cavern, Minowi said softly, "Even the haunted voices of past victims have grown silent. The canyon is satisfied for the time being, its thirst slaked by fresh blood. But it will be thirsty again soon enough."

"Long as it ain't 'til we're gone from here," Lone muttered. "And it'd be good if you held off any more talk like that when Jeth gets here. You know how it gives him the shivers."

Minowi smiled wanly. "Okay. I'll try to remember. But where is Jeth? Ought he not have been here by now?"

"Yeah, that's what I been thinkin'," Lone said, frowning. "Especially since he had to've heard all that shootin'. The only thing I can figure is . . ." He never finished, interrupted by the clopping sound of approaching hooves.

Minowi's smile widened. "What is another White Man's saying . . . Speak of the devil?"

Only her words turned out more prophetic than she ever could have guessed. Because when Jeth appeared, he wasn't alone. He showed up

315

bracketed by two men, the canyon over that particular stretch being wide enough for them to ride in three abreast.

The sight of the two strangers—slovenly yet mean-eyed and dangerous looking—would have been unsettling in and of itself. The way they were each holding a repeating rifle braced on one hip with the barrel tilted toward Jeth's head made it something a lot more. The dazed expression on Jeth's freshly bruised face, a thick worm of blood crawling out one corner of his mouth, only added to the menace on display.

They halted their mounts a dozen feet short of where Lone and Minowi were caught standing out in the open. Swinging his rifle lazily away from Jeth and leveling it instead on the pair now before him, Lyle Vallen's wide slash of a mouth twisted into a sneer, exposing the oversized choppers he was famous for, and said, "We ain't gonna waste time beatin' around the bush. We'll start with you two layin' down the rifle and scattergun, then you shuckin' your gun belt, Mr. Big Injun Scout."

There was no choice but to comply. Stiffly, their eyes all the while smoldering, Lone and Minowi did as instructed.

Vallen nodded approvingly. "Good. We've already lost enough hours and days foggin' your stubborn asses over half of Creation. So I'll cut to the rest of it: Where's the fancy brooch was among the loot this outlaw bunch stole off the train?"

Even though he was all too familiar with the brooch and had, in fact, removed it from Harriet's body just a few minutes ago when he examined her and Pierce to make sure they were dead, the question nevertheless caught Lone off guard. But before he could give any kind of response, Jeth beat him to it.

"Don't tell 'em a goddamned thing, Lone," the old teamster groaned through bloody lips. "They're hired mongrels working for Whitlock's weasel of a son Peter! Since they slipped up and told me that much, they can't afford to leave us alive! So no matter what they—"

Halloway swung his rifle in a hard backhand swat, laying the side of the barrel across Jeth's forehead, knocking him out of his saddle and sending him toppling loosely to the ground.

Lone took an involuntary half step forward, fingers curling claw-like at his sides, but was stopped by Minowi clutching his arm and a thrusting motion from Vallen's rifle. "Don't be a fool, I'll cut you in half!" Vallen snarled. "The old man's brains are muddled from us havin' to slap him around some. No percentage in us killin' you, not unless you give us no choice. All you *do* need to give us is that do-dad. Then we'll ride off and leave you . . . no horses, no guns, of course . . . But you'll have your lives so you

317

oughta be able to make it somewhere by the time we're long gone."

"Supposin' I told you we don't know where that lousy brooch is?" Lone rasped. "If you been followin' us like you say, then you know about the fracas at that farm last night and how these three barely got away with the skin on their backs. You think that left 'em time to gather up any of their loot?"

Vallen replied coldly, "What I think—no, make that what I know—is if they *didn't* have the brooch with 'em, then you wouldn't have took out after 'em so quick. The brooch is the main thing you been chasin' all along. Same as we been chasin' you to lift it out of your grubby paws once you finally caught up with it."

"Which brings us to the here and now," announced Halloway, swinging down from his saddle. "And as was said at the start, we ain't in no mood for beatin' around the bush."

"So you can hand the brooch over and take a chance at stayin' alive," Vallen re-stated, "or you can for certain die and we'll pluck it off whichever body we find it on."

"But there's one body," Halloway said thickly, advancing on Minowi with eyes gleaming and his mouth twisted lewdly, "that I aim to do some pluckin' at no matter what. Hell, I'll even settle for after she's dead."

"You filthy—" Lone spun on the vile dog only

318

to be met by the rifle muzzle ramming hard into his gut, knocking the wind out of him and bringing him to his knees.

"Knock it off, Hayden!" Vallen also came down off his mount. "We don't have time for that now."

"The hell we don't," Halloway growled without looking around. He reached out with his free hand and began fondling one of Minowi's breasts. "I been lookin' at and achin' for a taste of this copper skinned beauty too damned long to pass it up now. You can wait your turn or do whatever you want, but I'm gonna have me some."

With her left hand, while she endured Halloway's continued mauling and the feel of his slobbering lips nuzzling the side of her neck, Minowi pulled from the pocket of her skirt the brooch she'd placed there when Lone handed it to her earlier. She held it up, grunting in resistance to Halloway, crying out, "Here is what you seek! Take it. Take it and please leave us alone!"

Vallen stepped forward eagerly and reached for it. "Well now . . . ."

Halloway stopped long enough to turn his head and look. Then he turned back to Minowi, saying over his shoulder to his partner, "You go ahead and have your fun with that. But me, I got something a lot more—"

He never finished. Not that sentence or any other—not ever. The only thing more to come out of his mouth was a gout of blood and an odd, hollow roar as Minowi's right hand jammed the twin barrels of Paul Caldwell's derringer up under his jaw and triggered its remaining load. The top of Halloway's head exploded, spraying brain matter and skull fragments.

Splashed by this gore, Vallen backed away in shock—right into the fists of Lone, who came out of his doubled-over position in a seething rage. He pounded the big-toothed hombre to the ground and held him there, raining down more blows until Minowi pulled him off.

They stood together, leaning on each other for support, for a long time.

Until, his breathing leveled out now, Lone gestured to the derringer still clutched in Minowi's hand. "Where'd you get that stingy gun?"

"I picked it up back down the canyon, where the man you shot dropped it," Minowi answered. "I thought it might come in handy."

Lone's eyebrows lifted. "One of these days we're gonna have to have a talk about you snatchin' up other people's property. Next we'll get around to teachin' you about choosin' weapons that have more than two shots. But, then again," he said, raising one hand to wipe a smear of Halloway's blood off her cheek, "I reckon you've done pretty good with the ones you put to use."

Minowi looked up at him. "Whatever you say. You're the smart one, right?"

In that moment, Lone felt the urge to kiss her. But, after what she'd just gone through and with the dead body sprawled at their feet, he willed himself to hold off. Instead, husky-voiced, he said, "Looks like we still got plenty of work to do. I fear Jeth's gonna need some doctorin'. And we need to reach the telegraph office in McCook as soon as possible. There's a fella named Whitlock who's gonna be mighty interested in hearin' what this skunk we left alive has to spill . . ."

EPILOGUE

Lone, Jeth, Marshal Kent, and Roy Whitlock stood outside the McCook stage office, waiting for a fresh team to be hitched up. Jeth had one arm in a sling and a head bandage mostly covered by his hat thanks to the beating he'd received from Vallen and Halloway two days earlier. Whitlock had graduated from a crutch to a cane to assist walking due to the wound he'd received a week ago during the train robbery.

"Reckon us two half cripples," Jeth was saying, "can do enough leanin' on each other, if we have to, to make the stage ride back up to Ogallala and then the train trip on to Omaha."

"Still think you can make your daughter's weddin' in time?" Lone asked Whitlock.

"By the skin of my teeth, I'm hoping," replied the freight man. "Thankfully, I allowed all that extra time for what I thought would be an extended layover in Omaha. But thanks above all, to you and Jeth, whenever I do get there it will be with the special gift I so badly want to present Pauline."

"I'm bettin' that you just bein' there, especially when she hears all you went through, she'll see as the *most* special gift," said Jeth.

Whitlock's mouth spread in a guarded smile.

"I certainly want to believe that. I hope so. Especially now . . . now that she is my only child."

The man's voice turned bitter and broke a little at the end. He'd had plenty to be bitter about since shortly after arriving in town the previous day and learning of the scheme set in motion by his son—Peter having arrived with him—to confiscate the brooch, the Whitlock Pulse. Confronted by Vallen from behind his jail bars, Peter had wasted no time attempting denial but rather had lashed out at his father, spewing his litany of petty jealousy and spite and hate for all to see and hear.

The old man had stood like a rock, listening, showing no emotion. Until the whining pup ran out of things to say. Then, with a single backhanded sweep, Whitlock had delivered a cracking blow and declared the ingrate disowned and never welcome in his sight again. Peter had slunk away and was last seen riding out of town at dusk.

Hoping to take things back to a lighter level, Lone said, "How about you, Jeth? You still figurin' to go on and look up your kin in Iowa?"

"You bet. If I ain't welcome enough straight out, I figure my beat-up condition ought to earn me at least a healthy dose of sympathy. And I plan to soak it up for all it's worth."

Everybody had a chuckle over that.

Then Marshal Kent asked, "Before you leave out, are you sure nobody wants to press any more charges against that Vallen fella? Or, for that matter, Mr. Whitlock, against your—er, I mean against Peter?"

"All we want is to be shed of 'em," Lone said, answering for all. "Let 'em drift in the wind. Their ways will catch up with 'em soon enough."

"And my lawyer will be in touch about the distribution of any additional reward money resulting from bringing down the Pierce gang," said Whitlock. "You already know what was agreed on. A quarter each to the town and to the Keoughs. Another quarter for the Indian girl, Minowi, to be delivered according to her wishes. Lone is declining any share. So the remainder, then, goes to my company in Cheyenne, from where I will forward it to Jeth whenever he decides to light somewhere."

Jeth's gaze fell on Lone. "So where will you be headed, you independent cuss?"

"Still aimin' for North Platte, same as I was when I stopped at that waterin' station where this whole passel of trouble landed on me," Lone answered with a crooked grin.

"And what of the Indian girl?" asked Whitlock.

"Minowi's been stayin' out at the Keoughs. Been sittin' with Mary and especially with Sara. Sounds like she may stay for a while. Drawin' from her own past experiences seems to give Minowi a special touch for helpin' Sara come to grips with what she went through," Lone explained.

"She still figurin' to return to her people down in the Nations?"

"At some point, yeah. It's a gap she's gotta close. Won't be satisfied until she does."

Jeth eyed him closer. "No chance you're gonna go with her?"

Lone gave him a look. "Me goin' to spend time amongst a whole mess of Pawnee? I may have grown more tolerant with the passin' years, but how long you think it'd be before I started eyeballin' some of 'em and wonderin' if they was possibly kin to or had some other connection to those who killed my parents? What do you think would come next? No, that's a trip I'm afraid can't happen."

Jeth gave a small nod of understanding. "No, reckon not. I just wish . . ."

"What?"

"Nothing. Never mind." Jeth looked around abruptly. "Hey! How long does it take to get that team of nags hitched up anyway? What kind of stage line are you jehus runnin' here?"

Grinning again, Lone raised one hand in a wave to all and turned away. "So long, fellas. I've got my own transportation to see to . . . an ornery ol' gray stud named Ironsides. He's probably sick of

nice fresh stable hay and grain by now, wantin'
to chaw some half burnt prairie grass and kick
up a cloud of dust on a trail to where he don't
particularly care."

AUTHOR'S NOTE

Massacre Canyon is a real place in southwestern Nebraska. The history of how it got its name is reasonably accurate as related in the preceding story, though too briefly told. Also, I took some dramatic license with the time frame between the setting of this tale and the date of the actual battle.

There is much more to know about events leading up to the massacre, including speculation on a possible government conspiracy that allowed the clash between tribes to take place in order to encourage the Pawnees to abandon their Nebraska lands. For anyone interested in learning more, I encourage you to research the subject further via the internet or other sources.—*WD*

Center Point Large Print
600 Brooks Road / PO Box 1
Thorndike, ME 04986-0001 USA

(207) 568-3717

US & Canada:
1 800 929-9108
www.centerpointlargeprint.com